what we hide

Also by Marthe Jocelyn

Folly

How It Happened in Peach Hill

Would You

what we hide

marthe jocelyn

EMBER

Text copyright © 2014 by Marthe Jocelyn
Cover photographs copyright © 2014 by Nikki Smith/Arcangel Images (figures) and
Mark Owen/Arcangel Images (background)

All rights reserved. Published in the United States by Ember, an imprint of
Random House Children's Books, a division of Penguin Random House LLC,
New York. Originally published in hardcover in the United States by Wendy Lamb
Books, an imprint of Random House Children's Books, New York, in 2014.

Ember and the E colophon are registered trademarks of Penguin Random House LLC.

Visit us on the Web! randomhouseteens.com

Educators and librarians, for a variety of teaching tools,
visit us at RHTeachersLibrarians.com

The Library of Congress has cataloged the hardcover edition of this work as follows:
Jocelyn, Marthe.
What we hide / by Marthe Jocelyn. — First edition.
pages cm
Summary: Told from multiple viewpoints, high school junior Jenny of Philadelphia
spends a semester at a Quaker boarding school in Sheffield, England, near where her
brother is avoiding the Vietnam draft, and where everyone carries close-held secrets.
ISBN 978-0-385-73847-7 (trade) — ISBN 978-0-375-89465-7 (ebook)
[1. Interpersonal relations—Fiction. 2. Boarding schools—Fiction. 3. Schools—Fiction.
4. Secrets—Fiction. 5. Foreign study—Fiction. 6. Sheffield (England)—History—20th
century—Fiction. 7. Great Britain—History—Elizabeth II, 1952– —Fiction.] I. Title.
PZ7.J579Wh 2014
[Fic]—dc23
2013015146

ISBN 978-0-375-85544-3 (trade pbk.)

Printed in the United States of America

10 9 8 7 6 5 4 3 2 1

First Ember Edition 2015

for Maz
and
for Elena,
friends of my youth

jenn

So here we were, running away to save Tom's life.

And turning mine inside out.

If there hadn't been a war going on, my brother would have taken a year off before college and doodled down to Mexico in a van. But now it was college versus Vietnam. Unless he wanted to fake a mental disorder, but Dad said over his dead body was he having a son with *psycho* on his record and Mom said it would be *her* dead body if her son got sent to war. They didn't say those things with me in the room, but the heating vent in the upstairs hallway conveniently transmitted any words spoken in the kitchen, so I listened in as the discussions went on for weeks.

The original plan was Canada. Tom was leaving. So was his best friend, Matt, of course, but to a different place. That part was bad. Tom was my closest person on earth, but when Matt got his draft notice, it was almost worse, because it made me feel lucky in an awful kind of way. Our parents looked at every option to keep their son out of the army. At Matt's house they were proud for him to be a soldier, like his dad had been.

They told me at a Saturday breakfast. I held my spoon between two fingers, making it vibrate like a humming-bird's wing. The idea of Tom staying at home and attending the University of Pennsylvania had been abandoned weeks earlier. Not safe enough. Now Canada—all billion acres of it—was also too close.

"If he goes to college in England he'll take up residence on another *continent*." Dad's hand swept over to capture my rattling spoon. "At least temporarily. It slows down the whole process if his name comes up. The new lottery system still lets the boys go to college, but that could change at any time."

Did he know what he was talking about? Or was it pure hope?

"There's a rumor," said my mother, "that they'll end college deferment altogether. He'd be forced to join up. Every single month counts, as long as he's eligible."

"Maybe he'll meet a girl," Dad said. "If he married an English girl, he'd become a citizen of the United Kingdom, which is not involved in the war. He'd be safe forever."

"Does Tom know you're arranging his marriage?" I wanted Tom to be there so I could roll my eyes at him. This was almost funny. But Tom, typically, was still in bed. "And why did you keep the whole boy-wonder-goes-to-

2

Britain plan such a big fat secret? No one thought I'd care whether my brother suddenly moves across the ocean?"

"We didn't want you getting upset until we knew for certain."

But *Tom* had known for ages, adding foreign applications to the pile he'd done for American schools.

"And now it's decided?" Without me having a say? "Where exactly is he going?"

"The acceptance letter came yesterday," said Dad. "He'll be at Sheffield. A very fine university." His smugness made me want to grind my teeth.

"Isn't he clever." *For a pothead.* I drummed the spoon on my side of the table as many times as I could before Dad's hand stopped me. "And what about Matt?"

Mom folded her napkin and stood to clear the dishes. "It's . . . hard about Matt."

I knew she loved him too, and had ever since the boys started Little League in the third grade. He'd sat at this table for a thousand bowls of macaroni, a million fistfuls of popcorn. Mom's eyes caught mine, but then she looked away.

"Each family has to decide for itself," she said. "We can only do what *we* think is best. For us. For Tom."

"It's not fair," I said. "None of it."

"Matt will be leaving in a few weeks, just like your brother."

"*Just like?* That's the dumbest thing I ever heard! Tom goes to England and Matt goes to napalm bomb land? How is that the same?"

And what about *me*? Losing Tom *and* Matt? Who would I *be* without them? All my life I'd had two big boys to watch for clues, two boys teasing me, squishing me between them, agreeing that I was a flea and a pest and still the best sister ever.

"You look hideous," they'd say when I dressed up for a party.

"We'll kill him," they said when Jared Benner didn't show up for the tenth-grade dance.

So now it was me, Mom, and Dad. Dad's earnest legal cases. Mom gung ho about the Equal Rights Amendment and having what she called "a voice." She wasn't exactly a women's libber, but she did say "Thank goddess" instead of "god" to support the movement. I told my parents that school was *bor*ing, even if my friends Becca and Kelly were as entertaining as a soap opera. Boys and drama. Competitive crushes on Tom. I was more a background kind of person, not shy, exactly, but . . . undercover. Tom was sure of himself, the one who got noticed, the one who knew every time what to say, who to charm, what to do.

"I'm supposed to just carry on, pretending that Tom is not a draft dodger?"

"Don't use the word *dodger*," said Dad.

"I should say *evader*? Or you like *resister* better?"

"Shush!"

"Don't they track down draft dodgers and put them in prison?" I pushed my bowl of cereal sludge away. "And I'm supposed to invent a story for my friends that he's got flat feet or something?"

Not that making up stories would be any different from usual. I *had* to fabricate home drama now and then, just to have something to say.

"G'morning." Tom slouched into the room. Boxer shorts, T-shirt, hair standing up on one side. The bristling silence made him pay attention. "What?" When did he start having stubble in the morning? It made him look so arty.

"Your sister"—Mom poured him juice—"is having one of her moody mornings." She opened the oven, releasing the warm cinnamon-bun cloud saved just for Tom.

"What?" he said to me.

"*Moody?* You've been hiding this from me for how long? *Months?* And now I'm supposed to just *lie?* On *command?* As if my opinion means nothing?"

I left the room. What *was* my opinion?

"Jenn?" He found me later.

"I'm not talking to you. Traitor. Secret-keeper. Favorite child. Sister-leaver."

"I've refined the plan."

I pulled a pillow over my head. The bed jounced as he sat down.

"Really. You're going to like it."

"Mmmph."

"I told them that I'd only go over there if you came too. You should do a semester abroad, come to England, be my pal."

I dragged the pillow off my face and sat up. "What?"

He lay down next to me. "Yep."

"What did they say?"

"That you'd have to go to school. Of course. But . . ."

"*Three whole months?* They didn't say no?"

"They were actually sort of cool with it. They think it was their idea. An opportunity for mind-broadening. Good for the college applications. You can always leave if it's awful. Or maybe stay if you love it. Plus it makes *me* going more believable."

"Like, *boarding* school?"

"Yeah, we'll find someplace near Sheffield. You can pretend to be Jane Eyre."

"Didn't her best friend die of tuberculosis in the dormitory?"

"Look at the alternative: You. Mom. Dad. Here. Forever."

The summer suddenly got busy. Shopping, packing, planning, and goodbyes. The hum of *anything can happen*, which I'd never felt before. My friends were wild with envy. The only really awful part about leaving was Matt acting as if we weren't running away from him too. He cheerfully never mentioned the sinking ship, or the rat named Tom who was jumping clear.

I told Becca and Kelly not to come to the airport.

"Family." They knew to avoid the situation. I'd used that single word to create this dark mythology about my home life.

So the send-off was parents plus Matt.

Matt was on leave, going back in four days to Virginia to finish basic training, just as Tom would be sitting down for his first college lecture across the ocean.

Tom had obviously smoked a joint before leaving the house. He bought a bag of M&M's and ripped it open in the airport shop. He poured them down his throat, laughing. Matt poked Tom, trying to break the flow of candy. Matt was taller, with broader shoulders and more muscles. You'd think Tom was the scruffy, poetic type, but he was the sneakiest, quickest guy on the basketball court. He couldn't chew *and* laugh *and* swallow, though, so he was spitting out M&M's, laughing so hard he almost gagged. I bugged my eyes at Matt to pull Tom away, behind the magazines. All we needed was for Dad to launch into another lecture on responsibility.

Mom and Dad took turns hugging us goodbye, making us show them again that we had passports, tickets, contact info for Dad's colleague who was renting us a car, English pound notes, and traveler's checks. Matt scooped Tom and me together for a lump hug, hanging on as if it were the last time. His uniform was stiff against my cheek, hardly worn.

Tom punched him lightly on the arm. "Go, bro."

"You be the one goin'." Matt tapped him back.

And then Matt mussed my hair and leaned in to kiss me, almost right on the lips. "Don't be messin' with those English soccer boys," he said. I tried to laugh, but tears were splashing out, probably blotching everything. He caught my chin in his hand and looked straight into my eyes, his beautiful brown face too close for me to see all of it. "Be brave."

"You *tooo*."

One more little hug, Matt-smell practically killing me.

And that was goodbye.

Illington Hall was announced by a faded sign at the end of the drive. Tom drove the rental car like a maniac, usually remembering which side of the road we should be on. We bounced over a half mile of rutted lane from the main road to the columned entryway of an old manor house. Tall oak doors. Sheep grazing on the playing field out front.

Tom whistled. "We should be arriving in a brougham instead of this rattletrap," he said. "With a team of fine horses and a couple of footmen, eh what?"

I grinned out the window. It was a rare pleasure to impress Tom. I'd be living like a character in a novel, far from junior year in the suburbs. In England, I'd be the mysterious stranger, the American with an unknown past. Finally, *I'd* be the one with drama.

The word *Headmaster* was etched into a brass plate under the doorbell. In less than a minute, the huge door swung open.

"Tweed!" murmured Tom. "Patched elbows!"

"Welcome to Yorkshire!" The man's enormous hand clasped mine, the calluses on his palm like the pads on a dog's paw. "You must be our new American girl. Jenn, isn't it? Jolly good show." He actually said that! He shook Tom's hand, face radiant with hearty English cheer.

"Richard Woods. We use given names here, no 'Misters,' in keeping with the Quaker tradition. Do come in." The most perfect headmaster on earth. "Quite enterprising, getting yourselves all the way here from America!"

We followed him into what he called the Great Hall, meaning *great* as in big, not awesome, though it was kind of both. It had a cracked stone floor and gleaming wooden doors leading off in all directions. A grand staircase swept upward, wide marble treads worn into dips, guarded by a polished banister that looked better than a sledding hill for a speedy ride. Probably not allowed.

"I've got a check here from our father"—Tom brought out an envelope—"paying the big bucks to unload my sister."

Richard Woods chuckled. "How very American. Straight to business, eh?"

The headmaster's assistant was also his wife, Isobel. She was about half her husband's height, with slight buckteeth and a gentle voice. "Your trunk arrived this morning. It's up in your dormitory. Please feel free to look around," she said. "Most of the students won't arrive until this evening." She pointed to a corridor that would take us to a courtyard where we could see the classrooms. And a path that led into the woods.

"A lovely ramble at this time of year. In the spring we have the most beautiful bluebell grove in Yorkshire, but autumn has its own special marvels." *Mah-vels.*

"Well then," said Tom. "Let's go on a ramble." We shook hands again and set off.

We passed the kitchen—"God, I hope that's not your lunch we're smelling," said Tom—and stepped onto a flagstone terrace. "Pretty damn quaint! Your classrooms are the *stables*!"

A giddy thrill gripped my chest. "I've landed in some weird gothic novel."

"Let's find the woods. I've got a joint."

"How did you scrounge a joint? We're four thousand miles from your dealer!"

He turned down the rim of his knit hat, displaying a neat little row of joints.

"Ohmygod, Tom! What if you'd been caught?"

"Ah, but I wasn't."

"But . . . ohmygod! You could have been arrested or sent back or . . ."

"But I wasn't."

"You could have gone to Vietnam over a *joint*! You would have been blown to bits by a land mine because you're a pothead."

"And now that won't happen," said Tom. "Relax."

A sun-dappled path led through a rose garden turned jungle and into the shadows of deep woods beyond.

"Nice," said Tom. "Quick escape to nature when needed."

A low granite wall rimmed an old stone fountain just off the path. A busted-up angel stood in the middle, looking as if she'd been in a bar brawl. Half her nose was gone, as well as chunks of her cheek and shoulder, but her wings were intact, and one graceful hand rested on the head of a swan, which would have appeared to be swimming if there'd been water. The angel's other arm held an urn.

"Too bad it's not working," I said.

"She looks like she's pouring a pitcher of beer over someone's head."

"A sight you're familiar with?"

"Clearly the hangout." Tom kicked the dirt beside the fountain's edge. "A million butts."

I glanced around at the tangle of wild roses and overgrown ferns. Maybe this view would become as familiar as the tree outside my bedroom window at home.

"Let's go farther before I light the spliff," said Tom. "Don't want to get you kicked out before you've even unpacked your trunk."

A few more steps brought us into the real woods.

"It's called weed over here," Tom had said. "But *hash* is way more common."

"How do you know that already?"

"I checked. Key vocabulary for survival in a foreign land."

Tom lit the joint, but I only had one toke. I was already tingling just being here, didn't want to be stoned. Dots of light through the branches shone fat gold freckles on Tom's face. Something scuffled in the fallen leaves, making us both jump and then laugh ridiculously. A red squirrel tore across the path, so we jumped again and laughed some more. A blackbird began to sing on a low branch right over our heads, which seemed even funnier.

"These woods have seen their share of teen action," said

11

Tom. "Smoking a joint is the tip of the iceberg. I'll bet there's hot sex behind every tree on a midsummer's eve."

"Shhh." Hot sex. I hadn't been there yet. Kissing wasn't sex, and even that had happened only a few times at parties. I wished that half kissing Matt goodbye could mean something.

Birdcalls and tree creaks emphasized the quiet.

"It feels like . . . we're trespassing on ancient territory." I looked up through leaves. "Ghosts all around us. Can't you see Scottish warlords stomping through these woods? Or Roman soldiers setting up camp. Drying their battle togas after plodding through a heavy rain. Hacking off branches to make a fire."

"I don't think these trees are *Roman*, Jenn."

"Sharpening their blades, going on a rampage against the poor farmers."

"Mmm," said Tom. "Well. No soldier is marching here now."

We'd gotten all the way to this grove of trees and I'd never asked Tom point-blank what he felt about the army.

"Yeah," I said. "How about that?"

Tom closed his eyes and swayed slightly, more stoned than I'd realized. Or maybe I was. He licked his lips, opened his eyes, which glinted faintly pink.

"Better use eyedrops before we meet back up with the headmaster."

"I can't stop thinking about Matt," he said.

I had a flash of Tom and Matt shooting hoops in the driveway, Tom's skinny white shoulders jostling Matt's brown ones, fighting for the ball during the nine millionth game.

"And the twenty thousand other guys who don't have the brains or the balls or the cash to be a coward like me."

Was he a coward? Or was he was making a personal stand for peace, like Mom said, and he'd suck at being a soldier anyway? I tried to imagine him with the haircut Dad had often threatened to make him get, a military buzz instead of his bushy curls crammed under a black watch cap like some pirate.

"Shouldn't we go back?" I said. He sort of deserved to feel like crap. Tom had a spot at Sheffield University and Matt was going to war. What did we know, other than what was shown on TV? Mud. Helicopters. Scared villagers. Explosions. Corpses. Matt would see it all up close.

When the fountain came into sight again, there were two girls sitting on the rim. One of them whipped a cigarette behind her back while she checked us out. Her hair could only be called *tresses*, dark and luxuriant like those of a heroine on the cover of a romance novel. The not-smoking one had heavy eyeliner and short hair the color of orange juice.

"Uh-oh," I said to Tom, low. I wasn't ready for actual other kids. "No one was supposed to be here till tonight."

"Don't be silly. One of them might be your new best friend."

We couldn't walk past and pretend there weren't humans perched at the edge of the path. But stopping? Saying *Hi, I'm new*?

13

"Let old Tom handle this," said Tom. "Watch the master."

The smoker took a last deep drag of her cigarette and then ground it into the dirt with the toe of a pink wedge sandal, never taking her eyes off Tom.

"So this is where the action is." Tom hitched thumbs into his jeans pockets and smiled in that charming way that I only saw around strangers.

"Welcome to the Swamp."

Tom nodded toward the fountain. "Your guardian angel?"

She smirked. "New, eh?" The girl tucked a strand behind her ear, flirting.

"Jenn is," said Tom.

"American?" said the orange-haired girl.

"Uh-huh," drawled Tom.

"What form are you in?"

"Fifth," I said. Same as eleventh grade back home.

"Which dorm?" asked the other one.

"Jane Austen." Thank goddess I knew the answers so far.

"Us too." She tilted her head toward the school building. "Staying for dinner?" she said to Tom. The girls got up to go.

"Dunno," said Tom.

"I guess dinner means lunch," I muttered a translation. It being noon.

Tom watched her butt all the way up the path till she turned on purpose to catch him.

"A handsome brother goes a long way," he said.

"You vain pig." But I knew it was true.

* * *

"Goodness, did you get lost?" asked Isobel Woods. "Your mother rang all the way from Philadelphia to be certain you'd arrived safely!"

"Safe and . . . perhaps not quite sound," said Tom.

Isobel blinked. "You can clean up quickly in the lavatory and join the early birds in the dining hall."

"Tom," I whispered. "Maybe you should go."

He started to smile and then realized I meant it. "Seriously? You're ready to . . ."

He might have said *You're ready to say goodbye?* but instead he went, ". . . ready to leap off the rusting bridge into the cool green waters of your own life?"

I laughed in the same instant that my eyes stung with tears.

"Fine," he said. "Eat crap school food all by yourself. See if I care." He gave me a real squeeze. And zoomed away before I could change my mind.

Poof! New life began as the two girls from the fountain sidled up.

"That was truly heartwarming," said the dark-haired girl.

"Don't be a twat, Penelope." Orange Hair made a face. "I'm Kirsten. Sit with us. We'll fill you in on all the sordid details."

The ceiling in the dining hall was high, *high* above our heads, adorned with plaster curlicues and blossoms, and dotted with large blobs of jam and butter.

"There's a tradition of food fights at end of year," said

15

Kirsten. "Only there's no ladder tall enough to clean up after."

"Oh Lord," said Penelope. "Good old Hairy Mary hasn't changed a bit over the summer."

A woman in a crisp white uniform waited next to the only set table.

"Matron," whispered Kirsten. "Dormitory Nazi."

"Ah! You've met the new *gerrl*!" Hairy Mary's Scottish accent turned *girl* into *gerrl*. She joined us at the table. "*Verry* good."

"I'll thank you two to show Jenn around this afternoon. Allow her to become familiar with the regulations. Which include 'No hair dye or makeup,' Kirsten."

"Term doesn't begin till tomorrow," said Kirsten. As if her hair color would disappear overnight.

"You're going to start out being cheeky, are you?"

"Cheeky? Me?"

The food was truly disgusting. My friends at home were expecting vivid descriptions of horrible school food, but I now realized that this was all there'd be to eat. Potatoes like old candles, meat loaf like discount cat food, peas like grubby pellets of paste.

Hairy Mary chewed with concentration, emptying her plate with impressive efficiency. Penelope served herself one mouthful from each tureen. Kirsten had only potatoes, mashed flat, topped with globules of margarine and a hailstorm of salt. After the first bite, my stomach rolled over in panic. I might starve to death.

"Was that your boyfriend?" said Penelope.

"No, Tom's my brother."

"Very tasty," said Penelope.

"Interesting aroma." Kirsten, letting me know they'd sniffed the pot.

"He goes to Sheffield University," I said.

Penelope's eyebrows rose. No one said *So why isn't he going to war?*

"You *gerrls* are on your own now, until tea." Hairy Mary rose to leave. "It would be most responsible to attend to your unpacking."

"Ah!" said Kirsten. "But *are* we responsible?" She looked at Penelope and even cocked her head at me.

The matron turned away with a little *tsk* of exasperation.

"Good old Hairy Mary," sighed Kirsten.

"I'll unpack far enough to retrieve my jumper," said Penelope. "We can go into the village. Does *your* brother want to come, Kirsten? Where's he been hiding? He didn't eat."

"Oh, you know Luke. He hibernates at school."

"Wait till you see Luke." Penelope smirked at me. "Dead gorgeous! But quite standoffish."

"Let's go have chips for tea," said Kirsten. "Instead of mulch."

"I'm surprised you're not all the size of pencils," I said. "The food sucks."

"It would poison a hog," said Penelope. "The baked beans are like someone else's spew."

Spew must mean "puke." I was quickly assembling a glossary.

"The cook's name is Vera Diarrhea," said Kirsten. "Which tells you everything you need to know. She boils her moldy knickers in the tea urn, in case you're savoring the flavor."

"Let's go," said Penelope. "I want to see if the townie-boy selection has miraculously improved over the summer." She and Kirsten bounced from their chairs, scraped their plates into the bin, and headed for the door. Was I supposed to follow?

"Oh," said Kirsten. "You coming, Jenn?"

An afterthought.

But of course I was coming! What else would I do?

"It's Jenny, actually." Jenny sounded more English. "Call me Jenny."

"Do you *have* a boyfriend?" asked Penelope, on the way up the many stairs to the Austen dormitory. I had a flash of Matt's brown face, the black velvet buzz of hair, the half kiss, his startled face when I'd begun to leak tears against his chest at the airport.

"You *do*!" cried Penelope. "Are you . . . all *missing* him and heartbroken?"

"I . . . uh . . ." What did she want to hear? "I mean, yes, I'll miss him, of course, but . . . I'm in England, right? And he's not."

"I'm liking you more every minute," said Penelope.

Matt would never know. Illington Hall was on a different planet from where he was.

"Matt's older. Nearly four years," I said. "He's in Vietnam." The wobble in my voice sneaked out, bringing tears that I quickly blinked away.

Kirsten stopped on the stairs. "You mean he's a soldier? In the war?"

I nodded.

18

"Doesn't that make you bonkers? That he's in the army?"

"Yes," I said. Yes, yes, yes.

"I went to a protest last summer in Birmingham," said Kirsten. "One smart thing our prime minister did was stay out of that war. You must be . . . Oh my god, you poor thing."

"Mental," said Penelope.

I'd done it. They were impressed.

In the dorm, ten cots stood in two rows, almost like in the picture book about Madeline. A bare lightbulb dangled in the center of the ceiling. The gray wool blankets made my skin itch without my having to touch one. The dingy walls; tall, narrow windows; battered trunks; a glimpse of a huge tiled bathroom—it was *perfect*!

Penelope and Kirsten had claimed the two window beds and now expertly pinned up their gray blankets to block out the faint sun. Each pulled a duvet from the top of her trunk and transformed the cots into cozy nests. I watched with a diving heart. Everything in Kirsten's trunk seemed to be black. Penelope's clothes, flying in several directions as she dug deeper, might have belonged to the singer in a hippie blues band.

I realized that the clothing list we'd thought so hilarious back in Philadelphia would now be the cause of resounding humiliation. The list must have been printed in 1938 and never updated. Apparently the uniform regulations had been abandoned. But Mom and I had sewn labels in everything according to the rules: *4 dark skirts, preferably A-line . . . 4 white blouses with plain collars . . . 4 warm vests . . .*

19

I hadn't known what a vest was, other than the sleeveless sweaters that Grampy wore. "Undershirt, silly," said Mom. "You'll be grateful all winter."

The idea of a school uniform had been so appealing, but now that I was here . . . I'd look like a freaking idiot! Too late to pretend that my trunk had been lost. Could I explain to Mom what to send from home? She had the fashion sense of a missionary. And it must cost a fortune to ship clothes overseas. I'd have to wear my one pair of jeans until they shredded.

Shredded. Why not? I lifted the lid of my trunk just far enough to retrieve my toiletry kit and one garment, which turned out to be the navy one of *4 dark-coloured V-neck sweaters*. I rummaged through my mini bottles of shampoo and lotion. Nail scissors.

I quietly began to snip at the neckline and then at the cuffs and the bottom edge. Within minutes I'd created fringe. I gave the sweater a shake and pulled it on. Penelope had now changed her clothes four times. Kirsten's eye makeup was seriously enhanced.

"Great jumper!" Penelope ran her fingers along my newly fluffed hem.

Jumper means "sweater."

"Thanks," I said. "It's kind of my thing, *adapting*. Clothes and stuff."

"We get expelled for thumbing," said Kirsten. "But sometimes a lorry will give us a lift without us asking." *Thumbing* means "hitching," I noted. *Lorry* means "truck."

We walked the three long miles to town. They peppered

me with questions about the States. And Matt. We went into a pub where Penelope bought fags. *Fag* means "cigarette." I could have been writing entries for a phrase book. We went to a chip shop where Kirsten made me try malt vinegar. It looked like brown pee, but tasted sharp and delicious. *Chip* means "french fry." Penelope pounced on two local blokes she knew from last term, Robbie and Alec. *Blokes* means "guys."

"I dunno how you ever snogged either of them," said Kirsten. *Snog* means "kiss."

"Are you joking?" said Penelope. "Did you *see* Robbie's bum? But Alec should *not* have shaved his head."

"*Sooo,*" said Penelope as we headed back to the school. "Have you slept with him, this Matt bloke?"

"Well, yeah." In the same house, about a thousand times.

I used to squish right between Tom and Matt on the carpet in front of the television where they'd be watching *Get Smart* or *Hogan's Heroes*, with a plate of celery sticks dipped in Cheez Whiz and a foil bowl of popcorn. I'd lie there wriggling until the boys shifted just enough for my scrawny self to lie between them. Peanut Butter 'n' Jenny, they called it. Sometimes we'd fall asleep that way, waking up to find that Mom had covered us with a blanket and turned off the television.

"And?"

"What do you mean, *and?*" Treacherous ground for a virgin.

"You don't have to answer her," said Kirsten. "She'll keep poking away till you show her naked photos."

"No naked photos."

"I *mean* . . ." Penelope leaned in closer, bringing wafts of clove oil and No. 6 cigarettes. "You said he was black, right? So is it true about black blokes?"

"Oh." I aimed for a sassy grin. "I've never slept with a white guy, so how would I know?" True statement. For a change.

"Whoa."

A moment of silence while I climbed to the next rung in Penelope's estimation.

"Do you mind telling me about his hair?" she said. "How it *feels*?"

"Pen, *shut* it!" said Kirsten.

A car horn tooted. "Super-perfect timing!" called Kirsten. The art master, Leonard, was offering us a lift.

"Happy to be back?" he asked.

"Yes," said Penelope.

"And how are you liking it so far?" To me.

"Super!" I tried to sound like Kirsten. "Perfect."

"Isn't it grand." He invited us, with a sweep of his arm, to gaze on the autumn fields, spiky and golden as the sun smoldered near the end of its day. Penelope rolled her eyes and slouched down next to me in the backseat.

"So many greens," said Kirsten. "Endless."

"Suck-up," Penelope mouthed at me. *Grand* means "grand," I thought.

One hundred and twenty-two other students had arrived and were jammed into the front hallway in frenzied reunion, tripping over luggage and generally hurling themselves at each other in passionate embrace. Hairy Mary was corralling the younger forms, sending the boys off with a teacher called Kirby and marching the girls up the stairs. Kirsten and Penelope were instantly swallowed by a crowd of their real friends and I was the new girl again. Loads of kids in clusters of three or four, a sound track of unfamiliar accents and new words.

"Who are *you*?" The girl had a cloud of blond hair with a serious frizz situation.

"She's Jenny." Penelope was miraculously nearby. "Jenny, this is Oona. Sorry, Oona, Kurse and I have dibs. She's in Austen dorm, not Brontë."

"Won't take you long to be utterly sick of them," said Oona. "Penelope's mouth will drive you away in no time."

"Charming as ever, Oona."

A twinge of worry. What if I'd landed with the wrong people, right off the bat? Should I be avoiding Penelope? Or Oona? Possibly both?

But they had a distraction. "Wow, Nico! *Hallo!*"

"Is that fresh Mediterranean swarthiness?" Oona was practically salivating. The boy had a total honey tan, plus dark wavy hair and, oh my god, *green* eyes.

"This is Jenny." Penelope played her card. "New girl. American. Yes, she has a boyfriend, *and* he's a soldier in Vietnam being bombed in some jungle as we speak, which is deeply traumatic, as you can imagine. *Plus*, he's *black*, so even *you* pale—get it, *pale*?—by comparison. . . ."

Nico raised his eyebrows and shot me an awkward smile.
"Uh, hi."

Penelope had turned my one little lie into a whole drama. Which was exactly what I wanted, wasn't it?

And so term began. With me in disguise.

robbie

I knew before he did that he was queer. That's why I was watching him in the shop when he nicked the stupid mints. Mints, for Chrissake. Nothing else in the whole shop worth nicking? *He's new at this*, I thought. *Just trying it on. Maybe there's other stuff he'll try.* So I followed him. Good thing he didn't get stopped for the mints.

He was one of that boarding school lot. Easy to tell, even apart from being strangers. They had a style about them; you knew they didn't buy gear in this widge of a town. He was cute as hell, eyes like a girl's, great bum in jeans, hair falling every which way, like he'd just rolled over in the sack.

So I followed him along the main road. He was clipping it, shoulders up, till he took a quick look back and didn't see any coppers pulling their sticks on him for a packet of bleeding mints. Then he slowed down, hands in pockets, looking in windows, checking out the runners at Smyth Sports like any boy on a Saturday afternoon. A couple of girls came out of Bigelow's with ice creams, girls from his school. He ducked into a doorway that led up to the flat above the shop. He closed his eyes, like if he couldn't see *them*, they wouldn't notice *him*. And they didn't. They giggled on by, giving me the up and down as they passed.

I stepped in next to him and his eyes popped open.

"Hey," I said.

"Oh, uh, hi?" He glanced into the street.

"They're gone," I said. His face was even nicer up close. A bit tan, a few freckles, hair flopping across his eyes.

"Oh." He seemed freaked that I knew he'd been hiding from the girls.

"You want one?" I offered.

He shook his head. "I don't smoke."

I put the packet away. Didn't want ciggy breath if this was going to work out the way I hoped. "Have you got a mint?" I said.

He jerked back, the git, bumped into the doorframe, hitting the bell with his shoulder. We could hear it ring inside. We stared—*click*—into each other's eyes for half a second and then pelted along the road, laughing as if we'd broken a window at the very least, not just blipped a doorbell.

We turned off the shopping street, down Tupper's Lane and around the back of the chip shop where there's a picnic table outside. We dropped onto the benches, panting.

"You saw me?" he said. "Take the candy?"

"Yeah."

"I'm a tosser."

"Not really." I was going to add, *I only saw because I was staring at your bum*, but maybe it was too soon for that. "Chance."

"Lucky it was only you."

"Only me," I said.

"I didn't mean . . ."

"Yeah, I know."

"Hey, boys." Suze, from the chip shop doorway. "Table's for customers only."

"Yeah, yeah. We're off," I said. "Unless, do you want chips?"

"No," he said. "I should get back." He tapped his wrist where a watch would have been, if he'd had one. Funny how no one has watches except old men, but we all know what that means, tapping a wrist.

"I'll walk with you," I said. "I'm going that way."

He likely wouldn't know, not being from here, that there was nowhere out that road except the school or the woods, unless I was completely barmy and going to visit bubble-lips, cushion-hips Daisy Danforth at her dad's farm next to the school.

My brother Simon used to get with Daisy Danforth when I was little, around nine or ten, and him nearly four years older. We hiked out there one time toward the end of a summer term so he could meet her, despite the heat lying over us like a woolly blanket. I remember how suffering hot it was. Simon must have been in charge of me that

27

night, since I had to tag along with his pals Benj and Felix. Daisy was meant to be at the back of her meadow where it meets the school property and there's a grove of trees around a pond. It was dark by the time we got there, and no Daisy in sight.

But there were lanterns strung from trees and some of the teachers were having a swim. Men and women both, and every one of them stripped to the skinny. No wonder the school's got a reputation for being a bit of a loony bin.

"'Allo, 'allo, what have we here?" said Simon, quiet and laughing. This was his kind of heaven, and the others were pretty stoked too, all those bums gleaming and splashing. Even I could see the joke of it, naked grown-ups flitting about. Simon started cawing, harsh and phony, so they clambered out after a bit, grabbing for towels and hooting back and forth as they stumbled off through the trees like plump and pasty wood sprites.

"Our turn!"

Simon was out of his jeans and into the water bare-assed before you could say "Lick me." The rest of us were close behind, hurtling off the planks set up as a dock. The air being hot, I didn't expect the water to be frigid. Knocked the breath out of me. The pond was murky and reedy too, bloody scary in the dark. I scrambled up the bank—no towel—and back into my clothes, nearly crying with the shock. The others faked it a little longer but not much.

"Good thing Daisy didn't show," said Simon, shivering in spite of himself. "My nuts are the size of gooseberries."

"Like she'd ever touch your nuts," said Benj.

"Or know the difference," said Felix.

They shoved each other back and forth, my-prick's-bigger-than-yours-you-tosser sort of thing, and then, chilled through, we set off at a trot across the Danforth meadow toward town, crunching whatever was growing.

"Hey!" Simon stopped after only a few steps. "You've got some ales in your rucksack, haven't you, Felix?"

"Yeah."

"Then stop bleeding running, you eejit, you're making fizz!"

So then we all had to stop, and they opened the beer tins and soaked each other, as if we weren't wet enough already and covered in pond scum, and then they began slurping what was left.

That's when Daisy turned up, crashing through the stalks like a rhinoceros, waving a torch around as if she were trying to flag down an aeroplane.

"About time," said Simon.

"I couldn't find you," she whined. Lights from her house glinted faintly behind her. "Until I stopped to listen and heard a pack of rowdy yobs."

"Very funny." Simon circled her waist and let his hand slide all the way around to rub her titty.

"Ooh!" She swatted his hand away. "Give me a beer, would you? I'm parched."

Felix passed her the last one. Nobody mentioned there'd been some agitation, all of us greedy for the *pffft* and the wail. She got a full-face shower.

"Join the club," said Felix.

29

"Hey," said Simon. "The rites. Time for Robbie to take rites, what do you think?"

"What do you mean, *rites*?" I'd learned to not trust a single thing my brother said. "What for?" We were standing close, all of us, it being night in a field far from home.

"To be one of us," said Simon.

Benj belched a good one.

"What for?" I said.

"You have to pass a couple of skill-testing tests," said Simon. "And then you're a man."

"What kind of tests?" I said.

"First," said Benj.

"First," said Simon. "You've got to touch a girl's titty."

"*Bare* titty," said Benj.

Daisy sighed.

"Go on, then." She lifted her frilly top and pulled one pale, wobbling breast out of its cup. This was horrible. She grabbed my hand and pressed it to cover the brown nipple, squishy and soft with a tough nub in the middle. The boys whooped.

"I dunno why boys get such a thrill," said Daisy. "Fancy if I was a pig and had fourteen!" That set them off for a bit, so I could reclaim my hand and quietly scrape it against my jeans. But then Simon remembered he was inducting me into manhood.

"Round two," he said. "You've got to drink . . . something . . . that your mummy wouldn't like." He waggled his beer tin back and forth.

"The kid is nine, Si," said Felix.

30

"Nearly ten," I said. Having a sip of beer couldn't be as nasty as touching Daisy Danforth.

"Oh dear," said Simon. "Nanny Felix says no beer." His voice had shifted a bit, the signal to leave the room if we'd been at home. Benj belched again.

Simon undid his fly and turned away from Daisy, trying to piss through the little hole in the top of the tin. We could hear some tinkling but see his hand getting half of it. He swore up a storm but got enough in the tin to make him happy.

"Step up, Robbie," he said. "It's your big moment."

"Ooh, you never!" squealed Daisy.

"Zip your fly, man," said Felix, taking the pissed-in beer to free up Simon's hands.

I looked around, out across the black fields. Teeny squares of light from Daisy's house shone on the one side and from the boarding school on the other. Distant headlights flashed briefly on a curve, showing where the road must be. All the civilised world was out of earshot. They'd snare me in an instant if I tried to run.

"And after drinking piss?" I yelled. "I'll be a big man like you?"

Simon just laughed. "Drink up, sport." He waved at Felix to hand over the beer.

"Aw, Simon," said Daisy. "Does he have to?" She slid her hand into his jeans pocket and moved it around.

"Bugger off." Simon wriggled away. "Come on, Robbie. Hold him, Benj."

"I'll do it," I said. "No one has to hold me." I nodded to

Felix. He held the can to my lips and tipped it. Warm beer gushed into my mouth. Beer, not piss. Felix had done a switch. He whacked me on the back at the same instant, forcing me to gag. I'm pretty sure he winked as I leaned over to spit, but perhaps not. Simon was laughing too hard to notice a thing.

"Aw, you're a trouper, kid," said Daisy. "You want to feel under my skirt next time?"

"No thanks," I said. "Thanks anyway."

Benj punched my arm. Felix turned to the empty field and hurled the can as far as Scotland. Simon corralled my head with his arm. "My brother, the man, eh?"

I got randy when I was twelve, maybe a bit younger. Simon was out there bonking girls like he was a studhorse. He'd slide in late, crashing down on my bed, cigarettes and beer stinking his breath, and something else on his fingers that he wouldn't wash off.

He'd stick those fingers under my nose and whisper, "That's Carrie," or, "Take a whiff of Lanny." He'd moan, just thinking about it while he waited for sleep. "Oh baby," he'd say. Then he'd punch my shoulder, flop an arm across my back. "Your turn next, mate," he'd say. "You won't believe what's out there."

There weren't any books at our house, but who needed them with nightly installments of The Adventures of Simon the Rutter, and pretty good it sounded too. Once he'd snored off, I'd turn over and work myself to glory, with his back warm against mine and a towel in my hand.

Eventually, Simon took me along, pushing his girls at

me, telling them, "Go on, make the kid's night." That's when the worry started. I didn't like it much.

My first boy was an accident, me not realizing that's what I wanted, me not knowing that anyone did. I'd heard the words *queer* and *faggot* and *poofter* a million times, just other words for *ugly* or *yob* or *piss off*.

By fourteen I could get my own girls if I wanted, but Simon still took me along with his crowd, like a football mascot, or a clever dog, trying to get me a good bonking.

"Come on, kid, how about Lanny? She's got titties that'll stop your heart."

"I'm going to find my own someone for the first time," I finally told him. "I don't want one of yours."

Simon was meant to be at that party too, but he'd stuck me with Abigail and then pissed off because he had a date with Kath. Later, Kath had his first kid, my nephew, Jerry, but we didn't know that yet. Abigail was a dim cow, but loyal. While we waited in her garden for people to arrive—*why was I first?*—she began telling me how lovely my brother was and wasn't I lucky? Her brother was in prison for nicking a car.

A pack of Simon's mates turned up, shouting about football. Andrew, Benj, Dickie the Dick, and Felix, who was also Abigail's cousin, each of them trying to prove something.

The girls arrived in pairs, smoothing their hair, smelling of baby powder and lilacs, wearing shoes with teetery heels. Abigail rubbed my shoulder like she meant to polish it for inspection. The girls thought it was adorable to call me Simon's Brother.

"Ooh, Simon's Brother, 'bout time you showed up at Abigail's Naughty Parlour. Aren't you in for some fun?"

"Simon's Brother, are you as cheeky as Simon is?"

One of the oafs, Andrew, pushed me out of the way while demonstrating his recent match-winning save.

"Piss off, yob," I said.

"Ooh, Simon's Brother," he crooned at me. "A softie, eh?"

It was dark enough he couldn't see my blood rise. Felix slung an arm around me. "Not worth a black eye," he said. "Come on downstairs."

Abigail's parents let her use the cellar however she pleased. Simon told me she'd gone about filching chairs and sofa cushions from rubbish heaps, so it was one huge grotty den of lust down there.

The cellar routine was: first, drinking games; next, Truth or Dare. No one chose Truth, as it turned out. You were a wuss if you chose Truth. It was all about Dare.

It started pretty tame. Benj had to sing a Beatles song in his underpants. Abigail and Rachel had to trade shirts. Dickie had to drink Andrew's piss.

Then it was my turn.

"Make out for two minutes," said Andrew. "With another boy."

"Who the hell is going to do *that* with *him*?" said Benj.

"The good news is, not *you*, yob," I said, but I wanted to crawl under a mouldy cushion and stay there.

"For the cause." Felix stepped up. "Eh, Simon's Brother? But only if the lights are out."

"How will we know you did it?" asked Dickie the Dick. "If it's dark?"

"You'll know," said Felix. He snatched up Abigail's little purse from her lap and snapped it open while she squeaked and grabbed to get it back. He pulled out a lipstick tube and dropped the bag into Abigail's reaching hands. He took off the cap and twisted the colour up. No one laughed or made noise, all just staring. My blood *zimmed* like a fiddle in my ears.

Felix rolled the lipstick across his lips, like he was an expert, a girl, making his mouth look as if he'd sucked blood. He winked at me—big jolly jeers broke out all round—and pulled me over to stand in the middle of the room.

"Who's timing this?" His hand slid down my arm, burning through my shirt.

"Me, I will," said Dickie, showing us a nerdy light-up watch.

"Two minutes?" said Felix.

"Yeah!" They all were laughing now, jazzed up on our behalf.

"Lights," said Felix. His hand was still on my wrist, circling, not holding. The lights clicked off, a couple of girls giggled.

"Go," said Dickie, and I saw the flash of his watch face before it went out, leaving the room sealed in dark. Felix's hand left my wrist and cupped my bum, pulling me all the way close. I gasped, girls giggled again, but now I felt him hard inside his jeans, and nearly popped my own fly on the spot.

It happened so fast, his one hand at the back and the other sliding down the front, while his mouth found mine with no trouble in the pitch bloody black. He wasn't exactly kissing me, just smearing the lipstick back and forth on my lips and face, his slight moustache scraping my skin. His hand in front was trying to get past the elastic on my boxers. I'd have fallen over if he hadn't been holding me up. Rustling in the audience and whispers. Their dark was not the same as my dark. I opened my eyes, not knowing I'd closed them, all this happening together. My prick was about to fly off, so happy and hot. Felix's mouth devoured mine, tongue everywhere. Dickie's watch flashed and he shouted out, "Thirty seconds left!" I moaned and someone snickered.

He never got inside my boxers, but we were clamped together, and I came hard. He licked my lips and then licked my ear and whispered, "Not bad for a yob, eh?"

"Time!" yelled Dickie. The lights slapped on, my eyes snapped shut against the clapping and raucous laughter. I felt like a kid caught peeing in the teacher's garden.

"Way to go, Robbie!" Someone poked me.

"Your *face*, man!"

"He got you good. . . ."

Felix was heading up the cellar stairs, chugging a Coke. I tried not to shake, surrounded by a crowd of grinning faces. Abigail shoved a makeup mirror into my hand and I saw my face, like a baby's after eating spaghetti.

"That was wicked," said Abigail. "Can't wait to tell Simon."

I wanted a blanket to wear over my head. They were having a big cackle, calling me *queer boy* and *poofter*. I laughed along, letting Abigail rub off the red smears, and I knew it was true. I was a queer boy. I'd just found an unimagined bliss.

36

As promised, Abigail told it all to Simon. Did she think she'd score points for making him laugh? Simon smacked her, I heard later. "You think it's a joke?" he'd hollered. "My brother acts like a fairy and you think it's *funny*?"

He thundered home and slammed into our room, knocking his football trophies off the dresser top.

"I should cut your measly prick right off," he said. "It's not to be used for *boys*."

"What do you care? You use yours like a flippin' stir stick."

He came at me, only I ducked and he cracked his head on the bedstead. I was out of the room before he stood up. I came back the next day to hear from Auntie Pat that Lanny Giles was knocked up and Simon was on the hook to marry her.

I saw Felix from time to time, but only at a match or in the pub, always in a swarm of yobs. He never looked in my direction. I tried not to look in his.

After Felix I only kissed girls. Passing the time with girls was no problem. If Felix could disguise himself amongst the yobs, so could I. My mate Alec was reliable cover, always on the prowl. The boarding school girls were his idea. One little hussy named Penelope could wank us both off at the same time and never stop talking.

Then came Mint Boy.

I liked him. We chatted, me wondering when he'd figure

out there was nowhere I could be going, his school being the only destination.

He'd been there two years, starting in third form, his sister went there too, yes he knew Penelope, his dad was boss of some slogan-writing business, his mum was tired of her husband never being home, the history teacher was a tosser, the food was foul, he liked Procol Harum too, and then, "Where are you going, anyway?"

We'd cut across a field, one of Daisy Danforth's, and I had no excuse. It was getting on dusky. We were past the pond area, alongside some kind of a shed. I leaned against it, giving him the gaze, cupping myself for an instant, just long enough for him to notice. His pretty eyes went wide and he flinched. *Blew that*, I thought. But then he didn't move and I saw the flush creep up his neck. He glanced up at the school, as if to check if we were being watched from a window. I stepped around to the blind side of the shed, heart drumming. He followed.

"I never . . . ," he said.

One second later, we were kissing like crazy, hot mouths, teeth gnawing lips while we grabbed each others' bums and rocked and humped all the way to rocket launch.

I wanted to cry, I truly did. Better than winning a football match, better than any music, better by far than a girl. I held on to him for a minute more, and he was hugging me too, our faces buried in each other's necks, sweaty as hell.

A solemn gong sounded in the main building. He cursed and peeled himself off me, yanking his clothes straight, swiping his crazy hair off his face.

"Gotta go," he said. Then, "Wait. What's your name?"

"Robbie." My lips were chafed, burning.

"I'm Luke."

"Nice to meet you." We laughed, ordinary.

He slid his hand into his pocket and pulled out the packet of mints.

"I got these for you," he said. And then he left.

brenda

"You be a good girl, now, won't you?"

"Yes, Mr. Eggers." Brenda's jacket hood snagged on the door handle. She fumbled to tug it loose, hating the man's yellow eyeballs. How could he see to drive? He reached across the seat to help, but she wrenched the jacket free in time to avoid him touching her by accident.

"Cheerio!" Brenda jumped down, ignoring a tweak of pain in her ankle as she landed. The truck rattled off behind her but she didn't turn. *Urg. Blech.*

A face was pressed inside the window of the house, making fishy-mouth against the grimy glass. "May your little self never grow up to be a yellow-eyed, hairy-knuckled, mucus-spewing dragon." Brenda waggled her fingers like worms in front of the boy. His face disappeared and a second later the door opened.

"Hello, Auntie Bren!" shouted Christopher. "I saw you first!"

"Awesome child," said Brenda.

"Before Jerry. I saw you before Jerry did."

"No fair, Chrisfer!" Jerry was right behind him, shoving to get past, fists yanking on his brother's back pockets.

"Steady on." Brenda laid a hand on each shaggy head, steering the boys back inside. "I need a bicky, how about you?"

Kath peeked out from the kitchen, circles stained under her eyes. "Thank the sodding Lord you're here. I'm ready to smack heads together, I'm so fed up."

Brenda dropped her schoolbag beside the radiator in the hallway.

"How was your limo drive today?" asked Kath.

Their dad had arranged with Mr. Eggers to bring Brenda into town after lessons, seeing as he worked out at the school, digging and fixing, moving the rubbish bins around.

"First, there's the gurgling accent. And that little hiccupping cough," said Brenda. "And then the juicy clots that he loosens up, while I'm pretending not to notice that he's got to have a great green glob of mucus sitting in his mouth, waiting to spag it out the window, if he can get the window rolled down while he's driving like a yellow-eyed fiend along the York Road. . . . It was hideous, thank you for asking."

"Auntie Bren said bicky." Jerry banged his mother's bum with a small fist. "Bicky, bicky, bicky."

"He's treading on my last brain cell whenever he opens

41

his yapper," said Kath. Funny how quickly she could move when getting out of the house was the goal; snatching up keys, dumping coins from the Marmite jar on the back of the cooker, jamming arms into the sleeves of her denim jacket, slinging a purse over her shoulder. "We're out of biscuits."

"Biscuit!" demanded Jerry.

"Shut it," said Kath.

"All right," said Brenda. "Off you go, then. Jerry, let's have honey crackers instead."

Kath worked at Bigelow's every day from four till seven. Brenda stayed with the boys for those hours, before she went home to make supper for Dad. She wished more than anything she could be a boarder at Illington Hall instead of a day girl, even though she loved Christopher and Jerry like crazy. She secretly thought that she loved them more than Kath did. Her sister was such a grouch.

"You're my saviour, today, Bren, I kid you not. I was nearly one of those mothers you read about in the *Daily Express*. 'Mother of Two Sets Fire and Kills Tots.' I swear to god."

Brenda would have laughed except that she believed her. "Anything I should know?"

"Christopher pissed the bed, Jerry spewed his Cheerios all over the breakfast table, the telephone's been cut off, oh, and the greasy munter who is Jerry's father did *not* bother to mention the fact, which I heard from Suze at the chip shop, that his wedding to Lanny Giles is back on despite her miscarriage."

"Simon fecking Muldoon."

"The blighter."

Brenda ran her finger around the rim of the honey jar and licked it before screwing the lid back in place. "Thank your lucky stars, Kath. What if it were you?"

"Don't I know it? One bloody bonk got me Jerry. Imagine what hell a wedding night could bring!"

Brenda glanced around to make certain her nephew was not listening.

"I'm going down the Red Lion for a pint after work, all right? With Alison," Kath said. "Do me a favor? Give them a bath? Ta." The door banged shut and then opened again. "Oh, and Bren? Stay late Friday, would you? I've got something going on." Her eyebrows did a little dance to show Brenda there was a bloke involved.

"What if I do too?" said Brenda. Empty threat.

"It's Dad's dart night, so no asking him. All on you, sorry, love." Door shut.

Bugger. Why did Kath always get to be boss? Brenda rested a hip against the kitchen counter. Christopher came in to lean against her, kneading her tummy.

"Don't do that, Chris, I've told you."

"I like the squishy," he said.

"Well, I've plenty of that," she sighed. "But girls don't want boys playing with the blubbery bits, you hear me?"

He scooted off with his brother to smear honey on furniture. The little boys' bodies surprised her every time, the smallness of them under their clothes, tiny wiry arms and tough stick legs, so unlike the large lazy limbs of her friends at school, or the lumbering, slouching boys Brenda knew in town. She retrieved her schoolbag and rummaged through. She might as well get the reading done for English. They were just starting *Great Expectations*. She was swallowed up by Pip and Magwitch until Christopher came in to poke her.

"Auntie Bren? Jerry's been sick again. In the toy box."

One thing about Jerry being ill, the evening sped by. No wrestling, no spills, no fuss. "You're good as girls tonight, you are," said Brenda. But what with the bath and Kath stopping for two drinks instead of one, it was too late to worry about her dad's supper—he'd have got takeaway by now. She'd stop in and pick up chips for herself on the way home, thanks to Kath actually paying her. They had chips for tea at school on Tuesdays, so why shouldn't she?

The chip shop was packed this time of night. Brenda would have to wait her turn, it being only Suze and her dim helper, Gus. There was a table of boys near the door: Alec and a couple of others, one of them a stranger, and oh crap, the other was Robbie Muldoon. Brenda and Robbie usually pretended that his brother had not knocked up her sister. (If Jerry had been Kath's first, things might have been different, but Jerry being the second accident, it made her look like a slag, meaning that Simon fecking Muldoon got off scot-free and never paid support or nothing. "Could be anybody's!" Simon had protested.)

Most times, Robbie avoided Brenda—there not being a way to say you're sorry if you didn't have anything to do with what happened. But they were stuck till doomsday, related to each other because of his brother's prick. It didn't make sense.

So what was the smile for? Brenda waggled fingers at him and looked away quick, as if she'd spotted a friend. Only she couldn't move because she'd lose her place in line. When her gaze casually passed Robbie again, she blinked to see him holding out a chair, inviting her to sit down with him and his mates.

"You know Alec. And this is his mate from Albury High School. What's your name again?"

"Michael," said the boy, flushing. Dead fit, actually. Dark hair and crooked eyebrows, but looked straight at you, which was rare as a two-pound note.

"Sit down. Let me get you some chips." Robbie slipped off before she could say, *No, no, please don't, I want to go home and curl up in front of the telly.* She'd have to make chat now, with barely known boys. She'd pretend to be Penelope, that's what. She'd make them laugh.

"Haven't seen *you* before," she said to the dishy stranger.

"We lived in Leeds, but my dad got a new office here about awhile ago. So now we're here."

"What do you think?" she said. "Must feel squat after a town as big as Leeds."

"It's all right," he said. "The girls are pretty."

And then he flushed and she flushed and Alec went, *Ooh, baby,* and Robbie came back with the chips. It could have been awful but Brenda laughed and said, "They grow them cheeky in Leeds, don't they?" And he flushed again, but he laughed too and Robbie said, "What did I miss?"

"These two are practically snogging already," said Alec, before Michael gave him a poke.

Why was Robbie talking to her?

"Brenda's at the boarding school," Robbie said. "Illington. Did she say?"

"Ill Hall," she said. "For how you feel after dinner."

That got a laugh. She was doing brilliantly.

"You must be posh like Michael here," said Alec, "going to that place."

"Scholarship," said Brenda, cheeks heating up again.

"She's brainy," said Robbie. What did *he* know?

"I know a girl goes there," said Alec. "And *she* knows *me*, if you take my meaning. Name of Penelope." He made a rude little hand gesture. "Mean anything to you?"

"She's in my form," said Brenda.

"I met a kid last term," said Robbie. "I was going to ask about. Goes to your school." He dipped his chip in a puddle of vinegar. "His name, I think, was . . . Lou?"

"Luke?" said Brenda. "Long hair?"

"Yeah," said Robbie. "Luke. Is he back this term?"

"He's there. His sister is my mate Kirsten."

"Right," said Robbie. "That's the one."

"I heard about your brother," said Brenda. "And Lanny. Being back on."

"You and the entire county," said Robbie.

"Why's she doing it, now there's no baby?"

"We're all stumped," put in Alec. "He's like a bleeding horsefly, one twat to the next."

"Brenda knows that, you wanker," said Robbie.

"Oh. Right." Alec grinned, the twerp. What did he care what it meant to have two little boys.

"What?" said Michael. "Fill me in."

"His brother." Alec pointed at Robbie. "And *her* sister." He jabbed a chip through circled thumb and finger. Brenda would have liked to crack a plate over his head. "And Rob's yer uncle!" Alec cackled like a nutjob.

Robbie smacked Alec's hand, knocking the vinegar bottle off the table.

"That's it, boys!" called Suze from behind the counter. "Table's wanted. Out, you lot."

"Take the chips," said Robbie as Brenda snatched up her bag. "You've had hardly any."

"Ta." She folded the packet closed and held it, warm and oily, in her hand.

Outside she was going up the hill, the boys heading down.

"Nice chatting." Brenda still wondered why they had.

"Tell your friend Penelope hello from Alec." Alec cupped his nuts, letting his tongue hang out.

"Tosser," said Brenda.

"And that kid, Luke," said Robbie. "Say hello from Robbie." He pulled on a cap with a little visor, made him look like an American.

They started off, but Michael turned back before she'd even done zipping her jacket, what with balancing the chip packet in one hand, not wanting to squish it into her bag.

"Brenda," he said. He came close enough that she could see the pink in his cheeks even at twilight.

47

"Yeah?"

"I come here most nights at this time," he said. "Puts off going home."

"Yeah?"

"I wonder . . . maybe . . ."

The other boys were making noises, *ooeeee*, and *woooo*.

"Just, only . . . could I meet you again?"

A boy was asking to meet her. A boy with brown eyes, a sharp crease in his school uniform trousers, and a bit of dark fluff along his jaw. A boy nobody else knew, not her sister or the girls at school or anyone.

"Or, perhaps not here." He tipped his head toward the chip shop. "By the library, how about?"

Brenda nodded.

"Friday?" A nervous smile. "Can you come Friday?"

"Yes," she said.

Brenda waited with Penelope and Lilly, a new girl in the third form. Penelope was unnaturally quiet, slumped on the bench with eyes shut, head resting against the wall. Hairy Mary glanced at her watch about forty times, not liking how the doctor wasn't there yet.

"Is he always late?" asked Lilly. "Only we've got a quiz in maths."

"If Dr. Stern finds your throat to be infected, you'll be popped into sick bay," said Hairy Mary. "Not attempting to complete a quiz."

Brenda thought sick bay sounded wonderfully girl-school-y, as if there'd always be sunlight through white curtains, dishes of rice pudding, and cool, clean sheets. Someone tending you instead of the other way around.

The doctor strode along the corridor, smiled at the waiting patients, nodded at Hairy Mary, and banged through the clinic door as if announcing that rescue was at hand. The matron slipped in behind him with her clipboard.

"He's quite dishy, isn't he?" whispered Brenda. "For an older bloke. My family goes to Wallace, in town."

"Dishy, and he knows it," said Penelope. "You watch. He'll have your top off in under five minutes."

"I've only got a sore throat and a bit of a cough."

"No matter." Penelope shifted to a more alert position. "Why do you think we call him Dr. Sperm?"

"Ew," said Lilly. "That's gross."

"Trust me, a vast improvement over Death Breath who was here before. We only got Sperm last term."

Hairy Mary opened the clinic door. "Brenda? I believe you were first?" She settled herself at her little desk. "Go on in, the doctor's waiting."

Penelope shot Brenda a big, fat wink before closing her eyes again.

"Hallo. Brenda, is it? I've not seen you before, have I?" He'd changed from his wool jacket into a white coat with a stethoscope stuffed in the pocket.

"I'm a day girl," said Brenda. "I usually go to Dr. Wallace in town. Only I'm not often sick, so . . ."

"But today you've got a bit of a throat, have you? It's going around Illington like fleas on a dog. Let's have a look, shall we?"

Brenda sat where he told her to, tilted her head, opened

her mouth while he pointed a wee torch and flattened her tongue with the wooden depressor.

"Mmm," he said. "It's pretty pink, but no nasty white spots, so you're lucky there." He tugged out the stethoscope and fit it into his ears. "I'd like to have a listen, just to be sure. Could you"—he nodded at her blouse—"unbutton?"

Heat raced to her cheeks. Brenda undid her top two buttons, showing half her bra, which, thank goodness, was the pretty lilac one that Kath had given her last birthday.

He was warming the pad of the stethoscope by rubbing it on his sleeve. "Breathe normally to begin." His fingertips were colder than the instrument that he pressed against her chest, moving the disc, listening, pressing again.

"It would be more comfortable if you'd slip out of your blouse," said the doctor. "Instead of me poking around underneath it. I want to listen from the back as well."

Penelope's prediction of five minutes had been generous.

"You're not shy, are you?"

Her arm got caught coming out of the sleeve, and he held the shoulder so she could wriggle it off. Her tits suddenly seemed g*inor*mous.

"There we go," he said. "That makes the task easier for the doctor, doesn't it?"

Brenda felt the press of smooth metal, here, here, here, as the doctor listened. And then, whoa! His palm cupped her entire left tit, fingers grazing the nipple under its lilac sheath, making it stand up in surprise. Brenda jerked back on the chair, eyes springing open when she hadn't known they were closed.

50

"Oops-a-daisy," said the doctor. "I should have warned you I'd need to shift things a bit." His hand remained firmly in place, lifting the breast to press the stethoscope beneath it. Brenda shut her eyes again, ears buzzing. Did Penelope feign illness, she wondered, just to let him have a feel?

"Keep breathing." His voice seemed to be right next to her ear. She realized that her lungs were clamped shut as well as her eyes. "Good, that's better. Your chest is not congested. Matron will give you drops for the scratch in your throat, but you needn't miss any lessons."

Brenda buttoned up so quickly that she missed one and had a shirttail dangling, but never mind now. She opened the door to the hallway.

"Goodbye, Dr.—" She couldn't call him Sperm but couldn't remember for the moment what his name was. "Doctor." *Dr. Doctor.* She must sound a complete ninny.

The end of the week came finally. Part of Brenda wished more than ever that she could dump her books under a dormitory bed and toddle down the woods to sit with the smokers before tea and a night of fun with a throng of girls. The other part was thinking about her promise to meet Michael on a bench beside the library at half seven. What if Michael thought she was dull and fat? What if, up close, he was spotty and posh? What if, alone together, they neither of them was bold and funny as they'd been the night they'd met?

Ah well, Friday to get through first.

* * *

Leonard often showed them paintings when he taught history lessons, his true love being Art. "In good conscience, however"—he twiddled a piece of chalk between his fingers—"there are very few pictures of the Anglo-Boer War in South Africa that are not upon the battlefield, and these I do not wish to show in the classroom of a Quaker school."

"Here he goes," muttered Adrian, sitting behind Brenda. "Yoko bleeding Ono."

"I wish to keep you mindful," said Leonard, "of the words declared in 1661, by the Religious Society of Friends, to King Charles: 'We utterly deny all outward wars and strife and fightings with outward weapons, for any end or under any pretence whatsoever—'"

Nico put up his hand. "How can we learn history without knowing about the wars? Aren't wars what *make* history?"

Brenda wondered if there was a boy on earth who didn't think war was so almighty. Her little nephews made weapons out of sticks or shoes or forks. Nothing they liked better than bashing each other to bits.

"The battles themselves are not central to our understanding of history," said Leonard. "We need instead to consider the *cause* of strife. To reconstruct the world that allowed—"

Percy waved his hand and began to speak before Leonard was finished. "The *cause* of strife was the British Empire stomping around sticking its nose in wherever it wanted."

"A simplified version, perhaps," said Leonard, smiling.

"But colonialism was indeed a large contributor to the conflict in South Africa."

"Like the Americans now," said Percy. "In Vietnam. Big fat bullies."

"That is not colonialism so much as . . . an assumed right by the Americans to influence the politics in other nations," said Leonard. "A greed for territory and for power is not, as you say, limited to the British. But we're getting off-topic. We haven't time today for all of mankind's misguided wars."

"Point being," said Penelope. "*Man*kind. It's men who fight wars. And women who bring the bandages."

"Nicely put, Penelope." Leonard sat on the corner of his desk, still holding the chalk. "I would say women *and Quakers* who bring the bandages. And, sadly, it is not usually men who fight, but *boys*."

What if Michael had been wearing a uniform in the chip shop, the way Brenda's dad had been when he'd met her mum way back? Michael holding a rifle, likely upside down, cheeks flaring pink in confusion. He didn't seem the army type, did he? Not one of the ones who'd be strutting about with bravado in the muck of a training field for the manly love of it. But what did Brenda know about who Michael was?

Next to her, Jenny was leaning forward, hair falling like gold blinds to hide her face. Brenda saw that she was crying only because tears splashed onto Jenny's hands, lying flat on the scarred wood of the desktop. Brenda scrabbled to find a tissue in her bag, feeling a hot drip on her finger in the half second it took to pass the tissue over. Here she'd been, wittering on about far-fetched maybes while Jenny sat beside her with the real thing happening, her very own boyfriend being pelted by bullets or blasted with chemicals, and for what?

Jenny squeezed the tissue into a ball but didn't lift it to her eyes.

"Do you want to leave?" Brenda whispered. Jenny shook her head but then nodded, strands of hair shimmering.

"Leonard," said Brenda. "Jenny's unwell. May I take her to Matron?"

"What was *that* about?" Penelope asked later, on the way to maths. "Did she get the curse or something?"

"It was all the blather about war," said Brenda. "Made her feel dead sad about her boyfriend."

"Do you think he's real? Jenny's boyfriend?"

"Of course he's real!" An otherwise hadn't occurred to Brenda.

"She says so," said Penelope. "But she doesn't seem . . . I dunno . . . ex*peri*enced."

"Speaking of which." Who better to ask? "Could you give me some advice . . . ?"

What should Brenda wear? She'd not be home before the appointed hour, but she couldn't be seen in this rubbishy pleated school skirt. She'd have to nick something from Kath's closet while minding the little boys. That brought her to the next horror. Kath had a date. Brenda had no way to tell Michael she'd be late, never thought to ask for a telephone number. Not that she could ring his house! But waiting for Kath to stumble home . . . what if Michael got ticked off and was long gone?

Brenda prayed to a rarely glimpsed God that her sister might work out a fair trade on time for romantic interludes that evening, but Kath was in a temper, what else was new?

"Give me a break this once, Bren, with no cheek, right? How often do I get out with a fella, after all? I'll be back by bedtime."

Whose bedtime? But Kath was gone.

Brenda made fish sticks for their tea, with fat dollops of tartar sauce, carrot pennies, and a bag of crisps divided between them, exactly the same number each and the broken bits for Brenda. "That's the chips part of fish-and-chips," she said. "Crisps are called *chips* in America. There's a girl at my school from a place called Philadelphia." Full-of-filthia, Christopher turned that into, thinking himself very clever.

She sat them down to watch *Doctor Who*, even if it baffled them. She needed time to devise a plan while she nicked something to wear. Lucky that Kath was doughier than Brenda, what with two babies, so the jeans fit fine. And she found a burgundy top with a scoop neck and pretty buttons, not too snug. Shoes, though, *ugh*. Her trainers were dead tatty. Her sister's new lace-up high-heel boots sat on the closet floor. Kath's feet were a size bigger than Brenda's, easily fixed with an extra pair of socks.

"You look fancy," said Christopher, when Brenda interrupted telly time.

"Eye shadow," said Brenda.

"You look tall," said Jerry.

"Lip gloss." She got them started with pyjamas. "We're having a treat, you two, what's called a Jammie Walk. Only it's a secret. Once you've got these on, we'll do shoes and jackets. Top-secret Jammie Walk outside, even though it's nearly night. Oh, and hats. Hats are good for hiding."

Worked like a charm and she hadn't needed the marshmallow tactic. Mouldering in Kath's kitchen cupboard was half a packet of stale marshmallows, which Brenda stuck in her bag for later. They'd have to go the long way round, avoiding Bigelow's and the Red Lion on the high street, but no matter. Her trusty boys were ready for adventure.

Brenda's saunter was a bit uneasy in Kath's boots but she trundled on. What was a blister, compared with a *boy*? She spotted Michael on the bench as they turned the corner.

Brenda crouched down for a whispered conference. "See that boy? Looks ordinary, right? He's got one of the best disguises I've ever seen. In real life, he is the Mastermind of Magic. A very dangerous wizard, unless approached with care."

Jerry slid an arm around her thigh, and Christopher edged closer.

"I'm going over there to trick him into giving me the code," said Brenda. "And I'm trusting you to keep watch." She pointed to the library steps. "Up there. Do *not* be seen. Are you brave enough?"

They checked with each other and nodded at her. She

tucked a marshmallow into each little hand and nudged them onward.

"Auntie Bren?" said Christopher, very intent. "The code for what?"

The code for what? Michael had noticed them and raised a hand. "The code for making your mother happy," she said. "Now, scoot. I have to perform my mission. Do not come near us unless one of you is bleeding."

Michael grinned when she sat down. "Your kids?" he said. "Secret life?"

She laughed. "My sister's," she said. "Last-minute emergency."

"Do you need . . . Should we make it another time?"

"No, it's fine. They'll be fine for a bit."

They looked over at the steps, saw the boys settle into spy positions. She glanced at him and away. *Now* it was awkward. Exactly as she'd dreaded.

"Listen," he said. "I just . . . when we met at the chip shop . . . I thought, you know . . ."

Boys could talk for ages and say nothing, Penelope had coached. *"Don't wait for him. Boys are sissy. You make the move."* Pen would have had the kissing under way by now.

Lights on the high street gleamed in the dusk. The chip shop was doing a bang-up business, nobody noticing two people on a bench. Brenda closed her eyes and leaned forward. In less than a second, his mouth met hers. It worked! This was . . . smashing! She was getting off with a boy who had hair on his face! Her thighs went warm with the thrill of it. Wait till she told Penelope!

"Auntie Bren?" Christopher jiggled and waved like a demon puppet at the end of the bench. Michael twisted around to look, covering his crotch with his hands.

"Christopher! Sorry, gosh." Brenda jumped up. "Sorry, Michael. Duty calls, be right back." She whisked the boy up into her arms, trotting away from the bench. How much had he seen?

"Don't wobble me," he said. "I have to wee."

"Wee in the garden." She pointed to the scrap of earth next to the library steps. "It'll keep the villains away, if you do that."

She helped him tug down his pyjamas and assured him that yeah, showing a bare bum outside was odder than seeing a frog in britches, but if you had to wee . . .

"Did you get the code yet?" he asked. She tucked his little thing back in, got him set.

"Not yet," said Brenda. "Did you see I was trying?"

"Yeah," said Christopher. "Inside his mouth?"

"Yes," said Brenda. "Not much longer, I promise. Here." She put two more marshmallows into his hand. "Now go on back and look after your brother."

"I told them you're a wizard," said Brenda. It didn't seem right to dive straight back into kissing without a bit of chat first.

"I used to know some card tricks," said Michael.

"I hope proof won't be necessary," said Brenda. They had a laugh and he put his arm around her. That was nice, cozy, like they were friends already.

"Christopher is my middle name," he said. His other

hand was fiddling with her top, trying to slip his fingers under. She shifted a bit. He didn't seem to know exactly what he was groping for.

"Michael Christopher Stern. What's yours?"

"Oh!"

"Did something bite you?"

She could hear Hairy Mary's voice. *Dr. Sterrrn is running behind schedule.*

"No, sorry, I . . . maybe a fingernail . . ." She shuddered, without meaning to. Michael Stern, the doctor's son.

"It's awful," she said. "My middle name, I mean. I'm named for my dad's nan. Brenda Winifred Parson. Dad says we must have had a vicar for an ancestor, that's why *Parson*. Like *parsonage*, you know?" She was blathering, willing him to give up on the untucking activity. Should she tell him? *Your dad has seen me with my top off.* How would that go over as a first-date conversation? Brenda was never so happy to hear little boys giggling. Both of them this time, standing right there.

"We saw our mum," said Jerry. "I saw her first."

Brenda cranked her head around, and Michael's hands fell away.

"In a car." Christopher gestured vaguely down the road, to where lights twinkled in a row of houses. No car in sight.

"Can we have more marsheymals?" said Jerry.

"Was it really your mum?" *Let it be a mistake.*

"Mumm*eee*!" Jerry raced past Brenda toward, yes, his mother, striding across the library lawn with a thundering glare.

"She's going to wig out," said Brenda. "You've got to go."

"But I—"

"Go. I mean it."

Michael slipped around the corner of the library building. In the half second before Kath arrived and was slapping her face, Brenda wondered if he'd ever speak to her again.

"I saw you up here and thought I'd gone bonkers," said Kath. "Why would the boys be running around at night in their pyjamas?"

Brenda held a cold hand to her flaming cheek.

"Oh, because I left them in the care of a selfish, skanky slag, that's why!" Kath raised her hand again, well practised in using it, but Brenda ducked. "A slag who steals my bleeding clothes the moment she's alone in my closet!"

Christopher started to cry. "Is something wrong with you?" Kath gave him a shake. He shook his head and shivered.

"No thanks to your *minder*." Kath put her face close to Brenda's. "What were you *doing*, anyway? On a *bench*? With a randy flipping schoolboy?" She jerked her head at her sons. "How do you think I got these?"

As if Kath were anyone to listen to. A kiss and a cuddle wasn't the same as having it off, being stuck with a kid for all time. Jerry was the sweetest thing on earth, but Lord, no thank you.

"I'd smack you back," said Brenda. "Don't think I wouldn't. But it's not right. Your kids—"

"Oh, preach away, you righteous cow. Would you know the *right* thing if it conked you on the head? Keep this nonsense up and you'll be sitting next to me down the launderette wondering what hit you."

"That is the *last* place you'll find me! I'm taking A-level exams next year! Ever heard of those?"

Kath took a deep shaky breath. Brenda's point had landed like a dart.

"Right, then." Half Kath's wind power was gone. "You just remember. You're the one chance our family's got. The best thing our dad ever did was sign you up when Ill Hall offered scholarships for locals. You could be a nurse. Or a teacher. Move out of the council flats. Buy a car someday! So don't go wasting time with schoolboys on benches, you hear me?"

Brenda heard. She gazed into the darkened bushes that flanked the library building. Had Michael raced obediently off? Or was he hiding, hearing Kath too?

"You could actually *be* something. More than bleeding rubbish."

"That's the nicest thing you've ever said to me."

"And I want those boots back, you thieving cow." Kath put a hand on each boy's head, steering them into the evening gloom.

Christopher tugged free after a few steps and ran back.

He leaned against Brenda with all the force a six-year-old could muster, giving her middle a squeeze with skinny arms. She hugged him before nudging him off to join his mum. She wouldn't follow just yet. Let Kath get the boys to bed before Brenda crept in to fetch her shoes. She'd wait on the bench, let the wobbles subside.

"Brenda?" Michael loomed out of the shadows.

Ouch. He'd heard.

"Better than a radio play." He took the spot next to her. "Not meaning to make light. That was harsh, no question."

"Not quite what you want a new boy to hear. Family secrets."

"You held your own." He tapped her hand.

"The awful thing," said Brenda, "is that it's no different from any other day." Try coming up with an answer to that. Her ugliest colours on display.

"Not to sound daft, but I sometimes wish my parents would have a proper go at each other. Better than chilly quiet, where you can practically hear the scuttle of black beetles."

Brenda laughed. He was dead nice, this boy.

"We've got the whole hornet's nest," she said. "Buzzing like hell on the high street."

Did Michael's mother guess anything off about her husband? That'd be a mighty big black beetle to swallow.

"Let's go for a walk." Brenda reached for his hand. "Leave the insect world behind."

oona

Dearest friend-of-all-friends, my darling Sarah,

Oh, the woe in starting term without you! I'm in Brontë
dorm with Caroline, Esther Madwoman McKay, and Sally,
Tamsin, and Fiona from the fourth form, and a couple of
other nobodies. Tamsin smuggled back a pineapple from
Mauritius, which we ate last night after Lights-Out and I
have never tasted anything so divine. Penelope and Kirsten
are in Austen, of course, and they've got the new American
girl (sent from Philadelphia to represent North America in
place of you, but of course no one could replace you). Her
name is Jenny and she happens to have the most perfect
skin I've ever seen along with sort of golden hazel eyes
and terrible clothes. She clearly had the wrong idea about

Illington because she packed nothing other than dire school uniforms, which, needless to say, are rather useless here. She went to work with the scissors and now has a wardrobe consisting entirely of tatters, as if she inhabits a schoolgirl horror movie.

What was looming in my last letter is now distant past. Yes, I went to the Algarve in Portugal with my parents and my foul sisters for the final week of holiday. It was a très posh resort but deadly dull except for one small interlude on the last night, with a boy named Alexandre—that dre, not der, to indicate there was an ACCENT involved—but of course my brat sister Lizzie squealed on us before we'd even opened the nicked bottle of vodka, so that was that.

*But here I am, chattering on, and what you're really waiting for is . . . drumroll . . . **The Nico Report.***

Has he written to you himself? Has he rung you?? Whatever your answer to those salient questions, surely you will be riveted by an objective opinion. . . .

He arrived back from holiday with his mother in Italy— very tan, longer hair, possibly even taller and more handsome. Yes, you should be squirming. I'd send you a photograph but that would involve me taking one, which would mean approaching him, and as I am a mere mortal and he is a god, this is not a possibility. He spends all his time in the sixth form common room, which of course I am not permitted to enter unless invited by a sixth-former and that has not happened. His mates are still the rat-nosed Adrian and poor spotty No-Face (ticket to aforementioned common room). No-Face is so distinctly unmemorable, physically and personality-

wise, that I suspect Nico of selecting him as a friend for the sole purpose of highlighting his own particular gifts. Percy the brown toad also lurks about in their company but that may be a hallucination. The detail you have been waiting for? NO FEMALE COMPANION . . . as yet. Needless to say, there is plenty of competition for that position. You would be ready to decapitate Penelope, for instance, whose tops get smaller and smaller as she masquerades as a Love Child. Despite her soldier beau, the new girl, Jenny, asked me specifically on the way to Sunday meeting when Nico was walking ahead of us with his trusty sidekicks, Is the tall hot one attached? *Rest assured that I quickly informed her of his status as my best friend's boyfriend, and insisted that he is no doubt still mourning your departure.*

Will let you know when his tan fades.

Meanwhile, I must leave you for a while to turn my attention to the question of British Constitution and the fascinating question What is the role of the House of Lords? *Thank your Canadian soul that such matters no longer engage you.*

What's going on in Toronto? How was the reunion with your old sweetheart, Tony? Rawther short next to his English competition? Tell me all. Write back, you slag, or I will tie your knickers in a knot around your kneck. . . .

> *From the incomparable Oona-licious*
> *xxooxxoo*

*   *   *

Oops, just found this in my binder.

Will now continue . . .

Your (first? of many?) letter has finally arrived from Toronto, apparently overland via the Arctic Circle, considering how long it took to get here. Life is barren without you. But there are a few little scraps of gossip to pass along. . . .

Remember Jasper, the English master? He has become a total psuede, growing a straggly little goatee. Penelope had a blazing row with Adrian in the middle of tea and threw a cup at him. Esther supposedly got lost on the moors during half-day last Wednesday and wangled a lift home with a shepherd. Caroline was FINALLY blessed with her period. Percy continues his efforts to appear mysterious by scribbling away in his journal. Luke is as delicious and as cold as ever.

Food is still inedible. Speaking of which . . . must go scrounge some coffee from somewhere . . . Will I approach Nico the Great to borrow sugar? Stay tuned. . . .

Back. No coffee. Got sidetracked witnessing a morbidly embarrassing incident. A crowd of boys in the courtyard were teasing your beloved Nico *because apparently there was a review on the BBC at the weekend about his mother's most recent book and then some panel discussion about some of the more lurid scenes. Out of nowhere, Percy pipes up and says, "Yeah, I get what you mean about seeing your own mum through other people's eyes. My dad's a bit famous too."*

"Who's your dad?" asks Nico. Percy flushes seven shades of crimson and mumbles, "Mick Malloy."

So Adrian quacks out a nasty laugh. "*Dangerous stuff you're sniffing, mate. Mick Malloy is, like, thirty-two years old! And famous!*"

"He *is* pretty young," Percy says, not backing down, but looking as if he'd welcome the flagstones parting for his exit through to the centre of the earth. What a daft delusion! No one knew what to say.

LATER . . .

Last night was the Autumn Follies, aka the night where we are herded into the theatre to stand around listening to somebody's idea of young people's music while streamers dangle from the ceiling and the lights flicker from behind red and amber gels. I think five people danced: Billings, by himself, Susan Splat and the other weirdo in second form, and, of course, the exhibitionist Penelope with her current drooling sex toy, Adrian.

Attendance was mandatory. Anyone with a grain of self-respect headed to the top of the theatre seats and crouched as far into the shadows as possible to avoid the notice of the staff. Thus I found myself next to His Royal Highness, Nico.

After some wry witticisms, we strayed over to the topic that most consumes us both.

YOU.

"Have you heard from her?" he said.

"Only once! Today! How about you?"

"She's written a few letters."

"And have you answered?"

"I will."

You can put aside your worries right now because it would be hard to call a winner in the Who Misses Sarah Most Sweepstakes. I believe I still have a slight edge.

There goes the bell for tea. Fried Spam today.

That's all for now my dearest one,

Oona Ultimata

film titles

THE TERRIBLE SECRET HISTORY OF ILLINGTON HALL
by Percy Graham

HOW THE COOK KILLED THEM ALL
by Percy Malloy

CANNON FODDER
by Percy Graham Malloy

NEW-GIRL FIXATION
by Percy Graham

VISITING DAY MASSACRE
by P. G. Malloy

WHAT WE HIDE
by Percy Graham

penelope

Worst weekend ever.

It started out worst for different reasons from why it ended up worst, but it basically sucked eggs. Happened like this . . .

I'm down the Cellar with Adrian, Henry, Oona, a couple of other nobodies. Adrian and me, we both came to Illington on the same day when we were eleven. We've been friends, we've been enemies, we've had a few snog-fests, and we've gone weeks without speaking. He even knows bits about my family, which is saying a lot.

The Cellar, which in the olden days was the wine cave for this big old manor house, is for fifth form and up, to smoke and get away from the prats in lower forms. It's nearly pitch dark, so there's plenty beside smoking going on.

Oona has got the silliest jeans, her pride and joy. They've

got a Velcro fly, swear to god, meaning it's public knowledge every time she performs any fly-opening activity. We're down there, and I'm snogging with Adrian, since no one better is offering. Oona is tucked into a corner with Henry. Suddenly there's this ripping noise and it's Henry getting his hands into Oona's knickers.

Adrian stops the kiss and says, "What the hell?"

I laugh. "You've never met Oona's jeans? Oy, Henry! Having fun over there?"

"Piss off," mumbles Oona. Henry is huffing and scrumbling about like a great bear.

"Possibly you should take this somewhere else," I say. "The sound effects are a little much."

"Possibly you should get busy on your own side of the room," says Oona. "That being what you're good at."

"Piss off." Where does Velcro Access get the nerve to make comments to *me*?

"*You* piss off."

"Can we get back to it?" Henry grumbles.

"Penelope." Adrian slips a hand under my top.

"Not in the mood now." I pull his paw off my tit.

"Oh come on," he says. "I'm . . . you know . . ." He rams my hand on his stiffy.

"Too bad." I stand up, out of reach. "That slag is pissing me off."

"Tease," says Adrian.

"Slag?" says Oona. "That's a laugh, coming from you."

"The air in this cellar is making me sick," I say.

"You *are* sick, full stop," says Oona.

71

"Ha," I say. "And you've got a total genital fixation, with a side order of narcissism."

Oona is quiet for a moment while she tries to figure out what I said.

"You're an authority?" says Adrian. "Because your mother's in the nuthouse?"

That was low, very low. I shove his face into the smelly purple corduroy sofa cushion.

"Wait," Oona pipes up. "Your mother's in the nuthouse?"

"No surprise," says Henry. "Oona, can we get back to business?"

I'm boiling. I burst out of the Cellar and up the stairs. I punch the wall along the kitchen corridor maybe twenty times, scaring the crap out of Vera, the cook. I get to the Girls' Changing Room, sag onto a bench, and start to boohoohoo.

That's when Kirsten comes along. Kirsten has never seen me cry, so she's a tad surprised. I've never seen her cry either and if that day ever comes I'll be gobsmacked. What would she have to cry about? She's the coolest girl in school. The only thing wrong with her is that sometimes she knows it. I tell her I had a row with Adrian, but I don't mention the nuthouse. I want to *kill* Adrian.

"Why don't you come home with me tomorrow?" says Kurse. "My mum's coming to fetch us. She'll be thrilled to have an extra, she's always going on about meeting my mates. It's my birthday Saturday. Perfect timing."

Get away from this dump for a couple of nights? Eat some decent food?

"That'd be so nice, Kurse. Ta."

"I'll go ring her now, shall I?"

"Your brother won't mind, will he?"

She laughs. "Luke won't even notice."

Their mum, Ann, picks us up Friday after lessons. She's got a Range Rover that's a few years old but still a bloody nice car. Luke dives into the back, clutching a tattered copy of *Prince Caspian* and the bag of crisps his mum hands over. I'm beside him, bunching my knees behind the driver's seat. Kirsten sits up front with her mum, rolling her eyes at me, you know, gotta-keep-the-old-cow-company kind of thing. She's a lovely mum, though, not a cow. Her hair is kind of ruffled-Twiggy, only grey. Makeup is Mary Quant—dark liner, smoky lids—and you can see she shops at Biba, not Marks and Spencer. But she doesn't push it by trying to be cool.

"Thought I'd come before tea," she says. "Give you one extra plate of edible food."

"What are we having?" asks Kirsten.

"Whatever you like. Tomorrow's the birthday, so you'll get the menu you ordered, but tonight you can each vote."

"Fish-and-chips," says Luke.

"Pizza." Kirsten, one second behind.

"Up to you, then." Ann looks at me in the mirror.

"No fair," I say.

"That means she wants fish-and-chips," says Luke. "Otherwise she'd just say pizza with Kirsten."

73

"Aren't you clever," says Ann. "Fish-and-chips, then."

Kirsten sticks out her tongue at me, but she's only fooling.

The house is massive compared with mine. Kirsten gives me a tour while Luke goes to the chip shop. The kids have the upper floor all for themselves—a huge room each with slanted ceilings because it used to be the attic. They've got their own loo and shower up there too, only Kirsten says she uses her mother's bath because Luke is a nasty-hairy-smelly member of the male species. "Doesn't the phrase *hair follicle* just make you cringe?"

The parents have got a suite on the ground level, the bathroom and this other room that's called a closet, but some gizmo on the door lights it up when you walk in. It's the size of my bedroom at home, with just clothes in it. One side is for their dad's suits, with stacks of shirts all folded on shelves like in a department store. The other, messier side is Ann's stuff, mostly black. There's the faintest perfume, like *"Hey, remember last night? Remember the moon and the silvery stars?"* I know it sounds queer, but I'm almost not breathing in there, looking at the row of polished shoes on a tilted rack for easy viewing.

"Where's your dad?" I say.

"Dunno," says Kirsten. "He'll be here tomorrow, though, for my birthday. He shags off all the time, working or who knows, but he's good about birthdays."

"I . . . I just realized . . ." We leave the closet and the light goes out. "I don't have a present for you."

Kirsten laughs. "Please! It's just great that you're here." Perfect answer, as usual.

Ann's made a table cover out of newspaper and we dump all the chips and all the fish into a huge steaming mountain in the middle.

"Medieval," says Luke. We sprinkle on vinegar and salt, with mounds of ketchup dotting the foothills. We use the wooden spears from the chip shop.

"Good thing you got a big order," says Ann. "You're eating like it's the first food you've seen this month."

"It is," says Kirsten, blowing on a lump of cod. Ann peels off the crispy parts and just eats the fish inside. "You really wouldn't believe school food, Mum. You think we're joking."

"We're not joking," Luke and I say together. We laugh and tap spears. It's so bloody jolly I almost can't stand it.

"Where does your family live, Penelope?" says Ann.

"Bradford." I eat a chip. "A mum, a stepdad, an old cat, and no sibs. Unless you count Barney, who's the son of my stepdad. I'm not lucky that way, like Kurse and Luke."

"I wish you wouldn't call her Curse," says Ann.

"Your fault, Mum," says Kirsten. "You picked a name with no short form."

"Plus," says Luke, "it suits her." Kirsten rolls her eyes.

"Great name for a skinhead rocker," I say.

"But she is not a skinhead rocker," says Ann.

"Yet," says Kirsten.

I'd expected the kitchen to be all shiny, like in a magazine, but it's the opposite and even better. The cupboard doors are glass, with stacks of pretty plates and cups peeking through. There's an armchair in a nook by the window, covered in faded sunflower fabric, with a book open on

75

the seat. The table was probably built by peasants in the twelfth century, and the cooker is one of those huge black things that you can practically drive. The floor is painted a glowing red, the colour of apple skins in an advertisement. It's all so bleeding *pleasant* that I'm dying to steal their vodka or take off my shirt, just to shake it up a bit.

After the newspapers get bundled and stashed in the bin, Ann puts the kettle on. "Fish-and-chips is the best," she says. "No washing up after."

"What's for dessert?" asks Luke.

"Ice cream," says Ann. "With chocolate syrup to pour over." She puts out these crystal cup things that she claims are especially for sundaes.

"I bought them in New York last year," she says. "Aren't they so American?"

"Were you there on holiday? Did you go too?" I ask Kirsten.

"My parents went without us," she says. "Romantic getaway or some rubbish. They brought good presents, though."

There are three flavours to choose from. I have coffee, Kurse has chocolate, Luke has both, and Ann has none. We pour on fudge sauce, slurp it up.

I run my finger around the inside of the scalloped rim, because Luke is doing it too. I get every last smear before I stand up to clear. I cradle the crystal cup for one second and then purposely drop it. The floor is wood, so the glass doesn't shatter, but it bounces and cracks, a couple of chips flying off. Good sound effect. Ann stares, first down at the glass and then at me. I smack my hands to my mouth. "Oh-my-god-I'm-so-sorry-I-can't-believe-I-just-did-that-oh-my-god-I'm-so-sorry."

"That's okay," says Ann. She folds her napkin.

Kirsten's got a telly in her room, so we watch for a bit and then natter and then go to sleep like two teddy bears on a great big pillow.

"Ohhh, best part of being home," says Kirsten, when we wake up. "No bell for breakfast. Missing Saturday classes. No freezing floor between us and the toilet."

"No squishy Susan masturbating," I say.

"No Oona rattling on about Nico."

"No spongy eggs waiting in a tub on the table."

"I heard you talking," says Ann, coming in. "Breakfast in bed?"

"Yes, please!" I say, just as Kurse says, "No, we'll come down, Mum."

"Which?" says Ann.

"I hate bacon in my bed," says Kirsten.

"Right, then, how about I bring just tea and you come downstairs for food?"

"Ohmygod, Kurse, you have the nicest mother." I burrow into my warm tunnel of duvet. "I feel like a princess. And it's not even my birthday." I punch Kirsten's shoulder.

"Owww!"

"That's one," I say. "Fifteen more for sweet sixteen."

She flips over. "Don't you dare!"

"Not telling you when, though. I'll get you as the day wears on."

"I love being home for my birthday," she says.

"I'm always home for birthdays," I say. "August fourth. I'd rather be at school."

"It can't be that bad."

"You have no idea." She has no idea.

Fourteenth Birthday, by Penelope Fforde

Wake up on school time even without bells.

Go to the loo. Flush toilet before use. Flush toilet after use.

Listen to snoring in parents' room.

Go to living room, see useless oaf Barney on sofa, too lazy to go four steps to his bed at three in the morning.

Look in refrigerator, note emptiness on both sides of milk bottle.

Think, Hmmm, maybe they're planning a smash-up surprise party for later.

Right.

Pull out milk. Find a bowl. Grab CocoNuts.

Fill bowl, pour on milk, push Silky off chair, sit at table, take a spoonful.

Scream. Milk's gone off.

Dump cereal in bin. Kick chair.

Feed Silky.

Get dressed, white shorts and blue cami.

Lie on bed listening to Procol Harum, "A Whiter Shade of Pale." Wait for thumps telling me to turn down the record.

Thumps. Turn down record.

Put on trainers. Comb hair. Pause to notice hair as one blessing in life.

Enter Mum.

Hallo, sweetheart, happy birthday. Did you make a cuppa? Milk's off.

Oh dear. Would you mind going down to the shop? Dave'll be in a mood if there's no milk.

And we're off to a roaring start. . . .

I didn't have my fifteenth birthday at home. Mum was in the bin by then. I lasted three days last summer, alone with Dave and Barney (the Oaf), before I hitched a lift back up here and worked for Mr. Danforth on the farm one over from school. Prime bleeding stall-mucker I turned out to be. August fourth came and went.

Kirsten's family has endless birthday traditions.

"We're going to the seaside," she says.

"You're joking," I say. It's nearly October, for Chrissake. But after breakfast we bundle into the car and toddle off to Scarborough, to the boardwalk.

Jolly jolly jolly, is the theme of the day. Most of the shops along the beach have their shutters shut, but Luke brought a jolly ball that we kick around till his foot goes through it. We paddle, screaming, in the icy swirls that swamp our jolly bare feet. I give Kirsten nine more jolly birthday punches. Luke likes this activity and starts his own series, so she's getting it now from both sides. We eat jolly wieners on sticks and have jolly lemonades.

Home again, home again, jiggety jig. Luke zizzes next to

me in the backseat and I wish I could too, but that seems a bit rude.

"When is Dad getting here?" Kirsten wants to know.

"In time for supper."

"When's supper?" asks Kirsten.

Ann laughs and gives Kirsten a jolly swat with her scarf. We stop at a shop partway home called Top Drawer.

"I'll wait in the car," says Luke. "I know you're getting nasties."

Ann buys Kirsten a purple bra and some tights. She buys us both saucy knickers with lace bits.

"You don't have to," I say, but honestly they're dead nice and I'm touched. By the time we get back, it's nearly evening.

"Good birthday, eh?" says Kirsten.

I punch her and pretend it was mine too.

"He's here!" calls Ann.

"Dad!" Kirsten's down the stairs in a flash and Luke lopes along behind. I give them time for the mushy part and show up as Ann's pouring drinks.

"Hallo, I'm Geoffrey," he says. He's sort of an old Sean Connery type.

"Penelope." I shake his offered hand, as if I'm a new business associate.

"Ah yes," he says. "You're the one who draws so nicely. Didn't you do a portrait of Kirsten for last year's exhibit?"

I'm impressed that he remembers.

Kirsten's menu is duck breast—*duck* breast!—and something called risotto, which looks like rice pudding but

80

tastes cheesy and divine. Also salad with loads of cress, and a huge cake shaped like a tortoise, which is some kind of family joke. The inside is marbled and the outside has got thin chocolate wafers stuck on, to look like the shell. Ann made it herself, a flipping masterpiece.

I do the dishes with Luke, Ann being the cook, Kirsten being the birthday girl, and Geoffrey being the dad. No dad I ever met does dishes. No brother I ever met does dishes either, but Barney the Oaf is likely not a fair example. Or, maybe it's Luke who's weird.

We're back in Kirsten's room when we hear the unmistakable sound of pissed-off parents having a row downstairs, not quite shouting. Her dad is leaving, going back to the office apparently.

"What's up?" I say.

"Mum gets fed up with him working all the time, that's all."

"Like now, on a Saturday night?"

"Yeah." She seems not bothered.

Kirsten goes to sleep with her face on this old stuffed dog, grey with years. It's sweet she still has him on her bed, and sweet that she leaves him here, since we'd tease the crap out of her if she brought him to school. Little Woofy is too precious for that, with his tufts and straining-apart stitches.

It's warm in the bed, but I can hear Luke still twiddling about in his room, so I pull on socks and a flannel shirt of Kirsten's over my knickers, but making sure tits and legs are still on view. I go in to see if he nibbles.

He's at the desk, hunched over a notebook, drawing skeletons with all the parts labeled.

"Luke." I stand in the doorway. "Knock knock."

"Uh-huh." His eyes flit over my legs and he flushes, but he just hunches further over. "I'm doing bio."

I sit on the bed. His duvet cover is diamonds like Kirsten's, only navy.

"Kirby is such a wanker." Wrong thing to say, I guess, from the look on Luke's face. "I mean, isn't he?"

"Yeah, but . . ." Luke's Biro does this jiggly thing against the page. "You can't blame a teacher for the existence of biology."

He's a nerd in disguise, I should have known. Perfect like his sister. "I like skeletons," he says. "I like the shape of bones."

"Huh." I wrap the shirt around me better, might as well, since it's bloody freezing and he's clearly not getting heated. I sit there for a sec and he looks at me sideways.

"Anyway," I say, getting up. "Can't sleep, that's all."

"You don't have to go," he says, but he's lying. The desk lamp lights his shaggy hair. From behind he's got this glowing halo.

"Anyway," I say. "See you in the morning."

"Sleep tight," he says, like he's a bleeding mother or something.

"Yeah." Sheesh. That was illuminating.

Kirsten's got this old-fashioned seat-thing built under the window, with a nice cushion and a couple of woolly jumpers I can wrap around my legs. I sit looking out at the street where a faint drizzle is falling.

*   *   *

The last time I saw my mother, she was sitting by the window in the "common room" at St. Dymphna's Refuge. St. Dymphna was some teen virgin whose father slashed her head off while she was defending her purity. Somehow this qualifies her to be patron saint of nervous afflictions. That's what my mother is, nervously afflicted. *Seriously* nervously afflicted.

But she's calm there, she likes it. I used to think I'd driven her crazy somehow, and then I was bloody positive it was all Dave's fault. At St. Dymphna's they asked us to meet with a counsellor, but Dave never showed. They tried to make me believe that blame is dumb.

The Day My Mother Cracked Her Nut, by Penelope Fforde
   Wake up on school time even without bells.
   Go to the loo. Flush toilet before use. Flush toilet after use.
   Listen to snoring in parents' room.
   Go to living room, find Mum lying there as if she'd just tipped over to one side, hands folded in lap, eyes wide open.
   Lights on, nobody home. I suddenly get what that means.
   Silky's paw goes tap tap tap tap on Mum's wrist.
   She looks dead, and I sway. I kneel beside her, whisper, Mum? soft as a paw. She doesn't blink or twitch or swallow.
   Dave lumbers in, hair flat on one side, sticking up like autumn grass on the other.
   Jesus H. Christ, is she dead?
   Because my hand is on her arm, I feel what is not visible,

a slight but certain clenching of her entire nervous system at the sound of his voice.

Or was that me?

What comes next has more than one part. The crazed-Dave part where he shouts two inches from her face. The scared-me part where I cry. The scared-Dave part where he calls an ambulance. The brave-me part where I climb in next to her and stick around for all the rest of it. The wank-Dave part where he never goes to see her again. Where he pretends she died.

I hear Luke go to the loo, see the patch of hall carpet go dark when his light goes off. Unbelievably, I'm hungry again. There's definitely cake left, or a slice of duck. Maybe they've got a bag of crisps in a cupboard. I move carefully in the dark, not wanting to kick anything and wake the whole bloody house. Socks are good for silent shuffling. I slide my toe over the edge of each stair on the way down, so when I hit the ground I won't do that idiot lurch-thing and go flying. I pause at the bottom remembering which way to the kitchen. Along the hall past the row of happy family photos, edging through the dining room, so's not to smash my hip on some antique chair or topple some treasure. I slide my hand over the wall, find the switch, and—*bam!*—the light snaps on. Holy crap.

Ann is at the table hunched over the leftover cake, using a spoon to cram cake into her mouth. Frosting is smeared on her lips and crumbs are spraying everywhere. She's making a ravenous smacking sound. Her nightie is hitched up, so there's this white thigh as part of the picture. Her eyes bug out when she sees me, and she sort of spits cake onto what an hour ago was a warm, rosy floor. All this in a hideous half second before I jam off the light and turn to run. I hear a nasty gurgling, but I'm not waiting around. Kirsten's mother has been devoured by a scarygreedy-goblin version of herself.

I skid toward the stairs, knee crunching into the railing—*ow!*—tear upstairs, career into the bedroom, and dive onto the bed, sure my frantic heart will crack a rib. Kirsten jolts up like I'm a nightmare. "What the *hell?*"

"Oh, sorry. Sorry." What do I say to Kirsten? Does she have a clue that she is the spawn of a lunatic binge eater? Oh, crappity crap crap.

Clock on Kirsten's nightstand says 3:17, that's A-bleeding-M.

"What are you doing up?" Her eyes aren't even open.

I could tell her. I could smash another cup on the floor under her feet.

"I saw something."

She pulls a pillow over her head. "Tomorrow," comes muffling out.

Well, sure. You deserve one more night of sleep. Since you've just joined the nut club and need to rest up for a life of denial.

I stick my head back into the hallway. Ann must have run for cover. The quiet is practically crackling with *ominous*. Now what? Climb into bed and pretend it never happened? *"G'morning, Ann! Yeah, ta, slept fine. Lovely to have a weekend away from the dorm. . . ."*

Obviously time to leave.

Kirsten's rucksack is on her desk, full of homework. I rip a corner from a page in her notebook, slow, quiet rip. I use her eyeliner: *Had to go. See you at school. Ta.* I put it on the toilet seat with a toothbrush lying on top so there's no way she'll miss it.

I leave the door unlocked, because how am I going to lock it behind me? It's dark outside, but no psycho lurking in the bushes can be as creepy as the one in the kitchen. Why did it take me so long to notice something wrong?

And haven't I sworn not to hitchhike again? But here I am at three-thirty in the bloody morning ambling along the motorway praying for a lorry. Instead there's an angel on earth, shaped like a podgy woman named Jean who's coming back from looking after her sick old mum. She's grateful to have someone keep her awake for a couple of hours, because she has the morning shift at a grocery market.

"I don't have kids," she tells me. Then there's this minute of dead quiet, like she's inhaling a cigarette, except she's not smoking. This stretch of road is dark, and her face is lit by the dashboard, aglow with spots of red and green.

"I never even had sex," she says. "And look at me. Now it'll never happen."

"Well, I've had enough for both of us," I say. "And maybe your sick old mum as well." I think I might have gone too far but she laughs.

I tell her about tongue-kissing and hand jobs and blow jobs, and then about Kirsten, about *my* sick mum and even about Kirsten's mum's midnight feast.

"That poor, sad woman," says Jean. "We all have our secret sorrows, don't we? She sounds downright miserable."

Jean takes me all the way up the drive and around back into the courtyard. It's just past five. I figure I'll nap in the changing room rather than risk the stairs and Hairy Mary's supersonic hearing.

"Thanks for the lift."

"Well," says Jean, laughing, "you've certainly added to my vocabulary." She does a tidy three-point turn and zooms off.

I see a light in the kitchen. Vera D. is already cooking up today's slops. I tap on the door, making her jump, but then she stirs up cocoa in a pan just for me. I sit on a stool and slice the margarine, carving wedges off a great block and dropping them onto plates for the breakfast tables.

Sunday afternoon, Kirsten comes blowing into the dorm like a wind off the moors. She pulls up short at the vision of me lounging in knickers and tee.

"Whoa," she says. "You're here."

"I said I would be. Didn't you get my note?"

"You scared the crap out of me, Penelope! How the hell did you get back? My mother totally wigged out. Toe. Ta. Lee. I mean it."

I think, *That's an understatement.*

"I better zip down and tell her you're alive." She peels out of the room and I tweak the blanket masquerading as a curtain, enough to see Ann's car parked right below on the front sweep. She's having a chat with Richard, a perfectly normal woman passing the time of day with the head-master. No sign of Luke. He must have hauled himself back to his dorm without lingering, not giving two thoughts to what happened to the enchanting weekend guest.

Just pray Ann is too mortified to mention anything to Richard about me coming back on my own or I'll have quintuple detention for thumbing. Kirsten hops down the front steps and skids to a stop. My efforts to telepathically transmit a psychodrama defence appear to be successful. Richard departs with a wave, mother and daughter spiky heads meet for a moment, Ann glances up but can't possibly see me. And please, never wants to again.

Eventually Kirsten comes back upstairs. "How did you get here?"

"I hitched a ride."

"Can you imagine the *hell* shit my mother would be in if anything had happened?"

"I got picked up by a nice veiny-nosed lady whose mum was dying," I say. "Safe as anywhere on earth."

"Well, I was worried," she mutters. "Selfish cow."

"Hey, sorry," I say. "Really."

Kirsten glares at me. "That was whack, Pen. What happened?"

I find a thread to pull on my blanket.

"You can ditch my family," she says. "But you can't ditch

88

me. We're sisters here in the big happy parcel of kin who inhabit the Jane Austen dormitory."

I smile at her for that.

"I know you," she says. "Something happened."

"Nothing, I swear. Thank you for inviting me, Kurse."

"Did . . . did . . . you try something on with Luke?"

I start laughing so hard I nearly choke, only that reminds me of her mother spluttering cake so I stop.

"Nah," I say. "I think your brother is a bit light on his feet. How could he resist me otherwise?"

I'm making a joke, but Kirsten's eyes go skinny.

So then I know it's true and she knows too.

But she doesn't know everything.

illington vs. zoffton: cannon fodder

AN UNFINISHED SCRIPT
by Percy Graham

OPENING SHOT *is of a television showing the
logo and playing the theme music for the
BBC nightly news, cutting to an anchorman
beginning his report. Behind him are blurred
photos of school buildings as he mentions
them, intercut with shots of worried parents
and teachers.*

                    ANCHORMAN
          Our top story this evening concerns the
          disappearance of schoolboys from several
          educational establishments throughout
          the British Isles. Whole groups of boys
          seem to have evaporated into thin air
          in the past several days. There are now

more than one hundred missing youth between the ages of fourteen and eighteen
and NO trace whatsoever to indicate what
is behind this disturbing epidemic. We
expect to have an update on the morning
broadcast.

In other news . . .

CUT TO:

INT.: KIPLING DORMITORY AT ILLINGTON HALL
SCHOOL

*Six boys lie in their beds. It is an hour
past bedtime and most are asleep, but PERCY
is reading with a flashlight. A blinding
brightness blasts through the window followed
by a glowing gaseous mist that seeps in around
the window frames. PERCY jumps from his bed,
croaking an alarm, but even as his dorm mates
stir, it is too late. The gas overcomes every
boy in the room and one by one they turn to
speckled forms and fade into nothingness.*

CUT TO:

INT.: *undetermined time of day because this is
a planet with two suns. Setting is a military
laboratory on the planet Zoffton. Enormous
picture windows overlook a dense tropical
jungle. In front of the windows are ultra-
techno-telescopes attached to beeping machines
that generate data being transcribed by white-
jacketed clerks and scientists who all have
a third eye planted in the centre of their
foreheads and extralong earlobes.*

One by one, the schoolboys from Kipling dorm rematerialize on a circular platform in the centre of the laboratory. They are bewildered, sleepy, wear various pyjamas or boxer/T-shirt combinations. ADRIAN is naked.

The Zofftonites gather, some with clipboards, some with cameras or other recording devices not known on Earth.

>   ADRIAN
>   What the frick?

>   BOYS
>   (cluster together, facing the
>   alien examiners)
>   Where are we? What's going on? Oh my
>   god! They've got three eyes! etc.

>   PERCY
>   There was a . . . like, a poison gas,
>   it came through the windows, all kind
>   of . . . pink.

>   ADRIAN
>   (glaring at one of the peering
>   Zofftonites)
>   What are you staring at? Never seen such
>   a wondrous member, eh? Takes three eyes
>   to see the whole thing!

>   ZOFFTONITE
>   xxkXX#00)()()xxxch##0))))xx

>   HENRY
>   What's he saying?

ADRIAN steps out threateningly toward Zofftonites. They chatter to each other but are not alarmed. ADRIAN encounters an

*invisible force field and stumbles back. The
boys are prisoners.*

                    ADRIAN
        What do you want?

                    NICO
        What are we here for?

                    NO-FACE
        What are you going to do to us?

*The Zoffton scientists pass smoothly through
the force field and begin to examine the boys,
mumbling in their language, making notes on
electronic devices. Then they leave through
the invisible barrier with no hesitation.*

*A heap of clothing materializes in the centre
of the platform. Basic military uniforms:
green-grey trousers, T-shirt, and pocketed
jacket. A cap for each boy. Boots. Utility
belts. The boys dress.*

*General muttering: What are we doing here? And
where is here?*

*Boys are prodded into a line and herded off
platform through a passage to a weapons room
lined with racks of firearms, knives, and
other unfamiliar but obviously deadly weapons.
There is one Zofftonite at a desk, ready to
assist in their selections.*

                    ADRIAN
        This is more like it!

                    NICO
        You lot made a mistake. We didn't sign
        up for this. . . .

                    PERCY
    We're Quakers.

                    ADRIAN
    They don't bloody care, mate.

                    NO-FACE
    I'm not a Quaker.

*He brushes his fingers over rows of gleaming
weaponry.*

                    ADRIAN
    If you're not, then I'm not.

He also examines weapons more keenly.

                    NICO
    Knockout gas I get. But how were we
    transported?

                    PERCY
    Do they know they've kidnapped Quakers?
    We're not going to pick up weapons!

                    ARMORY ZOFFTONITE
    xx##0))((00#xxx- - #&()(&xx—

                    NICO
    They want us to be soldiers.

                    PERCY
    We don't know how to shoot guns! We
    don't know anything about this! Being in
    a war . . .

                    NICO
    I don't think that matters.

                    NO-FACE
    So we're supposed to choose our weapons?
    We can pick *anything*?

                        94

                    ADRIAN
              (*picking up a machine gun*)
        I'll blow their fecking brains out.

                    HENRY
        If they have brains.

                    PERCY
        They obviously have bigger brains than
        we do.

*ADRIAN and NO-FACE choose weapons. ARMORY
ZOFFTON selects weapons for reluctant boys.
As each is armed, he turns to speckles and
fades out.*

CUT TO:

EXT. THE JUNGLE

*Boys rematerialize in a cluster. They are in
a clearing surrounded by thickly overgrown
trees, vines, massive blossoms, etc.
Persistent bird and animal cries punctuate
scene.*

                    BOYS
        What the hell? Where are we? *etc.*

                    PERCY
        We're in the tropics.

                    NICO
        Hotter than Greece.

                    ADRIAN
        I could use a drink, mate.

                    NO-FACE
        Look in the packs.

                    NICO
        Maybe they've given us water.

They shrug out of packs and take a look. Each
has a canteen. Each opens, takes a swig, spits
violently.

                  NO-FACE
        Tastes like piss!

                  ADRIAN
        It IS!

He upends the canteen and a yellow stream
pours out.

                  HENRY
        Still better than school tea!

A flash of light and an explosion nearby. Boys
jump in panic, throw themselves to the ground
like they've seen in movies.

                   BOYS
        What the HELL? Somebody's shooting at
        us! Oh my god! etc.

Gunfire and explosions continue nearby, coming
closer. Boys grovel on the ground, crawling
for cover amongst the roots and blossoms.

                  PERCY
        Wait! Look! They're—points up to where
        military lab windows are glinting in
        sunshine—WATCHING US!

                  ADRIAN
             (hollering at windows)
        We're British flipping subjects, mate!
        You can't just zap us to some damn
        war zone in some other universe and

                     96

then observe us for your own bloody
entertainment!

                    NICO
Apparently they can.

                    PERCY
We're cannon fodder for aliens.
Welcome to war.

luke

Brenda told him there'd been a boy in town, sending hello. Luke shrugged as if, *What are you on about?*

But it had to be him, right? Had to be.

Luke had been waiting and waiting for this, not realizing how much. The name had been caught between his mouth and the pillow in a dark room with the door shut. Now he could *do* something, get dressed with a reason on Saturday morning, stop hiding at school and go find Robbie. *Robbie*. It had to be a message, using Brenda. Luke wondered, should he have asked her more questions, because even a few hours later his curiosity would be obvious, shout that he cared.

At the tea urn, no one else nearby, he said to Brenda, "That kid who said hey in town?"

"Watch it!" Brenda snapped down the lever. "You're about to spill over!"

Luke's mug was full, stewed tea foamy and lapping at the brim.

"What were you saying?"

Now it was not casual at all, Oona there waiting with her cup.

"Nothing," said Luke.

Getting dressed was harder than usual. At home, his sister would say "Cool" or "You're wearing that?" as the measure of Luke's fashion sense. On his own when it mattered? Hopeless.

Jeans—no choice there—but flared or not so much? He tried to remember the hem of Robbie's jeans. Which T-shirt? If he put on one with a band's name on it, what if Robbie didn't like the band? This was stupid, this was what girls did. The grey T-shirt, then. Keep it simple. Only it was blustery out and he'd need a jacket.

"Are you coming or not?" Adrian thwacked his arm. "Limo's waiting."

Gnarly Mr. Eggers had promised a one-way lift for anyone willing to sit next to rakes and bushels of manure in the back of the pickup. Was Luke going to stink as well as look stupid?

They passed a group of girls near the edge of town, including Kirsten and her lot, who all turned around when he waved, and waggled their bums, laughing like loonies. Losing Adrian and Nico took no time. To be honest, they lost Luke, but he didn't mind being dropped.

He stood alone on a corner in a remote Yorkshire village, his chest so full of hope and nerves that he could scarcely breathe, but with a ludicrous vacancy where a plan should be. Had he expected Robbie to stroll up out of nowhere, to clasp Luke's face in his hands and give him a soft, smoke-flavored kiss? *Move. Go somewhere.*

It was the same cashier in the shop where he'd nicked the mints, making Luke feel bold, standing by the magazines for ages. Long enough to read a silly "What Kind of Friend Are You?" quiz from start to finish, crap like, *You are walking along the street and you see your boyfriend sitting in a café with a really sexy bird. Do you: (a) go in to holler at him, and tell her to keep her hands off; (b) pretend you don't see but get revenge by playing the same game at a later date; (c) join them at the table to see what happens; (d) ignore them completely and never speak to him again.*

Luke checked the cover. *Jackie* magazine. His sister read this crap. He'd seen it before but never looked inside, why would he? Girls followed this advice? There were never any magazines about . . . the kind of boy Luke was. Or possibly there were, but where would he find them? Not for sale at Bigelow's or Loney Tobacco.

Tobacco. The taste of Robbie.

He was wasting time. *Get on with it.*

Luke paused for a second on the step where they'd met. He even looked at the doorbell, but now what?

Chip shop?

He should have gone there first.

At the picnic table outside, Robbie sat astride one of the benches, laughing, waving around a cigarette while he told some joke.

Bloody shock, having him suddenly there. Luke about keeled over. He forced his eyes to move from Robbie to the other boys. Jesus. Skinheads? Skulls nearly shaved, big boots, seriously tough-looking blokes. He almost turned around, would never have seen Robbie again, never even come back to town. For half a second he imagined himself at the window table in the library on a Saturday afternoon, tracing skeletons from the medical dictionary in the utter peace of a deserted school.

Somebody said, "Luke."

Not Robbie, but Robbie was watching now. Luke's eyes went *snap*, to find him first. For one brilliant electric second, Robbie looked back, before knocking ash off his cigarette and turning away his beautiful face.

"Luke!" Penelope was balancing chip packets, crossing the yard from the shop door. "Come sit with us. You can meet my friends."

Luke teetered on his heels, ready to run.

"Your sister's meeting me here. And Jenny. We've got a lift back to school. Want to come?" Penelope plonked the chips down and the boys tore into them.

"Vinegar?" said the younger fuzz-headed one.

Penelope lifted her T-shirt to reveal a bottle of malt vinegar shoved down the front of her jeans. "Be my guest, Alec." She shimmied her hips a little, let the boy reach in further than required to grasp the bottle. Luke had seen Penelope flirt with just about every boy at the school. He was probably the only one who didn't dream about her. The world must hold others like him, or there wouldn't be so many words for being this way. But none at school, he was pretty certain about that.

"Luke, this is Alec. Maybe you know these fellas already? Banger? Robbie?"

What kind of name was Banger?

Penelope perched on the end of the bench, her hip nudging Robbie's.

Alec said, "How do, mate?" mouth full.

"No," said Robbie. "Never met." He flicked away his cigarette and hunched over the chips, not a blink of interest in Luke.

Had Luke imagined everything? Was he in some bizarre Mick Malloy film where hallucinations made more sense than reality?

"I'm off," said Luke. Better to believe in an alternate universe than admit he was just the biggest reject. The biggest *queer* reject.

"Don't you want a lift back?" Penelope licked vinegar off a chip.

"No, I like to walk." He quick-turned and tramped up the little hill, skidding a bit on the cobbles, taking his red face and pricking eyes far away, fast. He was an effing idiot, panting now, way too hot in this stupid jacket that he never should have worn. Made him look like a . . . poofter. He tore it off and bundled it up, would have tossed it in some bin, except he'd need it for Meeting on Sunday. The biggest queer reject in an ugly jacket . . . Oh man, he was sweating all over, his neck damp and his face probably shiny. Eyes hot enough to melt out of their sockets. But he kept walking, the sodding jacket in a ball under his arm, thirst pressing, and Robbie's careless shrug burning a hole in his brain.

Up the high street, out the York Road. The town ended, the farms began just past the petrol station, where he heard his name called.

His feet and heart stopped together. He didn't dare turn around, certain he'd see only a vast field, empty but for mud and broken stalks. Then Robbie's hand was on his shoulder, puffing breaths showing that he'd been running to catch up, *running* to catch the big queer reject in the ugly jacket.

"You walk so fast," said Robbie. He took a sec, bent over. "I smoke too much maybe." He straightened, put his hands in the pockets of his jacket. "You surprised me back there. . . . I couldn't say . . . you know? In front of them."

Luke saw that he was waiting to be forgiven.

"S'all right." His voice croaked slightly, with so much wanting to rush out. "I get it."

"Ta for coming," said Robbie. "To find me."

"Ta for the message," Luke said. "The carrier pigeon."

Neither of them pretended not to understand.

"So here we are . . ." Robbie spread out his arms and laughed, *the nicest laugh*, Luke thought. "In the great wide open. For all the world to see, eh?"

"I don't care who sees," said Luke. He would have grabbed him right there, kissed him, *danced* with him even. Except for holding this jacket like a supreme twit.

"You'd better care," said Robbie. "That's why, before, I—" He tapped a finger to his lips, making a secret. "It'd

103

be stupid. There's yobs in town who cut up queers and eat them for dinner."

Luke flinched, hearing *queer* out loud.

"We'd be better off not queer and that's a fact."

"But—" said Luke.

"You hear me?" said Robbie. "If this . . . if we . . ."

Luke's heart stopped for the second time in three minutes. *We*, he'd said.

Robbie stepped closer, close enough to erase the rest of the universe. "We've got to be . . . quiet as bleeding cockroaches."

Luke nodded. Was he being asked or being told?

Robbie said, "Let's find a hidey-hole, shall we? For a minute?"

There was one weedy bloke in the window of the petrol station, didn't glance up as they circled round to the back, away from the cars barreling past, away from anyone with two eyes in his head. There were a couple of crates back there, some odd planks and bits of lumber. Nothing cozy. They weren't touching yet and the sun was hot. Luke's mouth was utterly dry. Was it going to happen again? What he'd imagined over and over?

Robbie leaned against the wall, casual, as if he were going to light a cigarette. He grinned, held his hands out, beckoned ever so slightly with his chin. Luke let go of the wrinkled, balled-up jacket and stepped into Robbie's arms.

They might have stayed and stayed, but a car honked out front and brought them back to their junky patch of earth. Robbie pulled a scrap of paper from his pocket, numbers written on it in green marker. "I wrote this out, in case we . . . in case I had to slip it to you, in secret. You could ring, maybe?"

"Can't we just say?" Luke took the paper. "Wednesday? It's our half-day. How about Wednesday?"

The breakfast toast was crisp and golden on Wednesdays after that; Luke's hair did exactly the right thing under a comb; he perfected his uniform of jeans and a T-shirt and traded two Procol Harum albums for use of Nico's suave Italian jacket. Even the sting of Adrian's towel flick was bearable; he had firm answers about Charles Dickens and decimal points and the floodplains of the Nile that he could not have fabricated on any other day of the week. No one noticed that Luke was accompanied by a flock of heavenly angels.

They avoided the chip shop. They mostly avoided town altogether. Robbie usually hiked all the way out to meet Luke in the school woods. And it wasn't all sex either. They both knew lots of lyrics and tried to stump each other, singing snatches, guessing. Same with programs on the telly, not so much with books. Luke quickly knew to steer clear of any questions about family, but that was fine by him. What did family have to do with this? With anything?

Once, there'd been a gaggle of girls who traipsed right past their spot in the woods. Then a scare one time in town when Banger and Alec had shouted Robbie's name. Luke peeled off and met up again later, Robbie a bit edgy, swivelling around every minute. But they'd been lucky and always careful. It was brilliant, really, until the day that Robbie did not appear where they'd arranged to meet, behind the shed that marked the border between the Danforth farm and the school woods. Luke had no chance to look for him on Saturday because of a school trip to Knaresborough Castle. And the next Wednesday, still no Robbie.

The paper with the number had stayed in Luke's pocket. He remembered, twice, to take it out on laundry day and put it back into clean jeans. Despite that precaution, the green ink became smeared with fingering, so Luke wouldn't know if that was a 9 or a 4, a 1 or a 7 . . . except that he'd memorized the number the very first day, and had it securely installed in his head. But dialling was a huge step past knowing the number. He carried shillings in his pocket for days, passing the telephone cubbie probably thirty times. Robbie didn't go to school. He had a dodgy sort of job with odd hours, delivering packages for a bloke he called the Ogre. No way to know when he'd be home. Ringing up and having the call answered by someone other than Robbie was unthinkable.

Even while he made excuses not to ring, Luke carried anguish like a coat of thistles, tearing his skin with every turn, believing Robbie's silence to be another message. This was different, and worse. He heard one phrase over and over: *"We'd be better off not queer and that's a fact."* Robbie was telling him, *Get normal.*

"Who would you choose, if it was shag only, no chatter?" Adrian was always posing these ridiculous questions.

"Diana Rigg," said Nico. *The Avengers.*

"In the *school*, you wanker!"

"Shag only?"

"Yeah."

"Penelope."

"Penelope."

"Penelope, as long as she can't open her mouth."

The whole dorm agreed. Easy for Luke to say *Uh-huh* and join the others.

"But what if you had to clock a full twenty-four hours of conversation before you could even touch her?"

A general groan about the impossible task and then a few opinions.

"Nico's going to say dibs on the American," said Adrian. "He hasn't got her yet."

"Yet," said Nico. "And since you don't know enough words to fill twenty-four hours, Ady, you're out of luck."

"I'd have to say Kirsten," said Henry. "She's very arty."

"Oh, well, I disqualify myself if my sister's in the running," said Luke. "That's obscene."

But he began to consider. He'd never given a girl a proper chance, had he? So how did he really *know*? Maybe girls were fine. He'd get off with a girl, prove this other thing was just a phase. Maybe everyone had to test it both ways and then it all settled into the right place. That wasn't the way it sounded, when he listened to Adrian and Nico, but who knew? Jesus, if Nico could be believed, he'd had his hand up girls' tops since first form. Nico was worse than Penelope as far as Luke could tell. Maybe he should ask Nico. Ha! Luke actually smiled for the first time in weeks. As if he could ever ask anyone anything. No one had advice for queers other than to stop being one. But he had a plan. He'd fix it.

He went to the Swamp after tea.

His sister said, "What the hell? You're coming with us?"

"Why not?" he said. "Are you charging a toll now?"

"You just never have, but yeah, come on." She linked her arm through his, being a mate. Good old Kirsten. Would she be this nice if she knew who he was?

But he was not going to be that anymore. That was the whole point. He'd already narrowed down the field of girls. Penelope was not even on the list, despite being the most likely to go along. Luke had a feeling she'd suss him out too quickly. She'd be too much even if he were crazy about girls. The girls in his own form: Caroline, Anna, Dot. Dot was kind of cute. Being Japanese she was slim and, Luke admitted, boyish, no big titties to grapple with. But Dot didn't go to the Swamp, so where could he ever talk to her in a way that would lead to . . . what he needed it to lead to? Oona had too much giggling going on. Fiona's mouth was kind of puffy, disgusting actually, the way she had shiny stuff smeared all over. Why did girls *do* that?

Did they really think that glossy goo upped their appeal? Maybe that was the whole problem? Luke wanted a mouth that looked like a mouth instead of an advert.

He'd meant to come along and join the chatter, only of course he didn't. He sat between Kirsten and Jenny, the American, with his hood pulled up and his hands clamped over his knees.

"Luke! Stop rocking!" Kirsten gently bonked her fist on his leg. "You're making me dizzy."

He stopped, not knowing he'd started.

"Thanks for bringing your lively brother to the party," said Penelope. "Haven't you got a riddle to share, Lukie-pie? Or a little song you'd like to sing?"

"I'm here as a social experiment," he managed to say. "Taking a look at the dark side of Ill Hall."

"Doesn't get much darker than this," said Jenny. "Except in there . . ." She nodded down the path toward the looming woods, which really did look spooky, silhouetted spikes against the purpling twilight sky.

"You used to be such a jolly little boy," said Kirsten. "Till you got all quiet and started doing the Houdini disappearing act."

"Houdini got tied up and untied," said Luke. "He didn't disappear."

"Well, you could use a little untying, Mr. Uptight."

"Aw, leave the poor kid alone," said Jenny. "It's his first time at the Swamp all term. No wonder he's scared."

If he was going to try to like a girl, Jenny might work. No lip stuff for starters. She'd been Nico's choice in Adrian's stupid game, after all. She must have something going for her.

When the bell rang for Cocoa, he touched her arm.

"Hey," he said. "Wait a moment, would you?"

She puzzled her eyebrows at him. "What?"

"Well, I . . . I just, I . . . maybe let the others go ahead?"

The others wandered out of sight up the path, leaving Luke and Jenny alone. There was a vague hooting somewhere, maybe an owl. Only the moonlight glowing, very romantic. Luke had never been alone with Jenny before, never had an actual conversation. Her accent wasn't as bad as the boys made it sound when they imitated her in the dorm.

"What?" she said again. "Did you want something?"

"I just . . ." Now or never. He put his hands on her shoulders and leaned forward and put his mouth on her mouth while she stared at him with eyes wide open before moving her head back with a little grunt of surprise.

"Hello?" she said.

"I like you," he said.

"Uh, how could you possibly know that?"

"I . . . I like your clothes." He touched the tattered collar of her blouse. Could he sound any more stupid?

She laughed. "Was this a dare?" She whipped around. "Is someone watching?"

Luke shook his head. "No, I swear."

Her head was shaking too, ever so slightly, rather baffled. She glanced up the path where the others had gone.

"Don't get me wrong," she said. "I'm flattered. But . . . you know I've got a boyfriend, right?"

110

"It *is* a dare, actually. I'm not supposed to say."

"Okay," she said, as if he'd asked a question. The *okay* was very American. She closed her eyes and tilted her face. "I'll let you try again."

He put his hands on her shoulders, just like before. He put his mouth on her mouth. Why wasn't it working? He was jinxing it, maybe, thinking about Robbie. It was a terrible kiss!

Jenny giggled and pulled back. "This is new, huh? Are you practicing for something, maybe?"

He let himself give the tiniest nod.

"I think you have to want to," she said. "A little motion would help, a little more enthusiasm?" She moved as if to touch him, but he dodged her hand. His pits were sticky, his face hot. He couldn't think what to say.

"I'm not exactly an expert," she said. "But don't worry, I'm sure you'll be fine at the moment. Come on, we're going to miss Cocoa. I won't tell anyone, I promise. Who's the lucky girl?"

Jenny winked at him the next morning, but Luke pretended not to see. It was mortifying. But worse, it likely meant what he didn't want it to mean. No question. So he barely noticed when Brenda came in and sat down at the next table. It was only that some of the girls were gasping, *What's wrong? You look terrible. Did Mr. Spag-a-lot Eggers make a pass?* And then her shaky voice telling the tale.

"There's a boy I know in town," she said. "He got awfully roughed up at the weekend. I've not been able to sleep, it was that horrible."

"What happened?" someone said.

"Was it the one you fancy?" said someone else.

"No, not him," said Brenda. "This boy got jumped by skinheads, kicked about and bashed up, but worse than the licking, they . . ."

Luke wasn't the only one who'd stopped eating to listen.

"They what?" said someone. Brenda was crying and couldn't answer.

"They . . . *painted* him," she whispered, after a bit. "They scraped his arms with a nail, and then they poured pink paint all over him."

"What the hell?"

"He's got these nasty scratches. . . ." Brenda faltered again. "Says *queer* right up his left arm, but they only got to *quee* on the right. Someone saw and called the coppers."

Luke put down his spoon. The porridge was foul. Like sucking on the spongy fungus that grew on the trunks of trees.

"His brother is the bugger who got my sister pregnant," said Brenda. "Which makes Robbie Jerry's uncle. I guess we're related, me being the auntie. So I doubt that Robbie's actually, you know"—her voice dropped—"a *fairy*. But someone was pissed off!"

Luke pushed back from the table ever so carefully. He carried his bowl to the bin and scraped it slowly, gently, as if handling a precious dish. The clang when it landed on the service trolley seemed louder than all the morning chatter in the room. Was everyone watching? Did everyone know? He fought the urge to tiptoe out of the dining

112

hall. *Don't be stupid*, he told himself. *That'd only draw at-tention. You may be queer, but you're not stupid. Or* quee, he thought. The spoonful of porridge rose in his throat. He went back to his chair, tea mug half full so he wouldn't slop with his shaking hand.

Luke did not know where Robbie lived. Or would he be in a hospital? It sounded bad. How do they get *paint* off? Jesus. Was his dad sitting by his bed, praying, maybe? No mum, he knew that much. An aunt, he was pretty certain. "It'd be like telling them I was dead," Robbie had said. He'd called his brother an idiot yob, but what did that mean? What had Luke said about Kirsten in the brief exchange on siblings? "*She's all right.*" With a shrug. Like she didn't matter much.

Luke looked around to where Kirsten sat at the maths teachers' table, smearing jam on bread while Penelope bab-bled in her ear. Would Kirsten sit beside Luke's bed in a hospital room if he were bashed and painted?

She must have felt his stare. She met his eyes and crossed hers at once, the way they both used to at the supper table, kids listening to their parents natter. He crossed his too, and smiled for half a second before he remembered. Rob-bie had been beaten up, cut up, covered in paint. Who the hell had *pink* paint?

He couldn't tell Kirsten. He hadn't had a true conversa-tion with her in about three years. He'd kept meaning to. But how could he just say, out of nowhere, *By the way, I like boys*?

One particular boy. He stood up, dumped his untasted

tea, touched the shillings in his pocket. He'd be late for Religious Studies. He would ring the green number now, just being a mate asking how was Robbie.

The phone was answered by a growly-voiced woman, Robbie's Aunt Pat, she said. He was over at the Harrogate District Hospital, she said, and when were her cursed nephews going to stop causing trouble, she'd like to know? Their mother must be spinning in her grave, what with Simon's fiancée finding him on the sofa with that tart from the hotel, and Robbie, well, Robbie! She couldn't bring herself to say that word aloud.

Harrogate was miles away. Eight, Luke saw, when he checked a map in the library, skipping the first lesson completely. He wondered if there was a bus from town. But town was already such a hike in the wrong direction, he might as well head toward Harrogate and put the walk to use. How long would it take? And what about getting back again? He supposed he could try thumbing, but what if he had trouble getting a lift? It might be quicker to walk.

All these stupid stones in the path, why couldn't anything be simple? But he'd already dumped his books, nicked Nico's black jacket, and set out down the back road to avoid being seen before he allowed himself to think, *I'm going.* And didn't Mr. Eggers come along right then, on his way to fetch bonemeal from a farm over that way? Didn't bother him, having a truant in the van. A bit of company makes the day go by.

Outside the hospital, Luke wished he smoked, something to make him inhale, a cloud to wash over his insides instead of this woodpecker having a furious go at his heart.

He asked which room, worried there'd be someone to stop him. But, "Third curtain on the left, love," said the chubby nurse gripping a water pitcher. It was a bit like the dorms at school, except the beds had dividers strung between them. Hidden somewhere was an old man making a snorty noise. Luke crept to the third curtain and moved it back with one finger.

Robbie's bed was tipped partway up. One eye was taped over with a medical patch, but the other stared from beneath a swollen violet lid. Robbie's bandaged arms flew up as if to fend off an intruder.

"Hey," said Luke. He pulled shut the curtain behind him and stepped nearer. Robbie looked . . . bad. Different, and bad. His skin was shiny pink, stretched-looking. They must have scrubbed the hell out of it to take off an entire flipping bucket of paint. Most of his hair was clipped off.

"Whadderyoudoonhere?" The sounds were not quite words.

"I got a lift," said Luke. "I was going to walk, but I didn't have to."

Robbie shook his head, like that's not what he meant. "Youshouldn."

Luke shrugged. He was here. He'd forgotten to bring anything. Flowers? Biscuits? What does a person bring to someone who's been beaten up? "Are you gasping for a cigarette?" he said. "I could get you some. Perhaps there's a machine."

Robbie shook his head again. "Mgonnaquit."

Luke wanted to sit but there was only the bed, and that seemed wrong.

"What happened?" he whispered. "Who did this?"

"Feknpricksiswho." Robbie's neck rolled slowly to one side, toward where the door was, beyond the curtain. "Youshouldnbehere," he said again. "Viciousbuggers-gonna . . ."

Luke glanced at Robbie's arms, heavily wrapped in gauze. He was curious to see the scratched letters. Plenty of time for that.

"Brenda was telling the other girls at school." Luke's fingertips tapped the sheet pulled taut over Robbie's feet. "I . . . I called the number you gave me. Your aunt said you were here . . . I left school, skipped Religion and Bio. I'm missing Drama now. I had to see you, I was going crazy, from the minute I heard, it was like pouring rain only on me. I wanted to tell you—"

Robbie's hands lifted to stop him yakking. "Look-likeshit."

"Me?" said Luke. "What about *you*?"

Every bit of Luke's skin tingled, as if *he* were the one rubbed raw. It was the brand-new bare-naked feeling of being himself. He tucked his arms around Robbie as best he could. After days of wondering, after the morning of screeching anxiety, Luke breathed in those few perfect seconds with the music of trolley wheels in the corridor, and his nose warm, in Robbie's neck.

jenny

The first letter I wrote to Matt, I struggled with how to begin. I crossed out *Dear Matt,* because how embarrassing was it to say *dear* on paper when I would never say it to his face? *Hi there! How're things?* A little too jaunty. He was in a war. Which made *Ahoy!* ridiculous. I skipped the salutation.

I thought of you tonight when my toes touched the hot-water bottle under the blanket and I wondered if you are freezing, like we are in Yorkshire, or steamy hot, the way I expect a jungle to be.

Complete drivel. Talking about the weather.

Funny how we're both so far away from home, only neither of us really got to choose. Does that make you mad? I never asked you in person, how you feel about the war and stuff. It didn't seem fair to ask, since your feelings weren't going to change anything.

How about I just tell you about the delightful school food, and we can have a contest: WHICH IS WORSE? Boarding School or Army? Entry #1: Breakfast today: poached eggs served in a tub of cloudy water. We were supposed to scoop them out, dripping, and plop them onto bread that was probably toasted last night. The eggs were as solid as baseballs, I swear.

Your turn!

xx Jenny

PS: I hope it's not too terrible there. I miss you.

For where to send it, I had to ring Tom.

Ring means "call."

The telephone booth was in the back hallway, under the stairs. You had to bend over to get in there, and then it was like *Doctor Who*'s time-travel spacecraft, with an enormous old-fashioned pay telephone acting as the instrument panel. The walls were an archive of doodles and penknife etchings from generations of homesick kids.

I used up too many shillings of my tiny weekly allowance, but it was worth it to hear Tom's voice. I tried ringing him pretty often but next-to-never found him in. This time, lucky.

"Way to support the troops, kid," he said. He had Matt's military address, but confessed he'd written only once. "What am I supposed to say?" He slipped into an English accent. "Oh bother! There was no cream for the porridge this morning! Most vexing, eh what? Killed any gooks lately?"

"Tom, don't say ugly stuff. I wrote about food too." I

118

traced my finger over a poem scratched into the wall of the booth. *Get Me. Out. Of Here.* "Maybe it will cheer him up for five minutes."

Tom was quiet, holding-his-breath quiet.

"Hello?" I said.

"Mmm-hmm."

"Are you *cry*ing?"

"No." He definitely had a crack in his voice. "I haven't written at all. I lied. Not even once."

"Oh, Tom." What was I supposed to say? "His life is in danger every single day. How are you going to feel if he . . . if he . . . gets injured? Send him a letter."

Hard to believe I'd been here over a month. Some days it was hard to believe it was *only* that long. Living in a dorm was like having a sleepover every night, sometimes claustrophobic but mostly great. I didn't mind anymore being naked in front of the whole crowd. Naked was normal. I examined the other bodies for dimply bits, tufts of hair, enviable curves. Having no sisters I'd never had a chance to see all this—except with my mother, who had been on a kick of not wearing a bra as some kind of women's libber ban-the-bra political statement, but with her I'd averted my eyes. At home in gym class, girls were extra modest, getting dressed behind curtains or under their towels. Kelly and Becca would have *died* to see me walk across a room with no clothes on.

And going to lessons wasn't like *school*. We sat at rickety

119

desks so old they had holes in the corners for *inkpots*. We had Russian classes with Sergei, who was rumored to be a self-exiled aristo, and he taught us French as well. We spoke in booming voices, as if calling across the icy barrens, and called everybody *tovarishch*, for "comrade." Biology and Physics were both with Kirby, who was the youngest teacher and played guitar every minute outside the classroom. It was clear by day two that the maths they were learning in England (*maths* means "math") was far beyond what we'd been doing in the States and the schedule was constructed so that I couldn't slip into class with third or fourth form either. Fran shrugged her Quakerly shoulders and let me not do it at all. That was brilliant! Jasper taught English, Phil taught Geography, Leonard taught History and Art, Richard the headmaster taught Religious Studies, a local dippy lady named Stormy came in twice a week to teach Dramatic Interpretations, and we had Malcolm for the dreaded British Constitution.

I got to the bottom of my trunk in my mission to make snipped art pieces of every single garment (except the underwear). I'd have to borrow clothes for Parent Visiting Day, when Mom and Dad were flying over just for the long weekend. I took my nail scissors to the Swamp one evening to cut Kirsten's orange hair. It had grown out so that the dark stripe at the roots made her look like a tiger. Her natural color was a coffee-no-milk brown, and we made her hair really spiky.

Nico taught me that the trick to breakfast was to make bacon sandwiches. Recipe: spread margarine over a piece of dry toast and fold around a clump of really greasy stuck-together bacon. School version of piggy in a blanket. Yum.

I could see time passing by watching Percy's notebook, which he had with him morning till night. The pages he'd written on were tatty and rippled with words, the untouched ones smooth and blank, waiting for his next inspiration. Sometimes he'd snicker and start scribbling in the middle of a conversation, dreadlocks trembling while he wrote. The other girls said Percy had a crush on me, but he was never shy or annoying, so who knows?

"He's your type," Penelope said. "As in, dark. Right?"

Ill Hall Lesson #29: don't rise to Penelope's bait.

"It makes me sick how the boys treat him," Kirsten said. "Luke told me Adrian soaked Percy's towel the other night, so he got out of the shower and had to freeze."

Percy never complained. He just sat there cackling and writing stuff down.

"What the hell?" Penelope would say. "Am I in your film?"

"What do you think?"

"Well, am I?"

"Do you want to be?"

"What's it about?"

"What do you think it's about?" He answered her every question with a question; it drove Penelope *mad*.

"What's it about?" I asked him.

"It's more than one little film," he said. "I'm creating an oeuvre. The Boarding School Chronicles."

We woke up one Friday to a whole lot of banging outside.

Kirsten sat straight up with a shout and we piled onto her bed to stare out the window. The Brontë girls crowded in to join us for the best view. The field of the farm next door was full of trucks and men.

"The Autumn Fair!" Everyone seemed thrilled to bits. It would be ready to open by evening and would stay all weekend. Even the teachers loved the Autumn Fair. Even *Richard* agreed that in the tradition of the great English novelist Thomas Hardy, such celebrations were a worthy rustic entertainment.

"Not sure why he's such a fan," said Kirsten. "The country fair in *The Mayor of Casterbridge* is where the bloke sells his wife and baby to a sailor, effectively ruining everyone's lives. I suppose Richard has faith that none of his students will sink so low."

"None of us are married," said Esther, in a typical moment of clarity.

"Right."

"Do you think he'll cancel Saturday lessons?" asked Oona. "He did that one time."

"You've conveniently forgotten why they were reinstated," said Kirsten. "The boys that year went to the cider booth at half past nine on Saturday morning and were completely sozzled by noon."

"In the meantime," came Hairy Mary's voice from the doorway, "*this* morning's lessons will proceed as scheduled. The bell for breakfast will ring in two minutes and I see altogether too many undergarments in the Jane Austen dormitory."

* * *

"What power does an unreliable narrator have upon a story?" asked Jasper. He jingled the change in his pockets and looked around the classroom. "Hmmm?"

His trademark *Hmmm?* was deeply irritating.

Fifth-form comments on Jasper:

Hmmm's like a deranged wasp.

Trousers like a butler.

Ear bristles like a privet hedge.

Goatee like a girl's pubes.

"How does the reader absorb what he is being told, before and then *after* he recognizes a narrator as being untrustworthy?"

Zero response in the fifth form. Nico was tipping his chair, rocking on the back two legs.

"Excuse me, Jasper?"

"Ah! Esther!"

"There's something I don't understand."

Esther was so dependably dorky that everyone kind of loved her. She could distract a teacher for an entire lesson, following some teeny-weeny point down a bumpy, shadowy path.

"Hmmm?"

"Well, it seems to me that each of us just sees the world, you know, the way we see it. Since we're each living our own story. So wouldn't that mean that—"

"Yes!" Nico landed his chair legs with a thud. "Sorry to interrupt, Esther, but—"

Esther's face was now the color of Plum Loco lip gloss. Getting attention from Nico might be enough to cause a seizure.

"I think about this all the time," said Nico. "Like, for instance, who is telling *this* story?"

"Which story?" Jasper seemed a bit bemused.

"*This* one!" said Nico. "The story of the English lesson on Friday morning in a shabby ex-stable that hasn't had the windows washed in a hundred years. We have"—he looked around—"sixteen stories in here, right? And all of them are true, right? According to the"—he twitched his fingers to show that he was quoting—"*narrators*. But all of them are unreliable, if you're one of the other fifteen people. So how can it be some literary genre, the unreliable narrator? There isn't anything else."

"That's heavy, man," said Adrian.

"I agree with Nico," I said. My turn to get the sunshine of that amazing smile. "*But* . . . isn't there a difference between someone telling a story from his—or her—point of view, and . . . and . . ." Suddenly I didn't want to finish the sentence.

"And purposely lying?" said Penelope.

"*Misdirection* is perhaps a more suitable term," said Jasper. "In the literary sense. And that brings us back, thank you, to the unreliable narrator."

By the end of the day the mood in the dormitories was practically giddy. The Autumn Fair was only a carousel, a miniature Ferris wheel, and a few tacky games booths, but you'd think we were off to Las Vegas. Richard made us wait until after tea and then he laid out the rules. There would be no drinking of alcoholic beverages, including hard cider. There would be no disrespectful language or behavior toward the townspeople. There was a curfew of nine o'clock for first through third forms, and ten o'clock for the rest of us. " 'Go then merrily!' " he said, quoting some antique poet.

"Luke's found a townie." Kirsten pointed to where her brother was chatting with a boy from the village. "How do people just start nattering to strangers? I can never do that."

"Watch and learn." Penelope flexed her muscles, as if she were going to demonstrate tree-cutting techniques. "Hey, Alec!" she called.

"That doesn't count," said Kirsten. "You already know that grimy lot."

I recognized Alec from my first day at Ill Hall. He'd been one of Penelope's boys in the chip shop. His head was still shaved, and when he grinned at Penelope we could see a new tattoo over his eyebrow, like a worm crawling across his face.

"Hallo, Pen," he said. I had the idea that maybe he couldn't pronounce her whole name. Two other boys were with him, neither of them with more hair than fuzz on a peach. It made them look like aliens, especially since the boys at school all had long hair. Wild hippie hair like Luke's, or soft brown waves like Nico's, falling across the eyes. These boys were weirdly clean. A bit scary. They all had tight pants, tidy sweaters, and boots with thick dangerous soles. One wore suspenders.

"I'm going to borrow a quid from my brother." Kirsten gave a quick wave, leaving me there with Penelope's conquests.

"This is Jenny," said Penelope. "She's from America."

"I hate Americans," said one of Alec's friends.

"America hates you," said Penelope. "So everybody's happy."

Lucky for us he thought that was funny, since he looked the type to chew his way through a car fender.

"I'm not really from America," I said. "I was born in Madagascar. That's an island off the coast of Africa. Lots of monkeys. My parents are monkey smugglers."

"What the hell?" said Alec.

"We only live in America for cover," I said. "The zoos over there are big clients. Sometimes they'll pay, like, half a million dollars for a rare monkey."

"A pregnant monkey," said Penelope. "Isn't that what you told me, Jenny?"

"Well, yeah," I said. "That's like getting two monkeys for the price of one. So the cost goes up."

"So you're rich," said the boy with navy-blue suspenders.

"I hate rich people," said the other one.

"And rich people hate you," said Penelope. "In America, everyone is rich."

"How the hell do you know?" said Alec.

"From when I was there last year," she said. "Right, Jenny?"

"Uh-huh."

"We went to this amazing ice cream parlor," said Penelope. "Where the film stars go. I brought home sundae cups as a souvenir."

"I remember," I said. "The night we met Robert Redford, who played the Sundance Kid."

"You're bonkers," said Alec.

A crowd of boys from school showed up, so we peeled away. Adrian, Henry, Nico, and some fourth-formers. Enough to surround us while our straight faces slipped into massive laughter.

We tried the tossing games, losing fistfuls of shillings. We ate sugar buns that looked better than they tasted. And then somehow it was Nico and me, the next two in line for the Ferris wheel, which was so small it had only six swinging chairs, each fitting two people. Probably made of tin. I asked myself afterward, did he plan to be next to me like that? Or was it spur of the moment? One certain thing is that Nico smelled delicious, like walking into your grammy's kitchen when she's baking spice cake.

He nudged me, sending vibes of *Hello there, it's you and me, kid!* the way big brothers do in movies, with a wide-open smile that makes you think you're the favorite. My own big brother was a little more jaded. The old carny guy held open the carriage door and Nico slid in after me, already fussing about the seat belt. As if a seat belt would do anything if the entire ride tipped over. Cool as anything, he draped his arm across the back of the seat so I could feel it there, warm and chummy—*Here we are, about to have fun!*

Our chair rocked forward, rolling the next one into

place beside the loading platform. Brenda and her townie boyfriend climbed in. I wanted to twist around to see who else was there, but then Nico might have taken his arm away. And I liked it where it was.

Finally the music started, crackling up from a speaker next to the operator, and the wheel creaked into motion. Nico tipped his chin toward the view of Illington Hall at twilight. "Picture postcard, eh?"

"They should take a photo from up here for their next brochure," I said. "And update the clothing list while they're at it."

His fingers ruffled the fringe at the neck of my sweater, making it feel as if a cat's whiskers were tickling my cheek. "I wondered why you wear these weirdo togs," he said. I was kind of queasy from being so close to Nico, and being up in the air right over the stench of burning gasoline from the Ferris wheel engine. And then he kissed me.

Right at the top of the wheel, in front of everyone in Yorkshire. A real kiss.

For a second I was just . . . gobsmacked, as they say in England. His lips were, oh, warm . . . His hand was cupping my face and even though the rest of me was thinking, *Yikes!* my lips were kissing him back and then his tongue was there at the same second that I heard hooting and clapping. I pulled away, with shivers creeping up my spine.

"Hey," said Nico. "Where you going? You've got a great mouth."

He leaned in again, but I said, "Wait, stop." No one had ever said that about my mouth before. No one this good-looking had ever been near me before. But our carriage was at the bottom of the cycle and we were practically face to face with Adrian and Henry. They were doing a slow clap, chanting, "Go, go, Nic-*Oh*! Go, go, Nic-*Oh*!"

I felt like a total dupe. I'd let him . . . Part of some dare or showing off, and I'd fallen, *plunk*, into the trap.

"You . . . you . . . sod!" I thunked him in the chest with my fist. Mostly it was so embarrassing because we'd been *really* kissing!

"Aw, come on, Jenny." He scooped his hand under my hair, cradling my neck with gentle fingers. "You can't blame me for them being idiots! Be fair!"

The ride slowed, thankfully us being the first ones off. The boys on the ground made sweeping bows as if welcoming a grand lady from a gilded coach. I would have stomped off in a mighty fit, but my path was blocked by Penelope.

"The worst thing," I told Percy and Kirsten later, "was trying to get away from the stupid boys and having Penelope smirk like I'd set out to make it happen."

"She's just jealous," said Kirsten. "Nico ignores her."

"Well, I wish he'd ignored me." I was lying.

"It's pretty much a law around here," said Percy. "That Nico gets what Nico wants."

Yeah, but what Nico wanted was to kiss me. *Me*. Even if it was partly showing off for those other jerks, Nico was the cutest boy who had ever even flirted with me, let alone . . . did stuff. . . . But because of Matt, I had to pretend I didn't care. I'd lied myself out of the chance to . . . to what?

* * *

Two or three times a week I used Assignments Hour to write a funny letter to friends in Philly, sometimes to Mom, or, most often, to Matt. I drew pictures of the teachers and told him gossip and included an entry in the gross-food contest. I tried not to think about what he was seeing. How he might be crawling around with enormous deadly spiders or lying sick with a tropical fever. Firing bullets at other boys far from home. Just plain miserably lonely and scared.

But still no letter back. Obviously Matt had better things to do with his evenings than write to friends' little sisters. As if *evening* had any meaning in war. As if he were lying on a couch after basketball practice instead of huddled in some bog with mosquitoes the size of bats, and bats the size of eagles. Evening probably meant that dark was coming, and dark in a jungle must be . . . I shuddered. Sometimes I'd wake up, imagining that it wasn't a dormitory around me, but a dark full of slithering ghosts and creeping invisible enemies and sudden noises that made your earlobes vibrate and your stomach twist and your eyes blink in gratitude that it was a noise and not an end. An explosion that scared you to bits instead of killing you was what you hoped for.

I'd got into the habit of Matt being almost a diary. I didn't even expect him to answer anymore. I tried not to think it meant he was dead. What was he supposed to say? War sucks?

I thought about him every day.

* * *

It was almost Halloween at home, but here they were collecting wood for a colossal bonfire on Guy Fawkes Day. On November fifth all of England celebrates the demise of some bloke who tried to blow up King James a few hundred years ago.

"The rule is to build the fire in the middle of the playing field," explained Kirsten, "so we don't burn the school down."

Middle of the playing field meant a long way to drag branches from the woods, but it was Kirsten's favorite night of the year, so she corralled her brother and a few other boys, including Nico without his shirt on, to do the major hauling. His shoulders were just about as broad as Matt's.

"Did you tell Matt about your liaison with Nico? Is that why he never writes?" Penelope was having a smoke. It was past dark and the last few of us were huddled together at the Swamp, keeping her company and waiting for the Cocoa bell.

"He's in Vietnam," I said. "Remember? It's not like there's regular mail service on the battlefield."

"I don't think Vietnam has battle*fields*," stuck in Percy. The boys in his dorm were being dicks again, while we were nice, plus full of gossip for his movies. "Vietnam has thick hideous jungles full of razor-edged elephant grass and teeming with poisonous snakes." He got up and hunched over, pretending to hold a rifle, darting crazy-looking eyes as he went into narrator mode: "The enemy, more deter-mined than fire ants, stake out the undergrowth, silently waiting for you to fall into a pit full of sharpened bamboo spikes guaranteed to rupture your innards and expose your intestines to—"

"Thanks, Percy," said Kirsten. "Very sensitive."

"I'm sure it's wretched," I said. "So how could he write that? He wouldn't want to bum me out with horrendous details. He not a whiner." He was the most uncomplaining person I'd ever met.

"But true love manages to conquer all?" Penelope needled. "Including interludes with tall Greek boys at your end? Including blatant silence?"

"I'm not going to answer that." I made my voice careless. "Who knows how anything turns out?"

The bell clanged, sounding mystical from this dis-tance. Penelope ditched her cigarette. It was generally agreed that Cocoa was Vera D's best offering and not one to miss.

Guy Fawkes night included a raging, and then a glowing, bonfire, a later-than-usual curfew, chocolate biscuits, silly dancing, and a starlit sky that seemed to reflect the spark-ing embers. All of it was ignored by the faculty who were off having their own party in the maths room.

Nico and I ended up, accidentally on purpose, on a bench in the tangled and neglected rose garden. What if I pre-tended to get a letter in which Matt broke up with me? I'd have to be heartbroken for a while, but then . . . Nico was *so* cute. I was letting him kiss me again, and it was . . . so *nice*, and took us from sitting on the tilting wooden bench to lying down on the mossy ground.

His hand was under my T-shirt, roaming around near my skipping heart. It slid around to the back and began to fiddle with the band of my bra. Except it was the bra with a hook at the front, under a tiny silk bow, so he wasn't making any progress. His kissing got sort of . . . distracted, him not being able to find the fastener. I heard a roar of laughter from the kids by the fire. I imagined for a second that they were watching us, laughing their heads off. That they all knew I was a big fat liar. The moss was suddenly damp and chilly.

"How do you undo this thing?" He sounded like a grumpy little boy grappling with the top of a cookie jar. *Nico gets what Nico wants.*

"You don't." I rolled away from him, scrambled up, brushing off dirt and leaves, tugging down my T-shirt. "Sorry," I said. "No cheap thrills here."

"Hey, wait." He was bent over, awkwardly getting up. "You can't just walk off!"

"Sorry. No, actually"—I had a flash of my mother's lib- ber jargon—"I'm *not* sorry. I'm . . . I'm . . . voicing my right to refuse."

"Is that another way of saying prickteaser?"

All I wanted was to not be there. Nothing clever, no smart words to end the conversation.

"G'bye," I said. "I made a mistake."

* * *

"Nico already has a girlfriend," said Penelope, back at the Swamp a few days later.

"Uh-huh." *She's delusional*, I thought. "And I have a boyfriend."

"Her name is Sarah and she left at the end of summer term, in July. Her parents wanted her to do her final year at home in Toronto. It was dead sad, them saying goodbye to each other. I'm sure he still thinks about her all the time."

"Despite," said Kirsten, "multiple efforts to distract him. From multiple sources, including one whose name begins with a *P*."

I laughed. Penelope scowled. "I'm only telling you so you don't go and compromise your true love with Matt for some futile attempt to seduce Nico."

"I appreciate your concern," I said. "Please stop being a nutjob. Nothing's going on."

"So why do you make a point of looking everywhere in the room except at him?"

She might have been a nutjob, but she paid attention.

"Kind of hard," said Penelope. "To break up with someone who's away fighting a war."

"I'm *not* breaking up with him!"

"Ohhh, so you have, like, an *open* relationship, the way the hippies do? Free love?"

"You're driving even *me* crazy," said Kirsten. "And I'm not the one under the microscope! Penelope, shut it!"

134

* * *

The letter came on a Monday, a heavy post day. Hairy Mary could barely keep order during distribution. The exotic stamps on my airmail envelope stood out, however, so I was surrounded at the Swamp. I wished I'd sneaked into a toilet stall to read alone, but they forced me to tear the flap and see Matt's boy-scrawl across the page.

Dear Jen-Jen, it began.

"Aren't you going to read it aloud?" said Penelope.

"Yeah, come on," said Oona.

"Nnn. Don't think so."

"Leave her alone," said Kirsten.

Sorry for not writing before. It's because the whole thing just stinks and I didn't want to fill up a letter with bad vibes or the lies I have to tell my mother. But I thought of you today when they served up breakfast. The eggs come in a powder that the cooks stir with water before pouring them into the pan. Re-vol-ting! We are definitely bad-food soul mates!

I feel like I'm ten years older just since getting here. I've seen stuff I could never tell anyone at home. Me and the other grunts (that's what we're called) eat more secrets than scrambled eggs. Last week the worst thing happened so far. Middle of the night, the VC (that's Vietcong—we have initials for everything) attacked our base, no fooling around, just bam bam bam, WE were the targets. The jungle is so close and dense, you can never see what's coming or who's out there. Anyway, our guys were ready or lucky or maybe it was just a few rogue soldiers on their side, but it was over pretty quick. The bad part was in the morning, going out to find the bodies, moving them, thinking about how it could have been us. Knowing they had mothers too, you know? Someone writing letters. And then the worst thing, we recognized one of them. It was Binh the barber, he was with our camp and we all knew him, but here he was VC all along, waiting to kill us.

Turns out we're not fighting for our country or any noble reason. We're fighting each day to get to the next day, and that's it.

What we're doing is terrible. This is a beautiful country. We've even been to the beach a couple of times. They've got palm trees crammed full of monkeys. You'd go wild for the monkeys. They wake us up screeching and laughing every day, like we're living in a zoo.

Even though I was kind of mad in the beginning, I know Tom did the right thing staying far away from Nam. I'll tell him to his face when I get out of here in 302 days.

Please write again. I'll try to be more cheerful next time!

> Your friend,
> Matt

"Does he still love you?" said Penelope.

I used the letter to fan my burning face. Matt was alive. Tears prickled up in an instant. He'd been under attack, he was scared silly, it was horrible, but he was alive. I had to call Tom. I had to be alone to read it again.

But the other, sneaky relief crept in too. This was *proof* that I had a boyfriend in Vietnam.

I had a flash of Matt hunched over this very page, thinking about me long enough to finish a letter. I could ignore the small, itching fact that it was likely only good manners that made him write to a girl who must now feel as far away and insignificant as his gym bag or his science trophies or his affection for *Star Trek*. I slipped the envelope into my English notebook and clasped it to my chest, holding what only I knew to be true.

"Ooh, she's gone all pink!" crooned Oona.

I didn't mind them laughing. Matt was alive.

brenda

"So. Your dad is Dr. Sperm."

"Stern," said Michael.

"Oops, yeah." Brenda's cheeks went hot as if she'd been slapped. "Stern."

"You're cute, all rosy like that. "

Rosy? Blazing, more like.

"Yes, he's my dad."

"Wow. I mean, I knew that. But how does it feel?"

"What do you mean?"

"Having a"—she adjusted a strap under her top with a little snap—"a *doctor*, for a dad? He sees a lot of naked people, right? He sticks his fingers lots of . . . *places*. So, how does it feel to watch him using the same fingers to . . . open a letter or pop a chip in his mouth?"

"He doesn't eat chips," said Michael. "He says they're greasy. I'm not supposed to have them either." His turn to blush, likely realizing what a prat he sounded. "But I do," he added quickly. "Whenever I want." He shoved in another chip as if to prove his daring. He was dead sweet, prat or no. Better a prat than a yob.

"Doctors see people naked," he said. "It's part of the job. I'd rather not think about it."

Brenda chewed on her lower lip, trying not to remember the doctor's hands on her bra.

"Funny job," she said at last. "Not the part about healing people. That's good, of course. But . . ."

"But what?"

"Oh, nothing."

He patted his hair again, but caught himself and quickly tugged on his collar instead. Could she ever tell him what had happened with his father?

Michael's collar was messed up. She reached over to fix it for him.

"I have to babysit at four," she said. "My sister's kids, who you saw that time." *Ages* ago, you gormless git. Where've you been?

She'd been back to the chip shop how many times? Ever so casual, wearing nice tops, putting up with Alec's remarks when she'd had the bad luck to bump into him. Today was to be Michael's last chance, she swore. And here he'd been, barely even sheepish, but dead sweet and paying for her chips!

"Let's not waste our time in this place," he said.

Brenda smashed the chip paper into an oil-stained ball. Her toss arced gracefully and dropped straight into the bin.

"Goal!" she cried. "Your turn."

He missed.

"Better luck next time."

They walked to the river, along the cinder path ending by a fence that protected the railway crossing. They leaned against that sturdy fence and began to kiss. He was a bit slurpy, Brenda remembered as soon as they started, just like last time. But so friendly, pausing to chat, playing with her hair, saying how the afternoon light tinted the river gold and how last winter he'd seen a whooper swan, had she ever?

But then he went for her buttons and it was like a cube of ice slipped down her front. All she could think about was Dr. Stern's confident hands.

"Stop," she said. "You have to stop."

He grabbed back his nervous fingers and shoved them into his pockets, stepping away but oddly bent, so she knew he had that embarrassing situation going on, boys getting hard if you even said the word *tit*, let alone had two real ones within arm's reach. Only she couldn't let him, could she? Wouldn't that be dead insulting, to have your dad touch your girlfriend more suavely than you? *Girlfriend?* That was pushing things a bit, eh?

"Sorry!" he said. "Didn't mean . . . You're just . . . so pretty."

"I have to go," she said. "My sister's got work. I'm ever so prompt since the muckup that night."

She hurried ahead along the path, letting him unbother himself, praying she hadn't ticked him off forever.

"Next week?" he called.

"Yes." She paused to smile back at him. Didn't want to scare him off with grumping. She'd decide later if she had the nerve to tell him that his dad was a bit pervy.

Tuesday, in the Girls' Changing Room, between morning lessons and dinner, Oona said, "Who wants to skip Brit Con this afternoon and go to the village instead?"

"I will," said Jenny. "I am completely hopeless with the inner workings of the British constitution."

"I'll come," said Brenda. "If we walk by the high school." Maybe she'd catch a peek of Michael, show him to the others, get their opinions whether he fancied her.

Going past the high school took ten extra minutes. A few boys were straggling back from the midday break, but no Michael in sight. Someone whacked Brenda on the bum, jumping into the road as she spun around. "What the hell!"

It was Alec, looking goofy with his skinhead hair and clodhopper boots along with the school uniform.

"Hands off!" snapped Brenda. "Or I'll cut them off."

Alec laughed. "Ooh, all Mikey's now, eh?"

"Piss off."

"You going to introduce me to your posh friends?"

"Oy," said Brenda. "What's the news about your mate, Robbie?"

"He's not *my* mate anymore," said Alec. "He's got *special* friends."

"But is he home from the hospital?"

Alec backed away at the sound of a bell ringing from the

141

school tower. "I'll see Mikey-boy in maths. Shall I pass him your"—he gave his hips a thrust—"regards?"

Oona giggled and Brenda swatted her.

"Don't encourage wankers," she said.

"Ooh." Alec moved off. "I'm so hurt."

"I'm parched," said Jenny. "Let's stop at the pub for a lemonade."

"Good idea." Oona swung her handbag on a long strap. "I need the loo."

They slammed through the door to the ladies' shrieking—more than they had to, Brenda knew—but laughing up a ruckus is one of those things it's easy to do with other girls. They must have mad fun in the dorm, while she was at home watching telly with her dad. Oona's mouth was stuffed with crisps, but she laughed so hard the crumbs spurted out, making the girls laugh all the harder.

Oona slipped straight into the first stall. Jenny and Brenda went to the mirror, did hair stuff and lip glossing, and called to Oona could she have a noisier piss? Oona made a wet farting sound, lips against her arm obviously, and that set them off again.

But then, in the mirror, Brenda saw a bulgy string shopping bag sitting inside the last stall, next to the toes of ugly beige granny shoes.

Oona flushed and breezed out, Velcro-zipping her jeans, smoothing her blouse. "That's better," she said. "I was brimming."

Brenda poked her to hush up, pointing to the feet. They'd been extra rude, thinking they were alone.

"Oops." Oona washed her hands, did her hair, glossed her lips, while Brenda crossed her eyes and Jenny banged her bum against the door, waiting. They all puffed out their cheeks to show how hard it was to keep quiet. The woman stayed in her stall.

"She's waiting for us to leave," whispered Jenny. "Maybe she's afraid of teenagers. It's called ephebiphobia."

"*I'm* afraid of old ladies in loos," said Oona. "Let's go."

Back in the bar, they let loose with demented giggling. The barman, Harry Hines, pinned them with the scowly eye.

"I'm going to buy tea bags," said Jenny, "soup packets, and cookies. I mean, biscuits. You coming or should I meet you later?"

"I forgot to go to the loo," said Brenda. "I'll catch you up at Bigelow's."

"I'll wait here," said Oona. "No cash. It'll only tick me off to watch you shop."

Brenda went back to the ladies'. The bag and feet were still there, exactly as before.

Brenda used the loo and flushed. Had the woman fallen asleep? Brenda coughed, ran the taps for a sec, watched the shoes. But then, a sort of a moan. Brenda froze. Had they been mucking about too much earlier to hear that sound?

"Hello?" said Brenda. "Is everything all right?"

Another little noise. Holy crap.

"Do you need help?"

Brenda's whole body got hot and right away chilled. Ghost trundling over her grave, as her gran always said.

143

"Hello?"

She tapped the stall door a couple of times. Nothing. Really not wanting to, she knelt down for a look under. String bag in front of her face holding a cabbage and a packet of PG Tips. She tried to nudge it aside, only it was wedged. The feet were . . . *Oh, gag me!* The feet were not flat on the floor the way they should be if the woman had been sitting up properly on the loo. They lolled over at the wrong angle.

Holy *flipping* crap.

Brenda crooked her neck and pushed her head farther under the door, horrified to recognize Mrs. Willis, who used to work at the post office till she had trouble with her ticker. The restroom door behind her *whapped* open and Brenda jerked up fast, giving herself an almighty smack on the skull.

"What the hell?"

Lucky it was Oona, but it must have looked pretty dodgy.

"She's having a fit or something in there."

Another of those scary wheezes.

"We can't stay here! That's horrible!" Oona walked right out.

"Cow!" Brenda scrambled up and went straight to Harry Hines. "Excuse me, but I think there's somebody dying in your lavatory."

He stared like she'd cursed his mother, but must have twigged from her face that she was not joking around. Brenda noticed that her hands were shaking like an old drunk's.

"Sylvie!" Harry yelled at the girl wiping a table. "Go in the lav and see what's up."

"You'll have to smash the door down," Brenda told Harry. "She could be dead by now."

"Lordy," said Sylvie. "Is it Mrs. Willis? I thought she'd slipped out on me. She usually leaves a bit extra."

They went into the loo.

"In there." Brenda pointed.

Sylvie crossed herself, being Irish. "Mrs. Willis?" she hollered. A faint wheeze in return.

"Saints be cursed." Sylvie tore out of the room. Brenda gazed down at those pathetic beige feet and whispered, just in case, "If you're going, Mrs. Willis, I hope you go easy. But hang on if you can, there'll be help coming." What if the last thing she ever bought was a cabbage? Made Brenda want to cry.

"Did you ring the doctor?" she asked Harry outside.

"Yeah." He was yanking the fire axe off the wall, sweat popping all over his forehead.

Jenny came in from the street just then, with her sack of supplies. "What's taking you?" she said. "I thought we were meeting at—" She gaped as Harry swung the axe over his shoulder.

"The police'll want to chat with you lot." Harry strode into the ladies', as if slashing down loo stalls was an everyday thing.

Jenny tugged on Brenda's arm. "What the *hell*?"

Brenda told her. "And! Oona's done a flit. If we talk to the sodding police, it'll come out that we've skived off school."

"We can't not stay," said Jenny. She was the opposite of Oona. "What's a detention compared with this?"

Four seconds later, two coppers hurtled into the bar, with Dr. Stern half a step behind. Brenda would swear her tits buzzed when he recognized her.

"Where's the patient?" he asked.

Jenny said, "Ladies' room," hopping over to hold open the door for the whole parade.

The first good bit was riding straight past Oona on the York Road, her with another mile to go. Next was coming up the school drive in the back of the police car, waving to No-Face and Nico kicking a football on the playing field. Penelope had caught sight from the dorm window and spread the word, bringing an audience to the front steps as Jenny and Brenda climbed out of the car. Richard had been telephoned and was there to speak with the coppers. The girls were to wait on the bench outside his office. Deep in Brenda's chest something burned, warm and steady. Mrs. Willis was on her way to hospital instead of to the morgue. Brenda felt pretty tip-top, thank you very much. Jenny was right, what was a detention compared with this?

"Shouldn't we agree on a story?" said Jenny.

"How about the truth?" said Brenda.

Jenny went in first and came out grinning three minutes later. "Your turn," she said. "I told him it was my idea. But he knows Oona skipped too." Her shopping bag bumped Brenda's knee, a reminder there'd be biscuits later, whatever happened.

Richard sat behind his desk, tapping his chin with both

146

his forefingers. Brenda had not been in his office before. Her tip-top feeling wavered as she absorbed the smooth wooden loveliness of the room. Richard was gazing at her and she had to gaze back, chin up, no fidgets.

"Is there anything you'd like to say?" asked Richard.

"Does my father have to know?" Brenda had a painful flash of Richard shaking hands with her dad, who'd be wearing his work gloves and have those rings of sweat he got under his arms from lugging mattresses out of the lorry all day. Could she lose her scholarship for skiving off? Her dad would strangle her with a bedspring.

"For now the story stays in this room," said Richard. "But I'd like to hear your reason for being at the Red Lion on a Tuesday during lessons."

"We shouldn't have been there," said Brenda. "I know that. But . . ."

Oh, but why? Be up front.

"But . . . we've got double Brit Con on Tuesdays. It can be as wretched as having chicken pox at Christmas."

Richard's face showed that he understood that much at least.

"But we *were* there. I found her, didn't I? Did the right thing, despite my sister saying I never do. Even the medics, they said she would've died in another few minutes, and then it would have been Sylvie, the server, who found her. Only too late. It was pretty ghastly even with her being alive."

Richard nodded, so Brenda kept going. "What I'm wondering is, does God let us do wrong things if they lead to doing right? I was skiving, which was wrong. But it was right that I was there to help Mrs. Willis. Wasn't it? And let's say there's a doctor who does a wrong thing in one part of his life but then does all the good of healing? Or Mrs. Willis, even, who has a drink too many most days. If she'd had her fit at home, she'd be dead right now. Her nip at lunchtime meant she was in the right spot for me to find her. So how can we ever know? Right or wrong?" Brenda stopped. She'd been rattling on.

Richard rubbed his thumb across his chin about thirty times. "There is a poem by Robert Frost," he finally said. "I would like to recite the last verse."

"All right, then."

" 'I shall be telling this with a sigh . . .' " He used the voice that made them crack up in Meeting, important and rumbling. " 'Somewhere ages and ages hence.' " He looked at her, as if to make certain she was paying attention. " 'Two roads diverged in a wood, and I—I took the one less traveled by; and that has made all the difference.' "

He went back to rubbing his chin.

"Oh." Brenda tried to sound impressed, but she was thinking, *Huh?* "That's a really nice poem, Richard. But could you explain a bit further?"

"I like to think that it means we should follow our hearts," he said. "That we may not understand our choices until we are looking back upon what they led us to."

"Do you think deep *all* the time?" Brenda asked.

Richard smiled and stood up, not even mentioning detention. "Happily for Mrs. Willis, your road converged with hers today."

Brenda felt that warmth again, as if she'd stepped into a patch of sunshine. "Yeah," she said. "She'll have a little more road to be looking back on. Because of me."

Richard drove a funny old Citroën that he said he'd bought twenty-four years ago. He collected Brenda after tea the next afternoon, said he'd take her to visit the woman she'd rescued. It felt dead strange to be sitting up front in the headmaster's car, in Isobel's usual spot, her things in the pocket: the eyeglass case, a tin of sour lemon drops, a crumpled tissue.

"I don't often think about the double lives of our day students," Richard was saying. "I thank you for reminding me how rich your experience is, steeped in the world of the town as well as that of Illington Hall."

"Ha," said Brenda. "*Rich* is the very last word I'd use. Nobody's got nothin' among the townies. Apart from the ones who run the hotel, perhaps, and a couple of blokes who make a lucky guess at the racetrack."

"You have a great deal more than you realize," said Richard. "Time will show that you have gathered much of value."

The headmaster announced that he would wait in the car while she was in the hospital. "Take your time," he said. "Be the neighbour you'd wish to have."

Brenda watched Mrs. Willis nap, quite grateful not to

find her awake. That might have been dead awkward, considering the knickers and such that Brenda had witnessed. She tore out a page from her history notebook and drew a cheery daisy with *Get Well Soon* scrawled over it.

The idea had come to her in the Citroën that she might ask about Robbie Muldoon while she was here. It had worked out nicely, Richard letting her do the visiting on her own.

Robbie's arms had just been rebandaged. "Stiff as pricks," he said. "Can't even bend at the elbows." He waved them about to prove it. "They're letting me out tonight."

"I don't suppose you'll say who did it," said Brenda.

"Don't suppose I will," he said. "Best for everyone if I didn't see."

"What if they go on and hurt someone else?"

"It was me they wanted," said Robbie.

She didn't quite have the pluck to ask, *Was it true what was scratched under those wrappings?* She'd never met a boy like that before.

"Well, ta-ta, then," said Brenda. "For now."

He lifted a long white arm. "Dead nice of you to come."

The elevator took an age. When the doors opened, Brenda was face to face with Dr. Sperm. Holy crap.

"Hello there." His smile was warm as mittens. Panic banged in her chest as she stepped in, staring at the numbers, anywhere but at him. Which road? A shadowy side path or the bright glare of a motorway with oncoming cars?

"You should know," said Brenda. "Your son Michael is a mate of mine."

"I didn't realize," said the doctor, "that he knew any girls."

"Oh yeah, we're good chums."

Now or never. "And I won't tell him you touched me, unless I hear you've done it to someone else at my school. Clear enough?"

The elevator dinged for the ground floor. Her face had never been as red as this, Brenda was certain. She let the doctor exit in front of her so she could go the other way.

oona

Hallo there, Toronto,

  BIG DRAMA!!! *I found a body in the ladies' toilet at the Red Lion!!!!!! Well, not actually expired, but nearly. Dead exciting! (Excuse the pun.) It was me and Brenda (roly-poly day girl, remember her?). You should have been there! The funny bit was that we were skiving at the time, with American Jenny, but all was well in the end. We totally saved the old bag's life and hardly got a wigging from Richard, just Early Bed for two nights. Jenny, by the way, seems to be getting the hang of Illington, though she made the fatal mistake of befriending Penelope at the outset, little knowing what inevitable woe awaits. Her peculiar fashion statement— the slashed-up uniforms—becomes ever more bizarre as the laundry does its share in turning every dangly bit into a* frayed rag (in the case of the blouses) or a knotted lump of lint (jumpers & skirts). But she goes along with American aplomb, thinking she's the coolest chick in the farmyard. She's mad on letter writing, mostly to her tragically military boyfriend in Vietnam. She milks it a bit, if you ask me, but she and Percy sit there scribbling away on what they apparently believe to be great works of art: his film script and her portfolio of love letters.

Last night, Kirby took a vanload of us to Leeds, to hear a band called Lindisfarne. Val Matron went as the other staff member (and speaking of members, I suspect that she is more than a little interested in that which belongs in Kirby's trousers).

It was me, Jenny, Carrie, Adrian, Percy (who wore a tie for some unfathomable reason), Henry, and . . . Nico!

I confess to looking rawther fetching in a new top from Marks and Sparks (defying their usual humble attempts at design and providing a flattering view of the upper-chest region). Adrian made several lewd comments, as did Henry (which was quite gratifying as we've had only one Cellar encounter since that heated display of affection after the Spring Fling dance last term). However, Gentleman Nico told them to shut their gobs, which was most noble of him. He can be dead sweet, can't he?

Wouldn't you know it, I was squished in next to him on the ride to Leeds, so we had the opportunity to discuss our mutual Canadian friend, i.e., you. We did, however, manage a couple of minutes of alternate discourse. Imagine that! Nico sat between Jenny and Percy on the way home, while Henry fell asleep and drooled on my scoop-neck top!

153

I have been on a beautification kick, using polish to stop biting nails and attempting to diet, which is not SO hard if you remember Vera D's exquisite cuisine. Kirsten smuggled an electric kettle to stash in the Girls' Changing Room so we can make tea or bouillon. I've been living on Oxo cubes and Tuc crackers.

> Much love from your friend with an actual waistline!

PS Band was brill!!!!!

TUESDAY

Hello, gorgeous and all the usual rather boring introductory crap . . .

Extra Bonus Feature! Today Only!
Genuine handwritten notes from
Odd Assortment of Cellar Dwellers (skiving off Assembly) . . .

SARAH!! Kirsten here. Austen dorm without you is not nearly as great as Brontë WITH you! Come baaaack! xxoo

Hi, this is me, Nico. Sorry I haven't written. We sure miss you.
I'll write soon on my own. Love you, N

How cold is Canada? Not as cold as the breakfast porridge I'm sure.
Cheers, Percy.

Kirsten says I have to say hello, so hello. Luke.

Hallo there, wish we'd been here together—you are talked about all the time! xx Jenny, "the new girl"

Hello, Oona again. Doesn't all that just toast your toes?

FOUR DAYS LATER

Whoops, just found this in Bio notebook, will send at once. xx

PPS Thanks for letter! Not long enough . . .

PPPS I don't actually see Nico as often as I mention him—I just assume you'll be interested. . . .

Whoops again, now writing from bedroom at home in Lowestoft, long weekend due to strep throat. I'd rather die than let Dr. Sperm touch my virginal being. . . .

Guess who rang up my first night back? To be completely honest, Nico rang me because I rang him first. Don't worry, it was all business, asking about getting a signed book from his mother for the camping trip raffle.

Otherwise, blah! Home! Nice for the first few meals and then deadly. More soon. xxxxxxxxooooooo

Still at HOME. BLAH.

BORED as HELL!

As much as school can be claustrophobic and the food

155

sickening, there's always something going on. I am PINING for entertainment.

Instead, I shall turn my attention to answering some of the one hundred and nine urgent questions in your last letter. . . .

Yes

No

Sometimes

Etc.

Ha ha, only joking!

I suppose I'm just avoiding the sticky matter of Nico's communication habits. . . .

We've been pretty occupied with A-level practice exams so that's one possible reason. . . . But yes, we've been spending a bit of time together. He's possibly my best male friend at the moment, so from the insider point of view, I'd say he's not writing because he's trying to face the fact that you aren't here, and staying in touch perhaps prolongs the pain?

Look for fun in merry old Toronto, since that's where you must remain. . . .

Anyway, must go,

Ta-ta for now
Oooooooona!

THURSDAY

Sparkling sunshine for your special day!
HAPPY BIRTHDAY TO YOU
HAPPY BIRTHDAY TO YOU

HAPPY BIRTHDAY, DEAR GRANNY,
HAPPY BIRTHDAY TO YOOOOOOU!

I thought particularly about your drastic aging during
Richard's uplifting poetic offering last Meeting, by some old
codger named Robert Herrick: Gather ye rosebuds while ye
may, Old time is still a-flying: And this same flower that
smiles to-day, To-morrow will be dying.

Cheerful, eh?

No time to linger but wanted to wish you many many
many happy returns of this memorable day. Thinking of you
from far far away . . .

xx a sp-OONA-ful of sugar . . .

(WAITING FOR SUNDAY MEETING)

Hi, Sarah,

Did you have a loverly birthday? Any particular wishes
you'd like to come true this year?

I wonder how much you think about us. I wonder if I'll
ever see you again. Perhaps when we're old ladies like our
mothers and drag our creaking limbs to a reunion, motoring
around the Lake District or something . . . Do we ever cross
your mind? Since Illington has no effect on your life anymore?
Are you possibly reunited with Tony?

Anyway, just saying hello.

Nico had a long weekend in the South of France with his
mother, did you know that?

Loads of things happening, can't write it all down, I'd be scribbling half the night. Sooo, just thinking about you. Sad you're so far away.

Cheerio,
Love you,
Oona

Dear Sarah,

This is actually quite an awkward letter to write, but I am going to come right out and say it. Even while you're hating me, I trust that once you stop shredding my photo to let it sink in, you will understand completely.

The truth is that Nico and I have become rather close over the past week, and by close I mean . . . We don't really talk that much but there's a sort of spiritual connection that doesn't need words to thrive. However, it now goes beyond the spiritual. Yes, it happened a while ago, but I couldn't quite bring myself to tell you right away. I admit he is the sexiest bloke I have ever met, let alone kissed, let alone the rest of it. It comes clear why you seemed to have a sudden interest in woodworking your last term. Who knew there was a lock conveniently located on the inside of the supply room?

This may be hard for you to read, but . . . you live in another country . . . and Nico has moved on. I happen to be the one he has moved on to.

In the beginning we both genuinely missed you so much that we had that as our common ground. Then we found out that we were having fun. I am totally in love and I think he feels the same way even if he hasn't said it yet. He wants to keep our relationship a secret for now, out of respect for you.

That's the story. Please write me when you're ready to find it in your heart to be happy for us.

> Your true friend, even though it may not feel like it right now,
> O

Sarah,

I don't really think all the name-calling was necessary. You left months ago! So it's not exactly a "heinous betrayal," is it? You claim you wouldn't care except that I lied to you, but aren't you actually lying to yourself? Nico says you were never really as close as you pretended to me, that he liked you, so he wasn't faking or anything, but it was a much bigger deal for you. So don't go around calling me a bitch when your idea of the relationship was just a tad inflated.

I know you're hurting, but don't take it out on me.

> Your friend, Oona

DURING BIO

Dear (I really mean it) Sarah,

Haven't heard from you, so I'm wondering . . . ?
I knew you'd be upset, but I couldn't call myself a friend if I didn't tell you the truth about what is happening.

Though I honestly expected you to be slightly more rational about it.

I'm in love with someone and so are you, but I'm here and you're not, so what did you suppose was going to happen?

Hurting you was the last thing we wanted, and believe me, Nico feels the guilt. He has been quite withdrawn lately.

Oona

BRONTË DORM, MIDNIGHT

Sarah,

A word of advice. Not wise to ring Nico yesterday on his birthday "for old times' sake." He's a little bruised by this whole transition, and it would be appreciated if you would avoid writing or trying to ring him again. I assure you that he is doing the right thing, but has no intention of grinding your face in it. So leave him alone, for your own mental health.

O.

FORGIVE ME PLEASE FORGIVE ME PLEASE
FORGIVE ME PLEASE FORGIVE

Dear Sarah,

I would be surprised if you've even opened the envelope after the contents of the last one.

I kneel before you in abject misery, begging your forgiveness.

Hurting and betraying you is the worst thing I've ever done and I see that even more clearly now that I've been hurt and betrayed myself.

Nico has revealed his true colours and they are ugly indeed. Even when he was with me, it turns out that I was not the only object of his attentions. He was also flirting and testing his charms with several others, beginning with Jenny-the-American-tart-with-a-boyfriend-at-war and moving on from there. Naturally, my meager appeal cannot compete with the apparent willingness of the entire female race.

I realize now he was only using me. He claims he never meant to get off with me and that I was just a little too available! As if he wasn't having a fondle-fest whenever he could!

Every minute that I see him panting after some slag is a minute of scalding pain for me. As much as you suffered when I betrayed you, at least you didn't have to watch.

Please please pleeeeeeeease consider my supplication for renewed friendship.

Yours forevermore,
Oona

nico

The news whisked through school on Monday morning that Jasper, the English master, had broken an ankle over the weekend, hiking in the Cotswolds. A nasty break that needed surgery, a metal pin, an extended stay in hospital. A supply teacher had been hired, her first assignment. She would begin today, taking over lessons on the regular schedule. Had anyone seen her? She'd gone into Richard's office before breakfast and had not yet emerged. Wasn't it awful about poor Jasper?

Nico and the other fifth-form boys were all faintly relieved about Jasper, none of them having finished the reading for the Monday quiz. By Wednesday, fifth-form opinion was mixed on the topic of Amy Storm, but no one gave poor Jasper another thought.

The girls said: *Too young to take seriously. Too bloody*

perky. Pretentious vocabulary. Trying to be everybody's best mate. Snooty voice. Tits as round as bleeding grapefruits. Do you think she has a boyfriend?

The boys said: *Hot.*

Nico did not like being one of a crowd, but he had to admit, Amy was hot. Extra hot today due to a dove-grey cashmere sweater snugly enhancing her young and perky body at the front of the chilly effing classroom in the bleakest corner of Yorkshire, where Nico could not believe that winter was only just beginning. Did he imagine that Amy seemed to smile in his direction more than anywhere else in the room? He tried to calculate; if she had gone to uni straight from school, with no work abroad or other do-gooder nonsense, she could be as young as twenty-three or twenty-four. Not *so* much older.

"I'm going to veer a little from what Jasper was planning." Amy tipped her head backward and shook out her long hair. Nico, watching closely, could almost feel the breeze on his own neck. "He wanted to focus for a few days on the important concept of *point of view*, and we'll do that. But I'm super excited to use a different text as the groundwork for our study. We're going to begin with a close look at the short story entitled 'Lady's Fancy.'"

Oh no. Anything but that.

"I'm sure you all know that this a-*may*-zing story was written by one of your very own Illington alumni"—her eyes sparkled at Nico—"under the pen name Miss Althea Neverly. And aren't we so lucky to have Miss Neverly's son right here in the room!"

Nico tipped his chair back very slowly. As if Nico being born five years after the story had been written had anything to do with anything. *As if the story was even worth discussing*, his mother would holler.

"Here we have a classic example of shifting points of view," said Amy. "Neatly layered in a masterful narrative that calls out for close analytical reading. You're in for a treat, my friends, if you are experiencing this story for the first time."

Nico rocked ever so slightly, willing his classmates to speak up.

"Excuse me, Amy?"

Thank you, Esther. Always willing to be the supreme nerd.

"Esther?"

"I don't know if you've run this past the headmaster? I mean, the story is in our anthology . . . and most of us have read it . . . but the school . . . well, it's not meant to be on the curriculum . . . you know, out of sensitivity to Nico."

Amy's glossy lips pouted like those of a birthday girl with a broken balloon. *Aw, diddums*, thought Nico. *Party over.*

"Not that it's not good," Esther hurried to add, with a quick look at Nico. He bestowed upon her his sexiest smile of gratitude, which caused an instant flush up her freckled neck. "But it's rather . . . out of bounds for discussion."

His mother had written the stupid story as a lark one weekend, with three university roommates each writing one too. They'd sent them all off to an American magazine with pseudonyms invented while under the influence of gin-and-lemonade cocktails. Thea's story had been accepted, the others had not. Thea Nevos had invented her nom de plume, Miss Althea Neverly, thinking it sounded gothic and hilarious and not Greek. Her friends were not surprised that her submission was chosen, but they were a bit miffed. More than miffed when her one silly story launched a career of deconstructing male assumption and mythology about writing by women, eventually making Thea Nevos an outspoken and foulmouthed celebrity on behalf of the new women's liberation movement.

"Janice never really got over it," Nico's mother said. "That's why she screwed your father a week after you were born. Hardly the behaviour of a woman defining sisterhood." She shrugged. "Of course back *then*, in the fifties? There was no such thing. It was up to us to define it. Possibly she was doing *exactly* what a *liberated* woman does."

Nico hated when she talked to him like that. He hated when she acted as if he were an adult, a peer, a pal, a woman, instead of a kid. *A boy kid, Mother, in case you hadn't noticed. And I'd rather not hear about your menstrual blood on radio programs either.*

Amy recovered quickly. "Come on, fifth formers. To revisit a classic is often to discover a new work! Each phase of our own maturity is marked by the ability to reinterpret what we have considered familiar, to adjust our point of view, to encounter . . . *revelation*." She slid her bum up onto the desk and crossed her legs, making Nico wonder what happened underneath the skirt. That would be a revelation worth looking into.

"Point of view from here a nice one," Adrian whispered, pissing Nico off that he'd been thinking the same thing.

But Amy was still chattering.

"I'm sure Nico is mature enough to handle a bit of literary appreciation! Since we're all *experts* on the Neverly tale, I want you to consider the character of Lady Rosalyn. Is she an archetypal victim? Or is she possibly what is now being referred to as a feminist icon? Does everyone know that word, *feminist*?" Amy's method of teaching clearly relied on a deep bucket of pseudopsychological insights. And now she was going to apply this phoney crap to Thea Nevos?

Nico imagined bashing a dent in his own forehead using the edge of the desk as an implement. He pictured his mother slowly raising her fingers in a cursing V at the shiny-faced Amy, her head giving its customary shake of disdain.

"Ah!" Amy clasped her hands together in front of her chest, making everything jiggle for a moment, distracting Nico just as he intended to interrupt the lecture.

"An enlightened source!" said Amy. "Nico?"

Young Thea did not waste time after the tiny flurry over her short story (told in the alternating voices of Lady Rosalyn and her child maidservant, Melly). She had quickly rewritten her thesis—"Reinterpreting the Gothic Novel"—as fiction, from the point of view of a vengeful female ghost. She was offered book deals from several different publishing houses and accepted two of them. Carefully balancing her academic intentions with a deft talent for ghostly murder mysteries, Thea wrote four more books in five years. She was suddenly a social darling, photographed at parties and climbing out of limousines.

Until the next phase of her notoriety: the out-of-wedlock conception of her son. ("*Wed*lock?" said Nico's mother. "*Doesn't the word just* scream *of something to be avoided?*") She referred to the father of her baby only as M, but did not flinch from recording the size of his penis or his love of maple syrup as a sex accessory. Thea Nevos was despised by anyone who didn't idolize her. The next book, promoted as strictly nonfiction, recorded her youth and the early years of motherhood, and quickly became a bestselling and irreverent "bible" for young parents.

"I can't listen to this," said Nico. He might as well go all the way. Ticket out of class, right? "You're spouting rubbish. She didn't know she was writing this destined-to-be-a-curriculum-hit type of story." That was his mother's phrase. *Curriculum-hit*, she'd sneer. *Big literary aspiration. The story is derivative, unmitigated crap.* "She whipped it off as a dare. For a magazine contest."

"I know that's the myth," said Amy. "But even if it's true, she came up with a super story! It has all the elements of an old ghost tale, with a 'new woman' agenda enmeshed in the echoes of a gothic literary tradition, challenging our preconceptions about—"

"She just needed the cash." Nico could hear his mother's irritated amusement. *I just needed the cash. I had my eye on a Volkswagen Beetle.*

The other kids laughed. He tipped his chair farther back, balancing.

Amy sighed. "You're not giving the author enough credit here, Nico. Is it too difficult for you to have an objective dialogue about what is possibly household scripture?"

Nico's chair legs hit the floor with a *thunk*.

"You're being intentionally rebarbative," said Amy. "I'm certain that your classmates take your mother's story more seriously than you do."

"Really?" Nico shrugged. "They look pretty bored to me."

Amy's cheeks were as pink as a girl's who has just been kissed. "You may go."

He nearly went. He'd purposely pissed her off so he could leave. But, "We just did this," he said. "With Jasper. The unreliable narrator."

"These narrators are *not* unreliable," insisted Amy. "That's what makes your mother's work so fascinating! She explores the same incidents through such different eyes. A woman chafing against the bonds of convention, and a girl in servitude who remains spiritually free, not yet trapped by expectations. Both perspectives are valid and reliable. They serve to enhance our—"

"In your version," he said. "From your *point of view*, 'Lady's Fancy' is some libber masterpiece. According to my mother, it is shite juvenilia. And I'm like, who cares? So whose point of view wins? What's the real story?" Would Amy take on the battle of a curse word spoken in class? Hands waved in the air, and she ignored the *shite*.

"There is no *one* story, is there?" Jenny did not look at Nico as she spoke. "Nobody *wins*."

"Except everyone claims to be telling the truth," said Penelope.

"Ah," said Amy. "The question that humans have tackled for centuries. What *is* truth?"

"That's what I mean," said Nico. "No such thing. Especially if you're talking about someone else. Nobody knows. It might not be lies, but it's not true either. It's the way the story is told, what gets emphasized. Or left out."

Amy's hair caught a sunbeam through the window, giving her a halo for a moment as she considered Nico. "You sound as though you've struggled a bit, being the subject of someone else's scrutiny," she said. "If a mere short story— 'Lady's Fancy'—is a problem for you, how do you feel about your mother's memoir?"

Amy picked up a book from her desk and Nico groaned aloud. He glimpsed his mother's public face for the ten thousandth time, mysterious behind dark glasses, fierce and beautiful in her youth. He slapped his palm onto the desk so hard that it stung for a moment. "You've got no right," he said, "yammering on about points of view, barging into people's lives as if it's part of some lesson, pretending you care about *truth*."

There was a deadly hush as he yanked open the door. He glanced back at the teacher, pale now, her glossy mouth sagging. She was holding the volume that he'd spent three years at Illington pretending did not exist. *Slam.*

Nico had made an effort, more than once or twice, to read *Raising Nicky*, but from chapter 3 and the moment

169

his parents met, it was excruciating. He liked the early bits, about his mother's idyllic childhood on the island of Spetsai with Nico's grandparents. Then, when Thea was nine, her Greek father, Leftaris, and her determined English mother, Rose, had joined a band of Quakers to form a commune in Yorkshire, peaceably sidestepping the war that loomed in Europe. Like hippies, but without the hair. And no love beads or silly clothes that would get in the way of a hammer or saw, since the centuries-old mansion they'd discovered needed to be nailed back together after decades of neglect. The book showed a photo of his grandfather transforming a stable into what was now the science classroom, sleeves rolled up on his stiff, collared shirt, a handkerchief tucked neatly into his pocket.

Nico's Papou and Granny Rose had helped to bring Illington Hall back from gothic ruin, and their daughter had grown up watching what could happen when social faith led to constructive action. After the war, they moved back to Greece, leaving Thea as a boarder to finish her education amongst her English friends.

Nico liked the chapter about the school, of course; descriptions of mandatory plunges in the frigid pond, séances to raise ghosts in the dormitories, and food cooked by a much-younger Vera, even worse back then because of war rationing.

When Thea lost her virginity (in the woodworking shed, with a discreetly unnamed boy—the first of dozens of lovers), that part turned out to be funny instead of mortifying because the teenage Thea was an entertaining literary character, barely related to the mother he knew. She had actually inspired him, if Nico told the absolute truth, to consider his own first time with a little more care than just the randy desperation he'd been feeling up till then. What if (as unlikely as it might seem) the event became part of his professional repertoire, the way his mother's had done?

Last spring he'd begun his mission: to have it off with a girl . . . poetically.

Even with the limited number of girls to choose from, Nico had eliminated Penelope off the top, for being a slag. He didn't intend to join a club. Kirsten was too good a friend. Esther, he'd have to face her baleful eyes for how long afterward? Fiona, Caroline, Oona: either silly or homely as hell. It came down to the Canadian girl, Sarah, to whom he'd not yet paid attention, but rather liked once he was noticing. She seemed to be wherever he looked, pulling her hair into a shining ponytail, snuggling into her afghan coat, filching sugar from the table and putting it in a little jar that she carried around just for that purpose, so she could sweeten tea made with the kettle in the Girls' Changing Room.

To launch his campaign, he cleverly bought a pound of sugar at Bigelow's in the village (along with a box of Durex). He and Sarah began to drink their tea together, from mugs they'd made in Pottery. Things moved along pretty quickly from kissing during walks down the woods to more serious rubbing and groping. Nico nicked a pillow from the infirmary and hid it under a clean tarpaulin in the woodworking shed, ready and waiting. But thanks to the spring crop of bluebells, which Sarah seemed to give him credit for, the closest they came was down the woods. They'd rolled around, humping through their jeans until Nico's had torn.

"Can I just . . . can we do it really?" he whispered.

"No chance," said Sarah.

They'd crushed teeny blue flowers like Roman fecking emperors and she finished him off by hand. Nico limped back to school so dishevelled that his dorm mates had broken into applause. Fine, let them think it had gone his way. Luckily, Sarah had gone back to Canada at the end of term without the truth coming out. But now, a full semester later, it was quite an effort to uphold his reputation while still trying to lose his virginity.

"Nico!" Amy laid a hand on his sleeve just as tea was finishing. "I'd like a word."

"Ooh." Henry and Adrian could be such holes. "What's the naughty boy done, eh?"

Nico's neck warmed as he stood to follow the teacher.

"Maybe you'll get spanked," said Adrian. Henry choked on his last swallow of tea.

Amy didn't stop outside the dining hall but led him into the dim and empty library. Her hair swung gently with every step, making him want to reach forward and grip a fistful, to feel the thickness, smell it maybe. *Jesus, mate, what are you thinking?*

"Nico, I am *so* sorry about what happened today. I spoke to the headmaster, and he . . ."

She deserved a bit of a raking, didn't she?

"Yeah, well, it's not really fair, is it? Sitting in a lesson, trying to *learn* something, suddenly having your private—"

"I don't blame you for leaving, even if it was . . . pretty rude, the way you did it." She sounded . . . tetchy, the way a girlfriend with hurt feelings might. The other blokes would love this—only he'd not be telling them.

"I'm just such a fan of your mother's work. She's so . . . almost *cosmic*, you know? She speaks directly to my inner-most . . ." Amy's fist pounding the swell above her heart caused a bounce under the cashmere that made Nico's prick stir.

"It's about my mother's *sex* life," he blurted. *Idiot*.

She reddened. "I'd been thinking how proud you must be . . . not considering how you might want to protect her privacy and—"

He'd never stood right next to her like this. He was taller than she was. Her hair rippled back from her forehead like on those virgins in Italian paintings. But she couldn't be a virgin, could she? He was now as hard as a bullet, which she would have noticed if she weren't looking straight into his eyes.

Might this be his chance?

"Of course I'm proud." He'd never said that before. And it was true. But it was also a pretty good line, wasn't it? Amy's worried face softened. "It's personal, though. That book. Not something I want . . . shown about. Or discussed."

"I just can't believe I'm standing here with the actual Nicky!" said Amy.

"It's Nico now," he said. "I'm not two."

"Well, that's certainly true! I'm certain your mum is proud of you too, all grown up! Not joking, I've read *Raising Nicky* five times. And I don't even have children! Your mother is the funniest, cleverest, most daring person!"

She laughed with her mouth open, the tip of her tongue showing between teeth. Was this an invitation? Was Nico dreaming, or did she want to get off with him?

The library door opened, giving Nico a half-second warning to step back before the overhead lights snapped on. Thank bloody god he hadn't leaned in to kiss her. He sat in the nearest chair, bulge safely hidden. Esther and Percy were here to set up for their twee little chess club.

"Right, then." Amy's voice was almost strident with perkiness. "We've got that sorted, haven't we?"

"Oh, hallo!" said Esther. "Didn't see you there in the dark."

"We're just setting things straight after the misunderstanding today," said Amy. Way too eager to explain, thought Nico. She was definitely hot for him. If he'd had five more minutes, who knows what could have happened?

He had a brief flash of Sarah, her eyebrows lifted in that skeptical way, reminding him to stay real. But Amy was real, wasn't she? Just because she was a teacher . . . admittedly quite an annoying teacher . . . but practically vibrating under that sweater, right?

Upstairs, Nico lingered in the bathroom. He was accustomed to girls looking at him. His mother's friends, even, always flirting. He was handsome, let's face it. *Handsome* being an old-fashioned word but exactly right for Nico's good cheekbones and perfect Grecian nose, his reliably wavy hair and clear tan skin. (There were no full-length mirrors in the boys' dorms, which Nico thought was a big mistake. Wouldn't it improve everyone's self-image if they spent a few minutes thinking about how to present themselves to the world?)

"The one thing you can thank your father for," said his mother. "Your face. I chose well. But it's only a bonus. Never the main thing."

He could recite in his sleep her list of qualities in a Good Man: Be surprising, funny, and fair. Listen. Take your time in bed. Don't be a baby, be a man.

With Sarah, he'd followed his mother's rules, tried to do things the right way. But she was gone, with no payoff. Was he supposed to start again every time, being thoughtful and surprising? Most girls were easily hooked with one cheesy smile and a couple of compliments. He could have Penelope any night of the week, and Oona shook her fanny at him every chance she got. Jenny had been a lost cause. Maybe he'd rushed it. But who could compete with a boyfriend in the army? And shouldn't they all be taking a lesson from that? Get it while, where, and whenever you can. Who wants to be choking to death on your own blood wishing you'd had more sex? *More* sex? *Any* sex!

Right in front of his nose . . . Nico was certain he was reading the signs from Amy as clear as the label on a packet of chewing gum: take off wrapper and put in mouth.

175

I can't believe you're thinking such shite, he could hear his mother say.

In bed, Nico lay on his stomach, using one pillow to wank against and the other over his head to muffle his moans. They heard each other all the time in Kipling dorm and usually pretended it wasn't happening. Sometimes they had to yell at No-Face about volume, but usually what happened under the duvet was ignored and allowed to stay under the duvet.

Tonight, though, as Nico drifted afterward, Adrian's voice croaked across the room, "Ameeeeee!" That had the tossers snorting and hee-hawing till the dorm monitor came in, telling them to bleeding well shut it.

Amy had dropped Miss Althea Neverly from her lesson plan, but that didn't stop the other boys from conducting a juvenile betting game, one that did not include Nico. He figured it out pretty quickly, watching Henry tallying points. Each time Amy glanced in Nico's direction, Henry made a mark on his page accompanied by a chorus of hissing and shuffling.

"You're all very lively today!" said Amy. "Am I missing something?"

Nico heard his name as part of a raunchy mutter from Adrian and willed himself not to turn around. He'd have been joking along if it were one of the others . . . but, honestly, it would never *be* one of the others, would it?

He had these moments where he couldn't understand what he was doing here. He expected his mother to ring up any second and tell him he'd passed the test, he'd shown his mettle in the foulest of circumstances, and he could come home now. He could go to day school in London and have the life he deserved. In any other situation, he would not be friends with these boys. How did someone like Adrian Mortimer end up as his best mate? He was good for a laugh and he'd try *any*thing, but seriously! Look at his tattered cuffs, hanging two inches above raw, bony wrists. Imagine him standing at the buffet after a film screening at Cannes! He'd likely shovel in the shrimp like a whale devouring plankton.

Nico glanced around, continuing the survey. Percy was an odd, skinny bloke, but with his own weirdly hip style. Those knotted dreadlocks were amazing, like the headdress of a tribal warlord. He didn't seem to care about the way Adrian bullied him to pulp, just kept humming along to some tune in his own dweeby head. But poor old No-Face, a local accent so thick he was practically speaking Bulgarian. What would No-Face do at a reception in Cambridge, watching Thea Nevos receive an honorary doctorate? Or Henry, meeting someone like that dolly bird Nico had fondled after the gallery opening his last weekend in London? Henry's pathetic effort at growing a moustache and goatee to cover his spots looked like a child's face paint at a fete.

If Thea Nevos hadn't gone to Illington, if his grandparents hadn't lifted hammers and dragged around pails of paint to help restore the place, this would not be the sort of school where Nico belonged. In his opinion. But his mother insisted that community living was an essential step on the road to manhood. Ha. Manhood.

"Nico?" Amy waved fingers in front of his nose. "You seem super distracted today."

The inevitable *ooh* from the yobs in the back row caused Amy to blink *and* blush.

"Excuse me, Amy?" said Penelope. "Can you tell us the name of the book that got Nico into such a snit yesterday?"

Foul little slag!

This time, Amy did *not* look at him. "We've decided," she said, "to keep that book out of classroom discussion."

"*We've* decided?" said Henry.

"But if you're keen to seek it out on your own—"

"No," said Nico.

"It's called *Raising Nicky*. Starring our very own—"

"Oh!" said Jenny. "My mom has that. I didn't realize . . ." She stared at Nico. "Oh, wow! Nicky equals Nico! Duh. That's wild. I read bits of that when it was lying around the house." She began to laugh. "Oh my god. That's *you*!"

Could he walk out of the lesson two days in a row? The whole room was shimmying to attention. How the hell could he stop this?

"Whoops," said Jenny, covering her mouth. "Sorry."

"Never take yourself too seriously," he heard his mother say. *"You'll only look foolish."* Why did he hear his mother's voice instead of his own?

"Hey," he said, shrugging. Not a care in the world. "You're the one who had to read it. No wonder you're sorry."

* * *

Nico nabbed Jenny after tea. "Are you going to the Swamp? May I walk with you?"

"I suppose," said Jenny. "Are you planning to buy my silence?"

"Do I have to?" he said. "*Buy* it?"

"Isn't this how blackmail begins?" she said. "One person knows something seriously damaging about the other person, and . . ."

It was already dark on the path to the woods, the branches clicking with cold as they swayed in the wind.

"It's a bit chilly for the Swamp," said Jenny. "Since neither of us smokes."

He nearly suggested the woodworking shed, but they went to sit in the library, where he had to think about Amy's sweater and the almost kiss.

"Do you really think, *seriously damaging*?" he said.

Jenny laughed. "Don't be daft." She said *daft* with an American accent, making it sound actually daft, like a bark. "I don't blame you, though, not wanting those oafs you live with to get their hands on a document that describes details about your potty training. I love when your mother says, 'Nico! If you're going to pee on the floor, please do it in the kitchen, where it's easy to clean!'"

"On the lino," he said. "I actually remember doing that. Hitting the black squares." His face sank to the table with his arms folded over his head.

"Oh, and when you pleaded for flowered underpants—I mean, knickers? And your mother bought them for you, thinking she was being all open-minded? *That* might haunt you for life."

"That never happened." He turned his head, speaking from under the tent of his arms. "I swear. An episode fabricated to take a stand against boy-girl stereotyping."

"You might just not remember," said Jenny. "You were only three. Or else your mother is a liar."

"Unreliable," he mumbled.

"Right," said Jenny. "Like with every other embarrassing incident?"

Nico winced.

"Aw, come on! I'm teasing you! Nobody really cares. Anyway, how are you going to stop them from reading it?"

Nico lifted his head. "I already took both copies, which my mother donated, from the library. I burned them down the woods. The book had been ex*punged* from Illington until Amy came along. Nobody even knew it existed."

"That's like Nazi censorship," said Jenny. "And it won't work for the ten million other copies out there in the world. But if you're trying to contain the mess within reach, I guess you'll have to steal Amy's copy too. Before Pen gets her sticky paws on it. If she hasn't already."

The Faculty Hallway was off-limits. Nico hadn't been here before. Bit shabby, wasn't it? Dingy light, grubby carpet. The student dormitories were quite flash by comparison, with their high ceilings and graceful moulding. Amy was apparently staying in Jasper's room during her time at Ill

180

Hall. How creepy was that? The door was smack in the middle of the row of the other single members of the teaching staff. Kirby, Fran, Beverly, and Jasper, all snuggled together.

His plan was to nick the book, since he didn't think she'd just hand it over. He tapped, face already warm. Movement inside. The door's handle seemed to stick a bit before the door swung open.

"Oh!" she said.

"Hallo," he managed.

Her hair was damp, as if she'd just had a shower. She was wearing a pink shirt and jeans. "You're not . . . Students aren't supposed to . . ." But she was opening the door wider, stepping out of the way. Inviting him *in*.

"This is kind of . . . urgent," he said. He looked straight into her eyes, following his mother's suggestion: *Direct eye contact makes a good first impression.* What was that scent? Not quite coconut. Almond bubble bath? Amy's fingers fidgeted, doing up a button, but too late. He'd seen the silky glimmer beneath, a wisp of lingerie. He imagined it with his fingertips, sliding over the round—

"Is this about the book?"

"Sort of." Now that he was here . . . was that why he was here?

There was one light on, a shaded lamp beside what Nico realized was the *bed*.

"Nico," said Amy. But instead of edging away, she moved toward him, as though the heat in his jeans was a giant magnet.

However many times he replayed the moment afterward, he couldn't be certain who started the kiss and how exactly they'd gone from standing to lying down. Though *lying down* made it sound pretty bloody peaceful, not the writhing storm that took them over.

Nico tried to be suave, willing himself to keep cool, keep *cool*. His hands tugged at her shirt with no luck, so he crazily cupped the soft denim over her bum, inhaling the sweet nutty smell warm from her body, hands roaming back up to her delicious titties in the same half minute. She made a little noise in her throat and he tried to swallow her face with his mouth. His balls were screaming hot, he'd never been this hard. She pressed her thigh exactly where . . . she moved . . . and *bam*—oh no! Please, *nooo*! He exploded, pulse after pulse, still zippered in.

Amy must have felt it though his jeans, mighty and useless. She sat up, lips and face chafed and swollen.

"Go," she said. "This didn't happen."

If only that were true. Nothing could be worse than this.

Nico stumbled into the Faculty Hallway, fists grinding into the sides of his face, wiping tears and punishing himself.

He was still a virgin. And he didn't have the book.

He skipped English the next day, told Adrian that Amy was beginning to piss him off. How could he arrange to never meet her again? Had he misread the signals so badly?

Had there *been* signals? Had he jumped on a moment that wasn't there? Oh god, her tits under that shirt . . . He wanted to cry all over again. What did she think of him?

He wasn't surprised when Kirby told him during Study Hall that the headmaster wanted a word. It was too small a school to play truant easily. It didn't occur to him, until he saw Amy's bum mincing away from Richard's office, that his crime might be more serious.

A copy of *Raising Nicky* lay on the grand wooden desk, like a tiny religious painting in a giant medieval frame.

"I understand there have been some fraught moments this week," said Richard. "Concerning your mother's book." He laid his palm over the jaunty font of the title.

"Mmm." Nico met the headmaster's gaze.

"And perhaps some other misguided actions as well?"

Had Nico been seen going into Amy's room? Had she made some kind of confession? What if she'd blamed him? How much did Richard know? Nico tried to clear his throat, but it was coated in silt.

What was the bleeding truth? *Whose point of view wins?*

"I just wish . . . ," said Nico. "I . . . don't think this book should be . . ."

Richard's hair was salted with grey. His eyes were grey also, watching Nico quite kindly. He was a decent bloke, if you could keep him off the poetry.

"Amy has suggested that her enthusiasm for your mother's work exceeded the parameters of a teacher's relationship with a pupil."

She did?

"Any misstep on your part, entering the Faculty Hall-way, for instance, will be overlooked on this occasion."

"Thank you." Nico's head buzzed with relief. She hadn't said anything. "Is this her copy of the book?" he asked. "Could I borrow it?" He almost said *sir*. It was a *sir* situation, but Quakers weren't sirs.

"It's mine," said Richard. He pushed it nearer. Nico could see now that it was an early edition, the blue paler, the corners slightly bashed. He flipped the pages and stopped at the dedication, written in his mother's oversized, emphatic hand.

Darling Richie,
    First time lasts forever.
        xx Thea

Holy shite! *First time?* Nico stared at the page and then clapped the book shut. Richard? With his mother?

He didn't dare look up. But he couldn't exactly leave either. Richard came around the desk, put a hand on Nico's shoulder.

"At Illington, we trust our students to behave in a manner that they will be proud of years hence. The result, naturally, is not always successful. But certain choices, made behind closed doors, are yours alone. You, Nico, are the author of your own tale."

What? Nico's brain was spinning.

"Please do not miss another lesson," said Richard. "You may go. I am two minutes late to ring the Night Bell."

Nico raced up the million stairs, two at a time, heart lighter with every step. There'd been no Richard wigging, perhaps would never be again. Richard—*Richie*—had bonked Nico's mother in the woodworking shed on page thirty-four of *Raising Nicky*.

Nico would have another chance. He'd get it right. It was only human to not hear the whole story every time. He flung open the door of Kipling dorm, sweating from the wild climb but shed of woe.

Each of his dorm mates sat on a bed, smirking. Every one of them was wearing a pair of girl's flowered knickers as a hat.

penelope

"Who's got parents coming at the weekend?" asks Oona at bathtime. "Both mine are. Of course."

Of course. Rub it in, along with the soap.

The two bathtubs get filled once each evening. Hairy Mary's got some complicated lottery system that decides which four girls share the First Baths, two in each. It would be bliss to have one of these alone. The water cascades out of an enormous faucet in the wall, filling the deep porcelain tubs that no doubt washed royal bottoms at some point in history. First Bath is heaven. Third, Fourth, Fifth Bath, the water turns to dishwater, blistered with soap scum, laced with hair.

I'm top of the list tonight, but so is Oona. She's with Kirsten in the other tub. I've got hot water up to my collarbone, trying not to poke my feet into Jenny, soaking in the Aqua Manda bubbles that she kindly donated to the cause.

"My mother will be here," says Kirsten.

"Mine too," Jenny says. "And Dad. Flying from the U.S.! They haven't seen the school yet, so it's a big fat deal. They're having a vacation after, in the Lake District. My brother's also coming, if he's not too behind with his essay on the epistolary novel." She squeezes the washcloth, drizzling droplets over her face. "What about you, Penelope?"

"Penelope's parents don't visit," Oona butts in.

"Oh," says Jenny. She blinks water out of her eyes. "How come?"

Three Words I Hate, by Penelope Fforde
Parent.
Visiting.
Day.

"Just the way it is." As if I'm going to tell her the whole sordid story in the bath.

"I suppose you're having Saturday tea with Kirsten?" says Oona. "Since you've already declined my mother's annual invitation?"

"Yeah, Pen, come have tea with us. It'll be fun."

"You don't think I've worn out my welcome with your family?"

Kirsten doesn't answer, remembering, even if she doesn't know why, that I was less than the perfect guest last time.

"Come for tea, you wombat."

"What happened?" Oona, dying to know. "Something about Luke?"

Kirsten slides down in the tub, dunking under to rinse off the crown of shampoo. Oona splashes her face, hiding the pout. Kirsten's head is sleek only a moment before the bristles pop up again.

"Where do people go, usually?" Jenny asks.

"The most expensive place," says Oona. "And you have to make your parents stop in at Bigelow's and load you up with food and snacks for the dorm. The week after Visiting Day is brilliant for trading."

I'd agree on that point. One perk of not having visiting parents is that even though you're forced to put up with the pity factor, the other kids get generous with the loot: biscuit packets and salted nuts and licorice. Leading up to and during the day, however, I do massive navigation. A leaky-canoe-above-the-waterfall level of navigation.

"You *can* go to the pub," says Kirsten. "The Red Lion."

"Right," says Jenny. "The place with the bodies in the bathroom." She can be dead funny sometimes.

"But really you should go to the Buckingham Hotel. Best scones in Yorkshire."

"I'm weirdly nervous," says Jenny. "About seeing them. My mom's going to have emotional fits about missing me."

"Yeah," says Kirsten. "That happens."

I'd like to say, *At least you've got a mother. A mother whose fits don't drive her to shave her head with the dog clipper to drown out the scary voices.* But that would make them all squirm the wrong way.

Caroline wanders in, starkers, from Brontë dorm. "Have you forgotten the thirty other girls waiting for baths?"

"Yeah, yeah." We climb out, wrap up, let the next lot

in. Brush teeth, comb out hair, smear on various lotions. Jenny has not invited me to tea on Saturday. Yet.

Plan B

Visiting day begins with Meeting, of course, so I slink my way amongst the arriving families and happen to end up on a bench between Jenny's brother and Oona's dad. The former, lovely. The latter, not so much.

"Remember me?" I say to Tom. He is dead cute close-up. Darker than his sister, no spots, wearing a flannel shirt that reeks of weed. Jenny taps his arm, makes him pay attention.

Richard welcomes the parents, recites his standby poem that starts, "When a friend calls to me from the road . . . ," and invites us to pause in silent contemplation. We hear what passes for the band—a cello, a violin, a clarinet, and a trumpet—playing some creaking melody composed by Curtis, the music master.

After Meeting, I stick close.

Jenny's mother's face glows from being in her favorite place on the planet—with her arm hooked through her daughter's. Jenny ignores me.

"You must be Jenny's mum. Welcome to England."

Jenny is obliged to say, "This is Penelope."

"It's so great to be here!" *Graaate.* "Which is your family?"

"My mum couldn't come today," I tell her in a low voice. "She's . . . not well."

"Oh, that's too bad! Would you like to join us for tea?"

189

Right on cue, all breathy and eager. "We'd love to get to know one of Jenny's new friends!" She speaks in exclamation points.

Tom lifts his eyebrow at me and I'm nodding, yes, I'd love to come, thank you, Mrs. . . . and I can't think of Jenny's last name, but it doesn't matter because she's giving me a hug, as if I'm beloved already. I have the evil thought, *What's this one hiding?* Kirsten's mother seemed nice to start with too.

Jenny pulls me aside before they toddle off for all the Show Your Work activities.

"You can come to tea," she says. "If you must. But don't mention Matt."

"Oh?"

"It's kind of a taboo topic. Everyone's really touchy about it. So, do me a favor?"

"Yeah." She's got me wondering.

I plan to spend the day on my bed, forgetting that families love to tour the dorms to get a taste of their child's home away from home, not bothering if they're interrupting someone else's *real* life. For me, this *is* home.

But I get curious enough to wander into Brontë while Esther is stashing her jumbo jar of Nutella. Esther's mother pokes around in the bathroom.

"Who's the poor girl who wears this nasty retainer?" she calls out.

"Don't touch anything! That's Oona's."

"I haven't met Oona yet, have I? Is she a friend?"

"She's not really friend material."

"Sweetie! That's a sad thing to say. What do you mean?"

"She's quite homely," Esther admits. "But she's boy crazy."

Esther glances at me and I gaze back without twitching.

"And what about you? Is there a boy you've got your eye on?"

"Mum!"

"It's a harmless question, Esther."

Does Esther's mother have the faintest clue how weird her daughter is? How she wears that floor-length cape from morning until night, apparently fending off the Dark Powers of Middle-earth? For which we're all grateful, naturally, but it hardly leads to romance.

I need a fag. I head for the Swamp. Two cigarettes later, who should turn up but Jenny's sexy brother. Brilliant. He grins when he sees me, offers a slim, hand-rolled entice-ment, and off we go a little deeper into the woods.

We get to the spot where a fallen tree gives us something to lean against. Tom lights the spliff and we pass it back and forth until it's gone and then we're facing each other.

"Is your mother as perfect as she seems?"

"Every bit and more," he says. "Except for a relentless attachment to optimism."

I hook my fingers through the belt loops of his jeans, tug-ging, playful, looking him in the eye.

"Good weed, eh?" he says.

"Yeah."

He's got a fleck of lint caught in the stubble on his chin, his lips are half smiling. "Um, what's going on here? Aren't you in the little-sister category?"

"Not if I can help it." I pull on the belt loops again.

191

"Wait a sec," he says. But it's not like he's resisting. He's a boy. Why would he say no?

In two seconds my hips are against his and same with our mouths. Am I really high or is he a great kisser? Maybe both. We're sort of swaying and kissing at the same time. There's some flowery word for this craving in my knickers, but I call it twat-ache. Tom, unlike any other boy I ever met, slides his hand into my pants and rubs exactly *there*, so I nearly faint and fall down. *He's* doing *me*, how's that for novelty? But after the full-body rush, I recover and find his zip. His turn.

We're back at the Swamp, me having another fag, when I ask him, "What's the deal with Jenny's boyfriend?"

"Who?"

"Is he really in Vietnam?"

"Uh . . ."

"Matt." I chuck my cigarette into the dirt. "Right?"

"Man, that was strong stuff," he says. "My dealer at Sheffield is actually Moroccan. Yes, Matt's in Vietnam." He rubs his eyeballs with the heels of his palms.

That's when Jenny comes huffing down the path like she's running for a bus. She skids to a halt, seeing us so chummy on the stone rim of the fountain.

"What the hell?" she says. I hope I appear to be purring.

"Hey," says Tom.

"You missed dinner," she says.

"Not really," I say.

"You look *cozy*." Making *cozy* sound poisonous.

"Uh." Typical male response from Tom.

I lift the hair off my neck and feel the breeze catch the curls, adding to what I hope Jenny recognizes as *dishevelment*. I didn't set out to piss her off. I *like* Jenny. But what makes her think she can manage the world?

"Penelope was just saying how much you miss your boyfriend," Tom says. Jenny looks at him and he looks at her.

"Matt," says Tom.

"I know his name." Jenny glares at me.

"I miss him too," says Tom. "Your boyfriend."

There is a slippery undercurrent here that isn't clear to me. Does it have to do with Matt being black? Or from not as posh a family? Or what?

"You are such . . . Penelope, you . . ." Jenny starts and stops. I can feel her steam whistle about to blow.

"There is *waaay* too much teen-girl nuance going on here," says Tom. "Are you two in a fight or something?"

"We weren't," says Jenny. "But we are now."

She turns and stomps away, trying to make her escape before I see how red her face is and how her eyes are wet.

Tom just shrugs goodbye at me and follows her. I guess I'm not surprised. I watch him catch up several yards along the path, but she wrenches herself out from under his brotherly arm. He tries again, she stops walking, he says something, she shakes her head and waves her hands about, they keep going. Neither of them bothers to look back in my direction. The chill from the stone under my bum spreads all the way through me. I'm really high. But

I'm really bloody low. So much for tea at the hotel. How the hell am I going to salvage this one?

It must be break between dinner and the afternoon program, because the courtyard is swarming. I skirt around the edges, avoiding the general cheer of chatting families, though when I look closely it's the parents chatting and the kids looking vague or haunted or embarrassed or all of the above. Nico's mother, the famous author, is wearing sunglasses. Percy's mum, wow, she's gorgeous, her dark skin glowing amongst all the pasty whites. Esther's dad has one of those beards that probably hosts a nest of wrens and a plate of macaroni.

I can't face the dorm. I slide into the kitchen. The weed and the loneliness have made me ravenous. Damn, I'd forgotten that they don't serve Vera's food to the parental masses, but a real dinner catered by a place in Harrogate. Scraps worth foraging for.

Two women in white jackets are rinsing glasses and stacking dirty plates into big bins. A man rattles the bins out to a van. I note the platters of leftovers covered in foil sitting on the counter. The strangers are like robots, no smiles, focused on getting the hell out, which they do pretty quickly.

Vera seems a bit dazed in the sudden quiet, wiping her hands down the front of her apron. The din of families in the courtyard comes through an open window.

"I've come to help tidy up," I say. She fetches me the ancient broom, no comment. I often appear in the kitchen at odd moments. She gathers up stray knives and spoons, wipes the counter with a damp grey rag. Very sanitary. My broom is not efficient, but I do my best. Near the food, I lift a corner of the tucked foil.

"You have no family today?" she asks. "No mother?"

No, I agree. No mother.

"Me also, I tell you already, yes? I have no mother. You hungry?"

She hands me a plate and lets me fill it myself. Little browned potatoes, slices of rare roast beef, slivers of carrots and parsnips tossed together in something sweet and gingery. It's the best food I've ever eaten off a school plate or maybe anywhere.

Vera watches me. "Good, yah?"

"No offence, Vera, but it's . . . in*cred*ible!"

She doesn't exactly smile but close.

"You think I don't know what they say?" She unwraps foil from another plate, revealing a Battenberg cake with glistening frosting. "You think I don't know what name they call me?"

Ouch. That cannot be a good feeling.

She shrugs. "How could be worse than Nazis?" Anytime I talk to Vera, she reminds me about the Nazis. "I get on a train," she says. "I leave mother and brother on platform. My father already is killed, betrayed by neighbour not liking Jews. I depart Prague and escape. I am fourteen years old. Why complain about stupid names?"

She trades my dirty plate for one holding a slab of pink and yellow cake.

"And then what happened?" I say. "What happened to your mother and your brother?"

"I never hear." She finds me a clean fork. "She was

195

wearing blue sweater with pearl buttons when we say goodbye. Brother was holding box with stamp collection."

I've been eating the cake so fast I'm practically drinking sugar, but now it lands in my stomach like a stone.

"It's a tradition," I say. "To complain about school food. That's what kids do. Don't take it personally."

"Good women feed us oranges and cocoa in Holland where we take boat to England. Good Quakers give me job in school. Cook before me is already gone. I must start right away to make food. How am I to learn cooking with no mother?"

She gives me the rest of the cake, which I carry like a precious baby up to Austen dormitory. Where Kirsten and Jenny are in a huddle on Kirsten's bed. It's one of those conversation-killing entrances and they don't have the grace to look guilty. I go to my locker and tuck the cake away.

"Something you want to say?" I ask. "Or just waiting for me to leave so you can stab me in in the back?"

"Look who's talking!" says Jenny. "Let's start with how I specifically asked you not to mention a particular something and you turned right around and opened your . . . Well, anyway. I guess you won't be joining us for tea."

"What'll you tell your mum?"

"I already told her"—Jenny slips into a perfect imitation of me when I explained my mother's absence—" 'She is . . . not well.' "

It's horrible.

"And then," says Jenny, "we could discuss how brothers are seriously off-limits!"

"Is that an American rule?"

"It's a worldwide rule for keeping your friends!"

"Penelope has a bit of a thing for other people's brothers," says Kirsten.

"I never touched your brother, Kurse, and I think you *know why*!"

She turns on me with a face I've never seen, eyes like a fiery dragon's. I've lost enough today. My hands fly up in apology. "Sorry!"

I want to say that certain brothers seem to have a thing for me too. I want to say what's wrong with taking it where you can find it? But Jenny is trying on Kirsten's clothes, her black pencil skirt and the turquoise Biba top, dressing for the Buckingham Hotel, leaving her snipped-up rags in a heap beside the bed.

I press my forehead against the window that looks over the drive. A parade of cars is nosing toward town, each car holding a family. There is only me to blame for where I am. There is only me.

jenny

When the letter finally came from Matt, I had this great idea. What if I kept getting letters? All it took was a tick beside my name for people to think I had post. The sheet was pinned on a board in the Great Hall during morning lessons. A quick, small pencil mark and my reputation was intact. Brilliant. I just let the stamped corner of the first envelope peek out from my notebook, and Oona or Penelope would notice, not that I was speaking to Penelope.

"Come on, tell us what he said!" Oona's thirst for romance was almost embarrassing.

I brushed off obvious nosiness with a distant gaze. Real letters came too, from my mom or from Kelly, red and blue markings shouting *Airmail*. Bundled together, who would know?

* * *

Penelope was still Queen of the Swamp—Percy's nickname—despite pissing off every single person at some point or another.

It was hard to admit that Tom had succumbed, but I did complain to Percy: "She says and does *anything* she wants to! Like no one ever taught her any manners."

"As if she's a toddler." Percy was good at listening. "It's very naughty to knock the jam pot onto the carpet or to poke hairpins into the butter, but she's still part of the family, so you clean up the mess and try not to leave jam pots or hairpins lying about."

"But then she finds a packet of matches. And burns down the house."

"Why aren't you pissed off at your brother?" said Percy.

"He's the one who . . . did whatever he did with her. She's just a pathological slag."

I *was* pissed off at Tom, but he was away on Planet Sheffield. Penelope was in my own dormitory. I never looked in her direction. I slept with my back to her bed under the window. And I'd been avoiding the Swamp for days. But where else was there to go? Especially tonight when we had a weirdly warm evening. I'd be missing that twilit half hour, listening to night birds, seeing the branches shift to monstrous silhouettes.

I spotted Penelope's white denim jacket from the top of the path, a perfect beacon. I took a second trail that circled away from the Swamp, bumpier, more scattered twigs and heaps of leaves. I hadn't approached the woods from this direction before, had no idea where or if the paths met up. What was I doing in the dim, creepy woods anyway? I just couldn't bear to go down to the Cellar by myself—what if people were making out? Or sit in the dorm looking like a lonely bunny when they all showed up at Bed Bell. I walked nearly on tiptoe, hearing small crackles in the hush, an occasional bird whistle. Yellow leaves fluttered and turned over like girls showing off the backs of their dresses. Maybe I'd find the shrine that the third form had reportedly built under a bush, a place for the fairies to come.

A boy laughed. I saw a flash of blue ahead, amongst the grays and greens. He wasn't a killer rapist because why would he be laughing? I crept off the path and peered around a tree, palms against the crinkled bark. There were two jackets, one blue, one darker. Two boys. I couldn't see who, but they were laughing again, and then . . . tussling. I inched from my tree to a thicker one, better for hiding behind.

Now they were snogging and bucking their hips, white hands gripping dark-clothed bodies. I could have walked right past without them noticing, they were going at it that hard. One wore a hoodie; neither face was visible.

The kiss went on and on. I pushed away from the tree trunk, palms welted in stripes, stumbled through the bracken, hearing myself pant. I somehow arrived on the path below the Swamp and pulled up short. No way could I go back past the boys, so there was only forward. I took a deep breath before breaking cover from the shadows, then stepped into the clearing, intending to pass the Swamp with an air of autumnal enchantment, hands in pockets, eyes toward the purple twilight.

"Look what the woods coughed up," said Penelope.

"Nymph wearing anorak," said Adrian.

"Jenny!" said Kirsten. "What are you doing?"

"Exploring." I tried to laugh.

"Hang out for a bit." Kirsten patted the stone ledge next to her. Nico and Penelope sat close by, twin demons staring at me. Oona was throwing dead leaves on Adrian, dodging his swatting hands.

"Nnn. Catch you later." I kept moving.

Who'd been kissing? I waited farther up, beside a hedge that framed the bedraggled rose garden. I'd see whoever appeared on either path. Night was blowing in quickly, swilling the violet sky, forcing the kids at the Swamp to think about curfew. It was Nico who ambled along first, with Adrian as sidekick and Oona right on their heels.

"The damsel doth await us." Adrian thought he was so funny.

"Ha ha." I kept an eye on the woods behind them.

Nico turned his head to follow my gaze just as Luke emerged from the trees. Blue jacket. Nico and Adrian looked at each other, big exaggerated *Aha!*, and turned to consider me.

"Luke?" murmured Nico.

"No." My mind leapt to a denim bum gripped by pale hands. "No, really!" I knew my face was flaming.

"What?" said Oona.

Luke paused at the Swamp, pretending to tip his sister

backward into the mucky fountain, sidestepping Penelope's attempt to retaliate. As if it were any ordinary day. And maybe it was, for Luke. Only for *me* a new notion had been startled out from under a rock. An invisible thing, suddenly catching the light. Luke and another boy.

They straggled up the path toward us.

"Hey, Luke," said Adrian. "There's a leaf in your hair. Just like the one in Jenny's."

My hand went to my head before I could stop it. No leaf. Adrian hooted. Oona bugged out her eyes. Penelope's went slitty, watching.

"Jenny?" said Luke.

"Jenny?" mocked Adrian, with a little shimmy to his hips.

"Jenny?" Nico was asking me, not believing.

I pushed through the bramble of bodies and hurried across the flagstones, praying with every step, *Don't trip, don't trip.*

I skipped Cocoa and sneaked into the bathroom to run a scalding bath before anyone could remind me that I was nowhere near the top of the list for First Bath. I went under, held my breath, whooshed up, went under again. It made me think of a news clip we'd seen on television before the Sunday mystery, of camouflaged soldiers in a swamp, with leaves and briars attached to their helmets, faces smeared with mud, only their heads above the murky water. Did Matt have to hide from the enemy like that? Was the enemy hiding from him the very same way?

Were we *all* hiding *all* the time, camouflaged by what other people expected to see? There was Luke, plain as day, letting assumptions keep him out of sight. Or in my case, a whole constructed person. But what was I hiding from? The nobody I felt like inside, or some other enemy? Was my disguise helping Luke's? Could his hurt mine?

I finally climbed out, not wanting to waste the bath-water, leaving it, still warm, for the girls now clattering up the million stairs, the chill driving them toward hot-water bottles like sheep. And even hotter in the Austen dormitory was the gossip tidbit of the night.

"Is it true?" gasped Caroline. "Oona said . . . you and *Luke*!"

I bent over, toweling my hair. "She's wrong."

"Nice try." Oona had sidled in from Brontë. "I was *there*!"

"Where exactly is *there*, Oona? You're just wrong."

Penelope came in, grabbed her toothbrush, headed for the bathroom.

"Pen?" called Caroline. "Did you hear about Jenny and Luke?"

"Penelope is ticked," said Oona. "She's been trying to get off with Luke for three terms."

"Stop." I pulled on flannel pajama pants and a sweat-shirt, cold all over despite the bath. "It's a lie."

Penelope stuck her head into the room, mouth foaming with toothpaste, pinning me with a look. A minute later she was back. "Mostly," she said, "I feel sorry for the poor soldier in Vietnam. Shouldn't *he* be the one we're thinking about tonight?"

"Ohmy*god*!" I said. "Why are you so quick to believe *Adrian* of all people, before even listening to me?"

Kirsten stood in the doorway.

"What was your rule again?" said Pen. "Concerning other people's brothers?"

Kirsten ignored her.

"Kirsten! I swear! I did *not* get off with Luke!"

Kirsten ignored me too.

I already had one fake boyfriend. Now there were two. Luke's secret . . . was his. I'd just pretend not to know. Even Penelope and Oona couldn't stir up a romance between us. But Matt was something else. I had to fix this. What if I said that Matt had realized his tour of duty was too long for me to wait, or maybe that he'd met someone else? Easier to lie than be straight, at this point. I'd tell one more and start fresh.

I got out a minute early from History the next morning, saying I needed the loo. I went straight to the sheet where the letters and parcels were listed. Today's letter would be the one. I'd have red eyes and not want to talk about it for a day.

I made a pencil stroke next to my name, thinking how the real me wanted to keep writing to Matt, how I'd have to figure out how to mail stuff without anyone knowing. He *needed* my letters, I knew he did. And if he wrote another one? If only.

"Do you have post?" Penelope stood next to me, Esther peering over her shoulder at the list.

"Yes," I said. "One."

Penelope was looking at my pencil.

"So." Luke was suddenly behind me at the tea urn after lunch. "You went for a walk down the woods by yourself."

It seemed as if the entire dining hall hushed as tea trickled into my mug. As if we'd stepped onstage.

"Yes. I did."

"And now there's this rumour going around."

"Yeah, crazy, right?" I stirred in sugar from the tin, slowly, slowly.

"I hope you don't . . ." He was whispering, no doubt feeling every eyeball and earhole in the room pulsing and stretching in our direction. "This has been a messed-up week," he said. "A kid I know got hurt because of a rumour. It's . . . I swear, I didn't say anything, you know, to make them think . . . Where did you go walking . . . ?"

His eyelashes were thick and dark, his eyes trying to pierce me. My chest was warm, like when Mom rubbed on Vicks for a cough.

Was he asking, *Had I seen him?*

"Rumors are dumb," I said.

He stuck out his lower lip and blew upward, fluttering his hair.

"No offence," he said. "You're really nice and everything. Especially after . . . that other time, when I was . . . But you're, you know, a friend of my sister . . . older . . ."

I leaned in and put my hand on his arm, ever so softly, not wanting to scare him away.

"Plus," I said, "I'm a girl."

He winced, but I held on. He didn't know enough to realize that most of what I said was not necessarily reliable. But I wanted my hand to explain that he could be with anyone he wanted, that I wouldn't tell. *Not* telling the truth was my specialty.

"Excuse me, lovebirds. Some of us need access to the tea urn." Adrian waved his mug in our faces. Luke jerked back, banging his hip against the table, setting off a massive wobble. Managing not to slosh my tea, I retreated right out of the dining hall, down the corridor to the Girls' Changing Room. I balanced my mug on the back of the sink and looked in the mirror, trying to see a person who could be trusted with a giant, dangerous secret.

I knew someone would show up at the Swamp before afternoon lessons. A feeble sun brightened what had started as a regular gray English day. I rubbed my eyes, jamming my fingernails into the corners, drumming up a sting.

"Hallo." Percy dropped down next to me on the edge of the fountain. "You look completely forlorn."

Kirsten sat on my other side. She'd forgiven me? She believed me about Luke? All the more reason to go ahead. I hugged my notebook, corner of envelope peeking out.

"I've heard from Matt."

"She heard from Matt," Kirsten announced. Penelope

and Adrian passed a cigarette back and forth. "But what's wrong?"

"He . . . he broke up with me."

"Oh no!" Kirsten and Percy lunged to embrace me, arms banging across my back.

"Lucky day for Lukey." Adrian dropped the cigarette and did a little butt-crushing dance.

"Shut it, Adrian," said Percy.

"Or Percy here." Adrian kicked Percy's boot. "He's having wet dreams about you every night."

"Shut it, Adrian," said Kirsten. "What did he say, Jenny? What's his reason?"

My eyes watered, she was being so sweet.

"When did you hear this news?" Penelope took another cigarette from behind her ear.

"My letter today."

"Really?" she said. "That's odd. Because when I asked Hairy Mary if I could take your post, she said your name must have got a tick by mistake, that you didn't have a letter after all."

Now I cried. Burning-hot angry tears poured out. I couldn't stop, and no one except Penelope knew why I was crying.

"Anyone got a packet of matches?" she said.

percy

The letter comes on a Wednesday by second post. A tick beside *Percy Graham* on the list in the hallway is so rare that he leans in till his nose nearly touches the page, making sure the mark is not misplaced from Luke Flanders above or Ben Hawthorne below.

Percy does not recognize the handwriting. But the stamp is a little Queen's head in cream on mulberry, announcing that the sender is in England. Inside, the letter had been written on a typewriter and signed with a scrawling *Mick* above more typed words in parentheses: *(Michael Malloy, your father).*

Percy stuffs the letter into his jeans pocket without reading it, and sits down right there on the stairs outside Matron's office, where the post is distributed. His chest is suddenly tight, and he wonders where he left his inhaler.

He'd better be able to breathe before he reads a letter from the dad not seen for nine years.

"Christ," says Adrian, purposely tripping over him. "Could you pick a worse spot, Chicken Boner?"

Percy Graham does not have his father's name, because, as his mother frequently reminds him, he does not have a father. She doesn't say it spitefully, nor exactly sadly, but rather the logical explanation of a fact.

She doesn't stint on facts. There was someone who had helped her make Percy. His name was Mick Malloy. He was that white-skinned fellow who came to Percy's sixth birthday party and held a camera the whole time. Maybe someday Percy would meet him again. He now worked as a film director and she'd even heard that he was quite a success. He sent money. But a father he was not.

The letter tells Percy—when he finally reads it down at the Swamp before tea—that he is about to see his father. This very weekend. Mick Malloy is coming to visit, Saturday at noon.

Roughly sixty-six hours from now.

Lessons, chess club, meals, sleep.

Percy has seen his father's films, of course. Five so far, at least twice each. (In forty years, when he owns a box set of Mick's life's work on DVD, Percy will know the films frame by frame, but at sixteen he relies on a version of passion to imprint them on his brain.)

The first time, and ever after, he'd gone to the cinema

alone, without telling his mother, using every bit of his pocket money for bus fare and ticket. He was overcome, there in the dark, with all the feelings he could never, not ever admit to anyone. The film itself, *Left Behind*, was scary, all right. That image of the kid's face at the window, when the audience knows that no one is coming back for him? Percy wept, gripping the flocked velveteen arms of his seat till the shuddering stopped. But even beyond that, he realized, last to stumble out of the cinema, he'd been hoping for . . . what if there'd been . . . a dedication, like there always was in a book? What if giant words had filled the screen for all the world to read: *For my son*.

At 12:37 p.m., Percy is hiding in the doorway of the Religious Studies classroom when his father climbs out of the passenger side of a van. So, someone else is driving. But the driver stays put and Percy can't see through the tinted windows. His father stretches, swinging arms above his head with fingers laced and palms flipped over to face the sky.

Oh god. Please don't anyone else be watching this. Please let him seem like a grown man. Percy is prepared to forgive almost anything, any film-world idiosyncrasies, but hope is dim that anyone else will be so kind.

Percy knows what Mick Malloy looks like. He has spent many hours of his life poring through newspapers and tabloids and film magazines on a hunt for one thing: photos or mentions of his father. He has seen him interviewed on the telly, so he's ready for the stammer and the eyebrow-raising-for-emphasis thing. Percy yearns to see the smile that Mick gave the interviewer Nicola Pettle when she asked him, "Any regrets?" and he'd answered, "I'd have liked to spend more time with my son," as if his son were a four-year-old waiting in the hotel nursery, instead of long-forgotten Percy, stashed in a boarding school.

Apart from the colour of their skins, and the hair—Mick's grows straight up, like a fine shag carpet, Percy's dangles in knotted dreads—Percy and his father look pretty much the same. Mick is pale and bony, Percy is dark and bony, both kind of short, though Percy hopes he's not done growing yet. He'd love to wake up one morning taller than Adrian, with genuine stubble on his chin and fists like a farmer's. "Get your vast stinking arse out of my road," he'd say to Adrian. "Or tell my knuckles why not. . . ."

Percy's brain zooms through all this while he watches Mick stretch. One of the worries in the last sixty-six hours has been what his father might wear. Percy's Mick file holds pictures of him in a velvet tuxedo, patched bell-bottoms, a kilt, a toga, a pink rabbit-skin coat, a sequined blazer, and a linen djellaba.

Today he seems to be in disguise, what he imagines a normal father might wear. *Thank you, God, if you exist and this might be proof.* Jeans instead of his favourite green suede trousers with suspenders. A T-shirt displaying neither curse words nor a tie-dye rainbow. A leather jacket with moderate fringe. Cowboy boots.

While Percy finishes up his prayer, his father clasps the

side mirror of the van, grabs one foot with the other hand, and bends a leg up behind him like a flamingo at rest. As he switches legs one minute later, Percy peels himself out of the doorway and dashes forward to prevent any further public body twisting.

Percy nearly chokes when he sees his father's eyes widen and brighten.

"Percy, m-m-mate, lovely to see you."

Back clap, back clap, sideways not-exactly-a-hug. Percy's heart thuds. He smells clove oil and sweat before his father pulls back.

"What a time we had getting to wherever the hell we are! This place is *bleeeak*! What a rat-shittle-ittle town! But *this*!" He glances around the courtyard. "*This* is perfect!" He looks up at the towers, his hands clasped, rocking back and forth on the heels of his boots. "Here we are, eh? And here *you* are, and just *look* at you! Chip off the old block, eh? And by chip, I m-m-mean *chip*, no fish included, blimey, you're as skinny as a noodle. The food is absolute shite, am I right? Well? Aren't you going to say hallo to dear old M-M-Mick?"

"Hallo," says Percy, mouth dry as crumbs.

It's a special year, won't happen again. Mick is exactly twice Percy's age. And Percy is the same age now—sixteen—that Mick was when Percy was born. Has Mick realized that?

"I talked to Alia," says Mick, quite still for a moment, feet flat on the ground.

"She knows?" says Percy. "That you're here?"

Mick sighs, as if revealing a hidden landscape beyond the means of language. Or is that only what Percy wants to think? Maybe it's just a sigh.

"Of course," says Mick. "She knows. She said to be sure you haven't outgrown your runners." He looks at Percy's feet and laughs. "You want to go shoe shopping?"

Percy shakes his head. He wants to throw up. He wants to sit someplace with his dad and tell him all the stuff he has imagined telling him for all these years. He wants to get through these five minutes and then this hour and then this day without looking like an idiot. He wants the kids in his dorm to see his famous father and go, *Whoa, dude, you weren't lying!* He wants no one at all to notice that this moment is a big fat hairy deal. . . . Is he really shaking all over, or is that just his heart slamming through his chest bone like a miner's pick?

"Who"—Mick stares across the courtyard while he rubs his fingers back and forth on the top of his head—"is that heaven-sent creature?"

Percy sees only the old bag who works in the kitchen.

"Where?" he says. "Who?"

"Her." Mick points. "The loveliest apparition that ever hobbled across a set. I need her. On film. *Need.*"

"You mean the cook? Vera?"

"That's her name? Vera?"

Percy wonders, is he watching genius at work? Is Mick as brilliant as the critics say? Or the most deranged tool to crawl out of the sand?

"Vera Diarrhea," says Percy. He knows it sounds bad.

But it's the only name he has for her. Mick's rubbing hand pauses as if it has encountered a thistle on his scalp.

"Percy," he says. "I've got pretty strong feelings about derision."

"Well, yeah." Percy shrinks a little. Crap. Foot wrong already.

"But it's likely bloody apt, right? She's the *cook*?"

Vera crosses from the storage shed to the kitchen door, banging a heavy bucket against her leg.

"I kind of love it." Mick looks at Percy. "What do they call you?" he says. "These teen gods of instantaneous pigeonholing and life wreckage? They've got some tag for you, don't they? Makes you squirm in the dark?"

Percy glances up at the windows of the Kipling dorm.

"Chinnbnrr," he mumbles.

"Eh?"

Percy can feel his shoulders hunching over, the Dormitory Defence System kicking into place.

"Dad," he says, trying it out.

His father glances toward the van. "M-M-Mick."

"Yeah, sorry, Mick."

Why didn't he just change his name, Percy wonders. Like, before he got famous? To something that didn't stop his tongue every single time?

"Look at this place!" Mick tips his head back. "What are those? Turrets? And all these m-m-massive filthy lead-paned windows! It's brilliant, Percy!"

Percy nods.

"The lane up from the York Road must be a mile long, with this grand old house perched at the end like a hal-

214

lucination. . . . Charlie!" he calls out. Someone emerges from the van, grinning and chewing gum at the same time. Charlie is female, it turns out, wearing a baseball cap over pigtails.

"Charlie, meet Percy. Percy, this is Charlie."

"Hey." Percy wonders, should he shake? But she's flashing a peace sign with the hand not gripping a clipboard. He tries a smile, but the combination of blue eyes and white teeth is making him dizzy. Is this Mick's girlfriend? His wife? Maybe Charlie is Percy's stepmother!

Mick hasn't paused. "See, Charlie? Do you believe what you're seeing, m-m-m-darlin'? Did you catch a gander at that old bird? Is this not everything we hoped for?"

Hoped for?

Percy wonders, in the second before she opens her mouth, what Charlie's voice will be like. Squeaky? Soft? But it's so husky you'd think she was horribly sick, except that she glowed with health, flipping a pigtail over her shoulder and gazing up at the windows in the tower above the music room.

"A tower! You couldn't have built better if you'd spent a million dollars." Husky, and American.

Suddenly, there are people in the courtyard. Dinner must be over—has *so* much time gone by already? It moved so slowly while he waited for the van, but now it gallops. Kids appear in droves, heading from the dining hall in the main building to all the ordinary Saturday-afternoon activities that do not include a father-son reunion or chatting with a beach bunny from California.

"Oh, oh, oh! I love it!" Mick actually spins, watching the

215

space around him go from empty to bustling in a matter of a single minute.

"Far out," says Charlie.

But then Nico and Adrian are standing right in front of Percy, like eager children.

"Hey, man," says Nico. He beams as though Percy is *his* son and has just won a prize at the science fair.

Nico, who knows how to conduct himself with grown-ups, extends a hand to Percy's father.

"Nico Nevos," he says. "I'm in Percy's dorm. And this is Adrian."

Adrian has a look of stupefaction, the direct cause of Percy becoming miraculously taller, his shoulders broader, his dreads thicker.

Mick lifts his eyebrows.

"We're mates of Percy's," says Nico. His eyes flick over to Charlie, widening in appreciation of a goddess standing in the Illington courtyard. "And you're Percy's . . ." Not a drop of brown blood between them, not to mention that Charlie is probably twenty-three and Mick looks barely older than that. Not evident parent material. "You're . . . with Percy?"

"Obviously, dude," says Adrian. "Since they're standing next to him, having a natter."

Charlie chuckles, throaty and dutiful.

Percy decides not to ridicule Adrian, just because it would be so simple.

"This is Mick," he says. "And Charlie." He loves how casual he sounds, as if he's been introducing them all his life, at film openings, tennis matches, art gallery exhibitions.

As if they're his. As if he hadn't got up at dawn to change his jersey nine times and sniff his pits and wash his feet just in case.

"Shall we go into town?" Percy's voice seems to have deepened. "We could have a snack at the hotel." (A *snack*? Has he ever used the word *snack* before?) "It's the only decent restaurant, really." (And how the hell does he know *that*?) "Unless you want fish-and-chips."

Nico and Adrian stare at him. *Who is he?* Percy can see them wondering. His muscles strain inside the sleeves of his jean jacket, his prick maybe doubles in size. He imagines that he has unsheathed a gleaming sword, or walked barefoot across a pit of burning skulls.

"Yeah, yeah," says Mick. "I'm starving. What'll it be, Charlie? Chips or champagne?"

Charlie's hand arrives on Percy's shoulder, a rare and exotic butterfly never before spotted in Yorkshire. He barely restrains a gasp of astonishment, stays utterly still so as not to frighten her off.

"It's a party, right, Percy? I'd say champagne, wouldn't you?"

Percy nods. To speak would be to choke. Adrian's neck is a gratifying shade of crimson.

"How about you boys?" Mick waves his arms as if to embrace Percy's whole world. "Want some edible nosh? I'll bet what you just swallowed was outright spew, am I right?"

Charlie's fingers twitch and take flight from Percy's shoulder. He knows that she knows that Mick should not have invited them.

"Wow, man, that'd be so cool," Adrian says.

But Nico grasps Adrian's sleeve. "No, sorry, we can't do that," he says.

"What? Why not?" Adrian is pissed.

"Because we can't." Nico jerks his head toward Percy. "He . . . you know . . . doesn't see his dad too often."

Percy feels a dangerous sting behind his eyes. He blinks, Nico soaring upward in his estimation.

"Fair enough," says Mick. "All too true." He puts an arm across Percy's back as if it lives there.

Adrian tugs himself free of Nico's hold. "But, sir?"

Mick laughs. "*Sir?* Try again, lad."

"I, er, love . . . well, all your films. I really do. That one, *Lucy's Secret*? I thought I'd croak when the doll turned out to be real. I love how you scare the shit out of us and then we think it's finally all over—*pow!*—you tighten the screws again! And then, in the final frame! The little shoe, next to the doll's smashed foot? Man!"

Mick nods. "You spotted that, eh?"

How many thousand times, Percy wonders, has Mick pretended that a fan was clever to notice some detail that he'd planted for the very purpose of making fans feel clever?

"Are you working on the next one?"

"That's what I'm doing here," says Mick. "Scouting locations. I've got another script ready to go. Ghosts in a girls' school."

"Awesome!" Adrian slaps his thighs in excitement.

That's what I'm doing here.

218

Percy wills himself not to flinch.

"Mick Malloy," says Charlie. "I'm hungry."

"Right, vanward ho!" says Mick. "Good to m-m-meet you, boys. Good to know Percy's got m-m-mates."

Percy sees Adrian's lips silently repeating *m-m-m*, as if learning a new trick. He wants to thank Nico for keeping Adrian on a leash. He wants, actually, to hug Nico, but settles for a peace sign.

Percy's mother, Alia Graham, was fourteen when she met the scrawny and hilarious Mick Malloy at the Silver Blades Roller Rink on a Saturday night in July. *Behind* the roller rink, to be completely accurate, and Alia prided herself on accuracy, then and now, sixteen years later. Alia was at Silver Blades for the first time, with her chum, Keisha, who had reported the terrible and tantalizing fact that if you wanted to practice snogging, the narrow alley sheltered by an overpass was the place to do it.

Alia was not especially yearning to practice snogging, but she was tired of being the only one who had not, so she borrowed roller skates from Tracy, who lived in the next-door apartment, and joined her friend at the bus stop, pausing to apply eye shadow before turning the corner into the high street.

"What did you bring *skates* for!" shrieked Keisha.

"My mother would have wondered otherwise," Alia said.

Mick was also there for the first time, because his mate Harry had told him it was a good place to meet girls of the sort who did not seem to mind mucking about without valentines and fairy lights. Mick was seriously in need of some mucking about. He had been class clown since primary school, always the friend and never the fondled, and he was about to bleeding well burst.

Alia and Mick returned to Silver Blades the following Saturday, but by the third week they were past needing the excuse—or the scrutiny. They were telling each other things that no one else would ever know, in between letting their hands—and then their tongues—wander deeper and deeper into forbidden territory.

When Alia finally admitted to her mother that she had missed three periods, she hardly had a chance to finish her sentence, let alone say goodbye to Mick Malloy. Alia's mother saw no reason to hesitate. She'd be damned if her daughter walked up Church Street showing a belly. Alia agreed to her parents' plan only on condition that her baby's father never be threatened or punished. Her parents agreed only on condition that Alia never see him again.

She flew to Antigua under cover of a story of a sick grandmother. The granny who met her at the little island airport showed as much vigour as a bandleader and didn't bother to scold. Having a baby wasn't such a terrible thing. Plenty of island girls did it. Granny Lala had been sixteen when she'd had Alia's mother. What did it matter? But she didn't want to know about the boy. Being white was enough to sentence him.

Alia wrote to Mick for months, never hearing a word

in return. Each morning, Alia lingered behind the beaded curtain, scrubbing the kitchen tabletop, until the postman came into the shop. She preferred to believe that Lala destroyed the letters rather than that they did not exist. She never asked.

When Percy was born, Alia used her own surname in case he grew up to have a stammer like his daddy. The baby's skin was as if he'd been dipped in caramel pudding, exactly midway between her own and what she remembered Mick's to be. His enormous eyes, his scrubby hair, his teeny fingers and poking-out ears . . . the enchantment was complete. She was fifteen and would not kiss anyone except her son for another twelve years.

Alia believed with all the broken bits of her heart that she'd used up her allotment of true love too early in life. What was left was to work hard and surprise them all with how much money a smart girl could accumulate.

She left the baby with her granny and walked every morning along the dusty road to All Saints Secondary School, in the opposite direction of the tourists on their way to float in the buoyant turquoise waves at Windward Beach or to see the old stockade in English Harbour.

Percy squalled and then toddled and then learned to read, always within a few yards of his great-grandmother's shop, where she sold general provisions to island people and home-steeped vanilla rum to tourists. Lala's shop was on the road that ran by Falmouth Harbour all the way to Nelson's Dockyard. Percy thought, when he was a child, that Nelson must be the man who sat at the gate to the marina, a man far older than Lala, with no teeth at all and parrot feathers stuck in the brim of his straw cap.

The sunshine ended when Percy was nearly six years old. Alia's father, laying bricks for the foundation of a house in Liverpool, stepped backward into a hole and conked himself out, tipping a barrow full of rubble and mashing up his leg. Alia packed up her little boy and flew to England to help nurse him, ready at last to forgive her parents for whisking her away from her own childhood.

Alia was unprepared for the shock to Percy of arriving in England. To her, it was coming home. She'd told him stories all his life, about the soothing mist and the quiet colour of grey, about the island so big there were places you could not see the sea but had tall, tall houses instead, where you might not know everyone and not everyone knew the story of you.

He had never worn boots, never touched wool, never nibbled liver. He had not smelled city rubbish, heard traffic, nor seen a sky the colour of knives.

Percy had no photographs of his island childhood, because there was no camera in Lala's house. There were dozens of pictures in existence, but none that he would ever see. The skinny boy with a beguiling smile was a popular subject for tourists who stopped to buy Lala's creamy homemade cheese or a jar of vanilla rum. If he scooped up one of the speckled chickens that ran every which way, he'd usually see a coin for his cuteness.

Percy's memories of faintly clattering palm leaves and white sunlight swiftly turned to dreams, barely recalled but mournfully missed. Later, he thought of them as scenes from movies, edited to the briefest repeating moments of hot dust under bare feet, black nets hauling glittering fish through blue water, Lala's voice singing over the whisper of evening rain.

In England, he noticed the incidence of fathers living with families behind the doors of the apartment building in Birmingham where he and his mother lived right next to her parents. He began to wonder as he never had before, where was his own daddy?

"But *why* doesn't he come?" he'd asked. "Do you think he loves me?"

He knew that Alia's answer was not intended to be cruel, but it wasn't what Percy wanted to hear. "How can a person love someone he doesn't know?" she said.

Despite his mother being correct about most things, in this case Percy wondered. His mother loved him utterly, but did she know him? Certainly not the part that became consumed with all things Mick Malloy.

Percy twiddles his fork, thinking the unthinkable. *Maybe the other boys should have come after all.* At least Adrian would have kept his fat mouth flapping and it wouldn't be so obvious that none of them—man, woman, or child— know what to say. What level of crazy had led Percy to fantasize a clasping fellowship with his father? For Mick's tender remorse, and his own simple words of profound forgiveness?

There'd been a bit of awe inside the van, noticing the mini refrigerator stocked with ginger beer and Coca-Cola, the telephone implanted in the dashboard, and the dozens of photos tacked up on the ceiling, recording a funny, sunny, brilliant life without Percy. There'd been getting stuck as a herd of sheep dawdled across the drive, then careering over cobbled village streets to the hotel, and examining a menu that offered devilled kidneys with nettle sauce and Yorkshire curd tart.

"Hamburgers all round," Mick tells the waiter. "With fried onions. And a bottle of your best bubbly."

Now what? Percy's mind skitters around, looking for a place to land where he'll be clever, at ease, and lovable. Useless endeavour.

"I'm going to take a piss," says Mick. "Back in a mo."

Oh god, oh god, now he is alone with the most beautiful girl he has ever seen and she's looking at him with eyes as sharp as the fork he's jamming through the tablecloth.

"I'm not your dad's girlfriend," says Charlie. "In case you were wondering. I met him because I was doing a paper about his films. At college. In the States."

"People *study* him?"

"After I saw *Left Behind*, I flipped out. And then *Lucy's Secret*. It was a big deal, getting permission, you know? To interview him. Transatlantic phone calls and everything. But he was great, chatty and friendly. Offered me a job, Just, you know, a gopher, really, starting out the way *he* did. *Lost Child* was my first, and then the one that comes out in the spring, *Cold Fingers*."

Percy sees Mick at the entrance to the restaurant, popping a mint into his mouth, leaning in close to say something to the hostess. Something that makes her laugh, putting a hand in front of her mouth. *Chatty and friendly.* The girl holds a menu like a shield across her chest. Charlie sees too. She keeps talking, faster and more quietly.

"I know it's weird," she says. "Today. Seeing him. Especially with me being here. I'll leave you alone after lunch. I don't think . . . he doesn't quite realize . . . Listen, every situation is different, but my parents divorced when I was nine, and even though they lived two blocks apart, I never felt like I was part of my dad's life, so I'm guessing . . ."

Percy slugs his ginger ale so the bubbles scorch his throat. This is what people mean when they use *American* as a derogatory adjective, this telling of stuff that isn't any of your business. Jenny, from Philadelphia, she's the same way, blurting out details about her mom's therapy or Esther McKay's tits.

"I just . . . my essay . . . it's especially meaningful now that I've met you."

Percy squints, to cut the glare of her sapphire eyes.

"It's probably really obvious to you," she says. "Of all people, right?"

What is she saying?

Percy's hand pats the pocket where his inhaler sits. "The kid?" he whispers. "There's always a kid." His lungs crowd his bumping heart. "Who goes missing."

Mick is sauntering back to the table, oblivious to the ladies who turn to follow the clicking of his cowboy boots.

225

"The lost child," says Charlie.

"It's not in my head?" Percy says. "You noticed it too?"

"Noticed?" Charlie's laugh involves a swish of golden hair and a glimpse of pink tongue. "It is seriously groovy meeting you! The title of my thesis"—she leans in, hurrying to finish—" 'The Missing Child in the Movies of Mick Malloy.' He doesn't even realize."

Charlie makes the bizarre excuse that Yorkshire bees are famous, and she's off to buy a jar of local honey. Mick pays for the meal and Percy wonders if he is getting the flu, the way his head is aching. They wander out to what the hotel calls a terrace—a bit of a porch, really—overlooking the muddy River Wharfe that runs through town.

"The girl was telling me," says Mick, "this used to be a stagecoach stop on the way from London to Edinburgh."

Jesus, thinks Percy. *Really? We're going to talk about local landmarks?*

"Last thing you care about, eh?" says Mick. "I know, I know, who gives a toss?" He drags one of the iron chairs to the railing, scraping it across the floor, leaving two long scratches. "Come on, let's sit," he says. "Bring over another chair." He puts his boots up on the railing, settling in.

Percy stares at the marks on the floor. His mother would flat out *die* of mortification. He picks up a chair with both hands and carries it over next to Mick's.

How long have they got before Charlie comes back? There's so much to wonder, to ask, to tell. Trying to sustain the appearance of cool is the hardest thing he has ever done.

"Turns out," says Mick, "that the school's finances are in a total cock-up. So your headm-m-master—he's a bit twee, eh?—he's dancing all over the idea of leasing the place out for the summer."

"To make your film, do you mean?"

"We spoke, on the telephone, but until I could see it, I had no idea it would be so fabulous."

"Ha," says Percy. "*Fabulous*. Not the word I'd choose . . . And I'm just thinking what Adrian would say."

Mick laughs, a merry laugh that sends a skewering thrill straight through Percy's chest. He has made his father laugh.

"Fabulous as a location for a horror flick. Possibly not as home sweet home," says Mick. "You've been there, how long?"

What dad doesn't know about his kid's school?

"Percy," says Mick, "I expect you'd like . . . a bit of a . . . father-son thing. But . . . look at m-m-me! I'm a total wanker."

Is Percy supposed to agree?

"I won't pretend it wasn't m-m-my fault," Mick says. "We were kids, you know? Never used a Durex. Did. Not. Have. A. Clue. . . . Her parents were livid, she told them she'd off herself if they went after m-m-me. She rang from the airport, gagging with sobs. Simple as that. Life over. You likely know all this, am I right?"

Did his mother's version count as knowing? Alia was the

calmest, most practical person Percy had ever met. The idea of her threatening suicide was ludicrous.

She never would have, Mick assures him. It was part of her instant survival plan. Scare them to bits, keep the baby, protect Mick from jail but agree to never see him again.

"And she never has, except the once. I think I wrote a hundred letters, never got one back. When she first came home to Birmingham, after your granddad got smashed up, Alia had a little party for your birthday. Her parents didn't come, being at the hospital. So . . ." He stops to rub his eyes like an old man. "She rang up, said you were there, turning six, as if I wouldn't remember. She said I could come just for a wee peek."

"And then?" says Percy. "After that?"

"I was just leaving for a crap film job," Mick says. "A little one, called *Silent Cry*. I was an AD. You know, assistant director? Which on those little flicks is code for having an extra copy of the script so when the director pours coffee over his, you're ready with the backup. But he had a bloody heart attack, second day of a three-week shoot. I stepped in to save them a few quid, rewrote the script, changed m-m-my life."

This stuff, Percy knows. Every time Mick's name is mentioned in the press, the story includes some variation of his miraculous beginning.

"I meant," says Percy. "I meant, after that, with *me*."

"Right." Mick swings his boots down from the railing and looks at him. "I did try, I swear. Only I was gone a lot. Alia was being a brain at law school, her parents were the gorgons at the gate. Not m-m-much chance. No chance, actually. It was always no, no, no. There was no *after that*. With you."

Percy wants to go along with the idea that in nine years there has been no single hour of time when he hasn't been hidden too far out of view for a paternal visit. But that's shite.

"How about your m-m-mum? Is she doing all right?" Mick's voice is quiet, as if Alia is nearby on the hotel terrace. "Is she, I dunno, happy? At least some of the time?"

Percy's throat takes a moment to work. He's wishing his father had fought for him, that his parents had fought for each other.

"She's got Cal now," he says.

"And he's a good bloke?"

Percy nods. "If you weren't looking for a school," he says. "If this film weren't happening . . ." He stops. Why ask a question when the answer will either be a lie or make you wince?

Mick slips off his left boot, yanks up a floppy sock, and pulls the boot on again.

"What we've got here," he says, "is the classic setup for a scene." He stands up and leans on the railing, gazing down at the river. "See why? We've got two characters, each wanting something very badly, but that *something* . . ." Mick rubs his head. "For each of them, that *something* is interfering with the other person's something. Do you see?"

Percy sees.

"I like to tell the actors secrets," says Mick, "just before

229

the camera rolls. I tell the girl that she has to avoid getting kissed during the scene. Whatever it takes. And I tell the m-m-man, 'Do not leave the room until you've kissed the girl.'"

So, am I the girl or the man? Percy wonders. He sure as shite doesn't feel like a man. But it's Mick who seems to be stepping around the crucial moment. Not a kiss, obviously. But a connection.

"So, here," says Mick. "We've got an arsehole of a dad, an accidental dad, preoccupied with work. In the room with . . ."

With who? Percy almost claps his hands over his ears but manages to shove them under his knees instead. Who's the other character?

"Bloody hell," says Mick.

"The other one is a boy," says Percy.

"Who wants a dad," says Mick.

All the imaginary conversations he'd had with his father during all the years—utter fiction. The wise words, the funny anecdotes, the manly tips that Percy had invented for Mick to pass along—complete made-up crap.

But. Percy waves at the van as it bounces away down the Illington drive. He realizes that whatever you'd call it—invention, wishful thinking, or brilliant observation— everything that Mick had said inside Percy's head in all those conversations . . . well, it was Percy who wrote those lines, right? All that knowledge was already there, just waiting to be summoned.

* * *

"So, Chicken Boner, why aren't you Percy Malloy?" Adrian asks, after Lights-Out.

"Just not," says Percy, after a pause. No better answer has occurred to him.

Kipling dorm is quiet for a long time, maybe fifteen minutes, before Adrian speaks again.

"G'night, m-m-mate."

revenge

A FILM SCRIPT
by PERCY GRAHAM

INT. KIPLING DORMITORY—EARLY MORNING

Cold light through uncurtained windows. Grey blankets on two rows of single cots cover boys waking up. A clanging bell is heard from downstairs, insistent. General moaning but no movement for a few moments. ADRIAN is the first to rise, pulling blanket off bed and wrapping himself before going to large communal dresser. His drawer is in the middle. HENRY and LUKE get up and stumble past, to loo, getting dressed, just part of the background.

>   ADRIAN
>   Colder than a witch's tit.

                        PERCY
              *(only eyes and nose can be
              seen above blanket, surrounded
              by his wild dreadlocks)*
If the coal miners are toiling away in
the depths of the earth to absolutely no
effect on the Kipling dorm, why do they
bother?

                        ADRIAN
Trust the Chicken Boner to think of the
miners. Bloody typical.

                        NICO
              (rolling over, half emerging)
I'd rather be the janitor in a morgue
than be a miner.
              *(He lies back down and pulls a
              pillow half over his head.)*
I'd rather unblock sewage pipes in
August than be a miner.

                        ADRIAN
              (dragging on jeans)
I'd rather be mashing up sheep pluck on
the line in a haggis factory than be a
miner.

                        PERCY
I'd rather be a—

                        NO-FACE
My uncle is a miner. So are my two
cousins, Terry and Phil. So you can all
shut your stinking yaps.

*NO-FACE flings back his duvet and skids across
the floor in his thick woolly socks.*

                        233

He EXITS to loo.

BEAT while boys absorb info. HENRY and LUKE
EXIT also, heading off to breakfast.

> NICO
> Should we have known that?
> *(He swings his feet to the*
> *cold floor and snatches them*
> *back.)*

> ADRIAN
> Was he wearing purple boxers?

> PERCY
> I feel like crap. Saying that about
> miners.

> ADRIAN
> You look like crap. And is it even true?
> Why is he at this school if his family's
> down the pit?

> NICO
> Lots of local kids at this school.
> Chance for a leg up in the world.

> PERCY
> Maybe he's got a clever-boy scholarship.

> ADRIAN
> This is No-Face we're talking about!

> NICO
> And why does he have that name anyway?
> He's got a face.

> ADRIAN
> *(hopping foot to foot because*
> *floor is as cold as an ice*
> *rink)*

Yeah, but—
>   *(He stops as No-Face comes*
>   *back in.)*

                    NO-FACE
Ice in the sink.

                    ADRIAN
Bloody miners. Sod the lot of them.

NO-FACE goes still. Easy for him, he's got
socks on.

NICO drops his pillow to the floor and
shuffles it under his feet and over to the
dresser.

                    NO-FACE
What did you just say?
>   *(He curls up his fists.)*

                    ADRIAN
Oh Christ.
>   *(yanking on socks)*
I was *joooking*, mate!

                    NO-FACE
It's not a bleedin' joke.

                    ADRIAN
Of course not. Nothing funny about it.
Do you see me laughing?

                    NO-FACE
Are you going to stop?

                    ADRIAN
Oh Christ. You're treading on my nerves,
No-Face.

NO-FACE

>Don't call me that.

BEAT. It is momentarily clear that despite having roomed with him for a couple of years, ADRIAN has no clue to NO-FACE's real name.

ADRIAN

>Would you prefer No-Prick?

NICO and PERCY jump out of the path as NO-FACE launches himself at ADRIAN, arms outstretched, hands aiming for the neck. ADRIAN stumbles against the dresser, getting stabbed in the back by a drawer knob at the same time that NO-FACE slams into his chest.

ADRIAN

>What the fu—

He ploughs NO-FACE with his open palm—wham—catching chin and nose together.

NICO AND PERCY

>Uhhhhhh!

Blood spurts from NO-FACE as he falls sideways onto a bed. KIRBY, the Chemistry teacher and dorm monitor, comes through the door.

KIRBY

>Adrian!

ADRIAN

>Hey, it wasn't me!

KIRBY

>I just watched you!

He leans over NO-FACE, whose nose is bubbling red snotty stuff.

ADRIAN

No, really! Back me up, lads!

NICO

First hit, No-Face.

PERCY

First hit, maybe, but . . . I mean . . .
to be fair, Adrian did say—

KIRBY

Don't stand about yammering! The boy is
bleeding all over the bed! Percy, soak
a towel in cold water. Nico, go fetch
Matron. And you—
     (He jabs a finger at ADRIAN.)
Go straight down to Richard's office and
explain what kind of a peace-loving
Quaker you are.

*PERCY, holding a small towel, tries to slip
around ADRIAN toward loo. ADRIAN, just outside
the doorway of the dorm, blocks PERCY's path
with a threatening smirk on his face. PERCY
pauses in resignation, no point pushing past.*

ADRIAN
     (whispering)
Was "back me up" too difficult a concept,
Chicken Boner? You just qualified for
some serious attention.

PERCY

That'll have to wait. I'm getting first
aid for your current victim.

KIRBY

Percy, cold water. Now.

                    PERCY
Could you move, please?

                    ADRIAN
Ooh, got some manly nuts when there's a
teacher in the room, eh?

                    PERCY
Piss off.

                    ADRIAN
Did I hear you right?
          (He puts a hand across PERCY's
          throat, pushing him to the
          wall, silent but scary.)

                    PERCY

Gags, blinks, blinks again . . . and morphs
into an avenging demon, muscles popping and
dreads aquiver. . . . His knee jerks up to
catch ADRIAN—wham—in the crotch. As ADRIAN
leans over in instant agony, PERCY head-bumps
him, grabs both his hands in one of his own
(the one not holding the towel). As quick
as Spider-Man, he binds ADRIAN's wrists. He
lifts him with a slow, spinning move like that
of a discus thrower, and hurls him over the
banister. ADRIAN falls nearly three floors to
the school lobby, but the rope holding his
wrists snaps him up short, to dangle just
above the floor. The dangling figure continues
to spin slowly. A close-up shows spittle and
rolling eyeballs. There's a weak, gurgling
moan.

PERCY flicks his towel to brush himself off
and heads to the loo.

Sound of exultant applause as kids emerge from all dormitories onto the landing to cheer their hero.

PERCY nods and smiles modestly as he returns to Kipling with cold-water towel.

The End

robbie

Lanny lost the first baby during the summer, but now she was knocked up again. If she liked my brother enough to have it off with him more than once, she deserved him, being a bit of a twittering dolly bird. But she came around one night when Simon was at work, telling me a wedding wasn't a wedding without the groom's brother and wouldn't I pretty please be there? She was a fence mender, she said. She knew Simon could be grumpy, but didn't I wish them well?

What I wished was to be rid of Simon Muldoon. Face-down on a bed of steaming rubbish would be my first choice, but seeing him married and moved into a council flat in Leeds was still worth celebrating.

Not as best man. No possible way of me fitting that bill. I'd be what they call an usher. Best man would be Felix. Ha. Joke's on Simon. Felix up from London where he worked in a nightclub hanging lights, making different colours flash onto a dance floor. Sounded dead exotic to us stuck carting boxes from one end of town to the other.

I wondered how would it be seeing Felix, now that I had Luke.

The church was out of the question, but Lanny's mum saved face, having them married at the parish hall and then a party at the Red Lion. Barmy, you ask me, seeing as Lanny might last two years before she came boohooing home. Two years? Two months would be a bleeding miracle worth calling the pope about. I was given a monkey suit with a waistcoat the colour of grape jelly, matching the bridesmaids' gowns. Everything rented and paid for with the sweat off Simon's arse from his night job pulling pints at the Red Lion.

All because of a shag.

Course, I'd had me lights clocked thanks to same, so the Muldoon brothers weren't too clever that way. They'd got me in the dark and from behind. First a grab around the neck, then a kick in the nuts so I was crippled with pain. They tied a knit cap over my head and zipped their lips except for grunts. If Simon had been there, I'd've known. But that doesn't mean it wasn't his idea. I'd bet ten quid one of them was Alec, him being frantic ugly on the topic of queers.

I told Luke I wished he could come to the wedding.

"Not bloody likely," he said.

"If you were a girl, it'd be all right."

"I'd like to see you dressed up as James Bond." He slid a hand under my shirt. "Tuxedo with lavender bits."

"Seems daft to bash me up for being queer and then prance about like poofters wearing something called a *cummerbund* on their wedding day, eh?"

"Your brother?" Luke caught my slip.

"His sort," I said.

My aunt Pat, being chums with Lanny's mum, had been baking sausage rolls by the dozen and organizing girls to serve at the supper in the pub.

"She was ticked when I told her the list," said Aunt Pat. "Brenda's coming, you know the one?"

"Kath's sister," I said.

"Ever such a good girl, she'll be a big help." She opened the oven door and slid in the next baking sheet. "But the high-and-mighty mother of the bride is taking exception to the . . . *prior connection*."

"She'd better get used to Simon's prior connections," I said. "Every girl in the village . . ."

"Too bloody true." Aunt Pat's splodgy fingers shaped raw pastry around little sausages. "Lanny will be wishing she'd run the other way before that baby's born, you mark my words."

No argument.

"If your mum hadn't passed on, may she rest in peace, your brother might've had a softer side." Aunt Pat scraped the last shreds of pastry from the bowl. No sausage left, so she made a lonely little tart shell, sprinkled with brown sugar, dotted with butter. "As for *you* . . ."

"What about me?"

"A little *too* soft, from what I've heard." She wagged her head back and forth, weary with the weight of her nephews, giving my long sleeves a particular look that made the scabbing cuts itch.

"That's crap," I said.

I'm the opposite of soft. You have to be, if you're the sort people hate.

Inside the parish hall Saturday noon, it was nippy as Norway. People kept their coats on, jiggled their feet. Lanny, being a bit dim, had me as one usher and Alec as the other. Alec looked even more of a prat than I did, gussied up. He kept scowling till I finally winked, making him yank sharp on Dickie's mum's arm, and her with a cane. Didn't look my way again. When everyone was settled on the folding chairs and the creaking had subsided, I sat next to my dad in the front row. What did he think, really, about his shiny new daughter? And what about Mum? Would she have been dolled up, looking grand and proud, a bit of lipstick? Or with a pout on, having a shadowed heart? Would wedding bells even be chiming if she were here? Like Aunt Pat said, there'd likely be a different sort of Simon.

I had a flash of Mum, working the jumble sale in this very hall. She never bothered with the pies or the potted plants, too many ladies making it a contest whose plum tart was juicier or whose geranium boasted the most blossoms. Mum liked to be at one of the junk tables.

"Here, Robber," she'd say. "See if you can find a lucky penny in one of these." I'd spend an age sliding my fingers into every wee pocket inside the ladies' handbags, chuffed to come up with the odd pence or two, along with bus tickets or buttons or safety pins. Then we'd move on to the books, looking for pressed leaves or scribbled notes. Once I found a hanky with a shiver of fancy scent. Might've belonged to a duchess, my mother said, the book being poems. And then, the best time, a ten-pound note, smooth as the day it was printed.

"Always worth looking." Mum combed her fingers through my hair, untangling the knots. "You never know what's inside."

Only we gave the money to the jumble, so the thrill didn't last long.

The service was short, because what could they say beyond, *We gather here today to sanctify the shag that can only lead to misery* . . . ? Not those words, but everyone was thinking it. Simon mumbled his *I do*. Lanny said hers and started to giggle till they got to the snogging part, which was over so quick the audience hissed, so we had to watch it again.

Outside after, Simon's mates had plenty to offer in the way of bedroom advice. Lanny just smiled, teetering a bit on her wedge-heel shoes. Had they ever *used* a bedroom? A sofa was likely the most plush they'd ever encountered. Simon caught sight of me, loitering like an idiot beyond the cluster of gooning yobs. If I'd been hoping for a big brotherly handshake, all crimes forgotten, I'd've been drenched in disappointment.

"You can piss off now," he said. "Done your duty. Sat a few twats in chairs. Big help. Ta."

"Simon!" Lanny linked her arm through mine. "Robbie's coming to the party, aren't you, sweetie? I want you to meet my cousin Elaine."

Harry the bartender had strung up Christmas lights at the Red Lion, early but cheery. The music was cranked on high, the Beatles playing "Two of Us." Very bleeding romantic.

Aunt Pat bustled back and forth, laying out plates of cut-up cheese, rows of biscuits, tray after tray of sausage rolls, baskets of crisps, bowls of nuts. Brenda was slicing pork pies, another girl stuck plastic forks in mugs and stacked serviettes.

Harry was laughing it up, everybody's friend for a change. Not often he had forty extra customers dead keen on getting blind drunk enough to forget it ever happened.

"No, lad!" He nudged Simon out from behind the bar. "It's your wedding day, nod nod, wink wink. You're not to be pulling pints. You're to be drinking them!"

"You won't send me home with a lousy drunk on my wedding night, will you?" Lanny was flushed and pretty, tits big and round. Simon always said she'd got the best ones. Tits get bigger when a girl is knocked up, right? Simon'd be in heaven till the rest of her caught up.

I stood next to me dad while he nattered on with Mr. Darrow, a nosy old codger, the two of them slurring a bit already.

"Simon's second, eh?" Mr. Darrow had a voice like fingers

245

scraping a screen door. "Or is there a third and a fourth Muldoon brat out there that none of us knows about?"

"No need to be sarky," said Dad. "As if your Sharon didn't stop off at the church on her way to the maternity ward."

Mr. Darrow showed us a few grey teeth. "And her mother before her, truth be told. I'd've never . . . if she hadn't been . . ."

"And that's a fact," said Dad.

"You were the lucky one," Mr. Darrow told Dad. "Your Aileen was a prize."

"Lucky for how long?" Dad rubbed his eyebrows. "Barely ten years."

"Well, your pup Simon didn't get stuck his first time, did he? With that lass who works at Bigelow's and her young 'un."

"There is a God after all," said Dad. "But the little boy is bright as a button and twice as clever, I'll say that. A scrap of sunshine in a dark room."

"That's a grandpa talking!" Mr. Darrow shuffled off to find his wife.

Surprised as hell, I asked Dad. "Have you seen him?"

"Seen who?"

"Little Jerry. That Kath has. Didn't know you'd ever met him."

Dad glanced around like a thief checking for coppers. "You won't say to Simon?"

I shook my head, not a bleeding chance.

"I pop by some Sundays," he said. "Take the boys in the road to kick the ball while Kath has her tea. She's a snapping turtle, that one. But Jerry . . ." He got quite a foolish look on his old face. "He's a corker." Nice for him, I thought. There wouldn't be grandkids from any time *I* spent in the sack.

"Mum's the word, eh?"

"Secret's safe with me."

Second Dad shock of the day, he said, "You've got a hairy handful of secrets, haven't you?" He laid a palm on my sleeve, patting ever so gently. "Does it hurt, lad?"

He'd never said a word about what happened, not one. Not while he rolled cigarettes beside my hospital bed, or when he fetched me home, or anytime since. He picked a crowded pub on his son's wedding day?

"Not anymore." My scabs were instantly itchy, but scratching would mean blood. No way would I cough up extra cash for the rental shirt.

Dad waggled his empty glass at me and toddled to the bar for another drink.

"Here you are!" Lanny pounced. "This is *Elaine*! My cousin from Scunthorpe, I was telling you about?"

Elaine from Scunthorpe was a bridesmaid, livid purple from titline down. She was endowed as roundly as Lanny, honey-coloured ringlets fixed on the side of her head with a violet paper blossom as big as a turnip.

"Hallo," I said.

"Didn't I tell you?" Lanny gushed to her cousin. "Even dishier than Simon! Go on, get cozy! See you later!"

I was stuck. Elaine was a grinner. I'd've sidled off, only I spotted Banger and Alec watching me over their pints.

"Well, darlin'," I said. "Think you've got a dance in you?"

My timing was terrible. The Beatles had just started "The Long and Winding Road," an eternal three minutes and thirty-eight seconds with my arms around Elaine from Scunthorpe, my nose itching in her sticky curls, my hips bumping close enough to hers to seem randy and keen.

The song finally ended. "That was . . . lovely." She sighed. Her eyes slid over to catch Lanny's, the bride perched on her husband's knee. The cousins would be off to the loo, if I played it right, girls always needing to discuss events as they unfold.

"Nice locket." I tapped the crap charm that rested on the doughy swell of her tits, running my fingers up her neck for the benefit of Banger, who had such an ugly mug he probably bonked his bulldog.

"*Eeep!*" squealed Elaine.

"Fancy a bite?" I tipped my head at the food table.

"I'm on a diet," she said.

Was I meant to say *You look fine to me*?

"Robbie, may I borrow Elaine for a mo?" Lanny, about ruddy time. "Don't go anywhere. We'll be right back."

I'd've nipped out and gone home, only a hand cupped my bum just long enough to show it meant to be there.

"Buy you a pint?" said Felix. He didn't need to be standing so close. "If you're done with the lady-killing portion of the afternoon?"

I laughed. Felix had always been a star at noticing. We stepped into an alcove by the coat stand, letting the girls go right past when they came out of the ladies'. They'd found another purple girl, so Elaine was occupied for a minute or two.

"What the hell, eh?" Felix meant Simon and Lanny.

The Beatles were strumming "Let It Be," the speaker right over my head. Lanny got Simon up to sway with her where tables were pushed aside. We leaned against the wall, watching. Lanny stopped dancing to tug at the crown-thing in her fancy updo. Simon tipped a paper cup to his mouth, while his new mother-in-law helped the bride.

"*Ow!*" Lanny pulled away. "Leave off!" But her mum unhooked the little tiara, along with only a few strands of Lanny's hair. Simon drained the cup and smashed it flat between his palms.

"You couldn't pay me enough," I said. "You couldn't buy me a van or a house or a holiday in . . ." I tried to think of the craziest destination. "In Morocco."

Felix grinned. "Me neither."

He was so close I could smell him. I nearly teared up, thinking how I had Luke because of him. This was *Felix*. If anyone knew me, he did. Better than Luke, even, because how could Luke ever suss what my house was like, what an arse of a brother I'd had me whole life?

"Was it Simon?" I said. "Was it him, told them to do it?"

Felix put his empty pint glass on a table. "Smoke?"

"No, ta. I've stopped for a bit."

He lit one for himself. "Step outside?"

Yeah, better outside, despite the chill.

"What I heard . . . ," he began.

249

"Yeah, what did you hear?" I rolled my shoulders.

"What I heard," said Felix, "is that no one knew about you."

"No one did? I'm baffled."

"Until," said Felix.

He took a pull and spoke as smoke streamed out. "Until a girl from that school told Alec, and Alec asked your brother was it on to show you what's what."

"A girl?"

"Some bird out to get you?"

Only one bird at Ill Hall who even knew me, apart from Brenda. I pictured Penelope with her hand on Alec's zipper, calling me queer last time I'd said no.

I wished I'd taken a smoke.

"You've got someone, haven't you?" said Felix. "A boyfriend."

"Yes."

He dropped his fag and crushed it under his heel. "In London," he said, "it's like a different bleeding planet. No questions asked. Just be who you are."

I checked his face. Was he joking?

"You'll get there," he said. "Or somewhere else that's not here."

"Not until I've mashed my brother like an old banana."

"And what would be the point of that?"

No point, I knew. Simon had more friends than I did.

"Just to hit him," I said. "Break something, maybe."

Felix had a pencil out, writing his London number on a scrap. "Use it," he said. "Whenever you need to. You ready for that pint yet?"

"Hallo." Brenda slapped a slice of pork pie on a paper plate and added a pickle. "You hungry?"

"No. Ta."

"Getting rowdy, eh?" She passed the plate to the next person in line. The music *was* louder, now that she mentioned it. The room had got smoky, more people dancing, including Elaine, thank god, with Alec, poor seconds. Raucous laughter hooted from the darts room.

I'd've liked to ask Brenda about Penelope. But what exactly? And how would Brenda know anything?

"My dad," I said.

"Eh?"

"He visits?"

"My sister, you mean?" She reached around my shoulder, handing over another plate. "Yeah, well, Jerry, more like."

"I didn't realize," I said.

Brenda gave a big, smiling sigh. "He's dead sweet, is Jerry. Calls me Auntie Bren."

"I'm Uncle Robber," I told her. "They're the cops and I'm the Robber."

Felix came back with two pints. "Cheers." He knocked his glass against mine, a wee *clink*.

"One of the boys from my school is here," said Brenda. "Will it matter he sneaked in to use the loo?" She jerked her thumb toward the end of the bar.

I just about pissed my drawers. *Luke.* I did a stupid dance step, toward him, back again, sideways away from Brenda. Felix caught on in less than a second, giving Luke the up and down. "Are you begging to have your nuts severed? Letting him in here?"

I quick-scanned the pub to see where Simon was. Must be in the darts room. I slid up next to Luke, his face sweet and sly, full of surprising me. But I wrecked it, didn't I?

"What are you thinking?" I touched my hand to his hip, fingers reaching skin under his jersey. "You can't be here." His crazy hair tickling my cheek. "You've got to go." Moving my hand away felt like tearing off a plaster. "You could get hurt." *Hurt*. Too small a word to sum it up, a lifetime of pinches and jabs, being shoved against every wall you ever passed, hair lit by matches, bangs to the ears, spag down the neck. Knuckles cracking against jawbone, the heel of a hand ramming an eye socket, the point of a knife slicing so slickly the skin doesn't bleed or yelp with pain for several seconds until so many cuts up the arm are running with blood and spelling out who you are. Which is hurt.

"Is it because of him?" Luke was looking at Felix. "Is he . . . ?"

He was jealous! "No, really," I said. "Thinking of you."

His eyes shifted just before a body pressed into me from behind. Something hard jabbed at my bum. Luke's face went scared as hell.

Alec's voice growled, "You like it this way, pricklicker?"

Banger's goofy hiccup of a laugh. "Up the arse!"

I wrenched myself around, brought my knee up fast. Alec dropped the bottle he'd been poking at me as my blow caught him precisely in the knackers and sent him straight to the floor amidst the shattered glass. My kneecap glowed with the sting of excellent impact. Banger backed right off. The party went hush, apart from the Beatles

252

strumming away and the crackle of a Christmas bulb giving up its last light.

"Excuse us."

I spun around to see Felix moving Luke toward the door.

"Show's over," called Harry from behind the bar. "Plenty of beer still in the taps."

Alec was crawling to his feet, using Banger as a ladder.

"Take it outside, lads." Harry handed a broom to Aunt Pat, for the broken glass.

Alec spat on the floor, tried to straighten himself. No way was I stepping into the alley with this lot. They'd cream me. Felix hadn't come back. I'd go out the front, find him and Luke.

But, "Hey, poofter."

I paused half a second.

"I'm looking at a dead faggot," said Alec behind me. Banger hiccupped.

Time to leave the party. Time to leave the village.

The door opened and in rolled Felix. How had he done it, all these years? None of them had a clue. Harry turned up the music, the din was on again.

"Oy!" The groom himself. "Haven't you pissed off yet?" He stank of whisky, head on a tilt like it was too loose to hold upright.

"Just leaving," I said.

Simon blinked at Alec. "Whatsa matter? You look like you've been kicked in the nuts."

Banger laughed like it was the funniest thing ever. "Your brother bolloxed him!"

Felix slung an arm around Simon, dragging him away from his sidekicks.

"A toast!" he called out. "To Mr. and Mrs. Muldoon!"

A faint cheer went up, mostly drowned out by the Beatles.

"And all the baby Muldoons!" said Felix. "May they keep on coming! Lanny! Bring that baby belly over here!"

"You!" Simon pointed at me. "Don't talk to my *wife*. And stay clear of my *kids*. You hear? No son of mine is having a queer boy for an uncle."

"Oh, Jerry's yours now, is he?" Brenda jumped in before I could even open my mouth. "After four years of pretending he doesn't exist? I'll tell my sister you've said as much. Ready to kick in a few quid for his Wheaties, are you?"

"You fat, stupid cow—" Simon swayed in front of Brenda. "You keep your mouth shut or I'll shut it for you." One of his hands tipped a bowl of dip, mucking up his cuff, leaving a puddle on the table.

"Simon?" Lanny tugged on Simon's jacket, her creamy tits nearly spilling out of their basket. "Steady on. Let's not get rowdy, right? Robbie!" she said. "Elaine's been looking for you!"

"Elaine. Her dress was purple, right?" Where had Felix put Luke?

"Oh you!" Lanny gave me a push, gleefully tipping me against a chair. "I was hoping she'd be your type!"

"My type?" I said.

Felix looked sharp my way, warning me not to say what I was thinking. *My type is the boy who just left the bar.* I wasn't quite so daft as that, pinning a target on Luke's back.

But I wouldn't insult the bride either.

"I've learnt a lesson from my brother," I said. "Leave the pretty girls alone, unless you're ready to play papa."

Simon swung hard, but it was an easy duck. I'd have loved to thump him, I really would. Only it couldn't end well, him having a pub full of yobby mates ready to do battle. And like Felix had said, what for? Simon was about to fall down all by himself.

"He's all yours," I said to Lanny. "An empty bleeding handbag."

Brenda came around the food table to slip an arm about my shoulders.

"Ta," I said.

Felix was there, and Brenda. Aunt Pat sidled over, broom in hand. Even Dad, nearby.

I had my own ragged army.

And something worth fighting for.

jenny

At home, it was the day after Thanksgiving. Usually there'd be platters of leftovers, except . . . I wondered who Mom cooked for, if not for us? No Thanksgiving in England. The Pilgrims *escaped* this country! They were giving thanks for landing somewhere that promised liberty for all, currently upheld by the United States Armed Forces. Was Matt having turkey in Vietnam?

My mother's method of roasting a turkey is to wrap it in bacon like an Egyptian mummy. The oven would be on from before breakfast until we were driven insane by the smell, midafternoon when people arrived for the feast. But Tom and I, we always tried to outsneak each other, nabbing the strips of bacon before anyone else had a chance.

* * *

No smell of turkey bacon came out of the tubs delivered from the kitchen of Ill Hall at Friday dinner. Meat loaf again, boiled spuds, wizened peas. In the dorm afterward, I sat on my bed, crazy homesick. Not for my parents. They'd just been here for the whole of Visiting Day weekend. And I'd be home in only three weeks! My semester abroad, already over! So what was missing? My bedroom? My Philly friends?

I pictured the reunion with Becca and Kelly, each of us draped over an armchair in Kelly's rec room. What would I tell them? *The food was terrible! Even worse than we ever guessed. Living in a dorm was awesome, friends day and night. The teachers, we called them by their first names, it was so evolved and cool. In the summer, there'll be skinny-dipping in the pond. This one guy, Nico, you wouldn't believe the color of his eyes! And my best friend of the boys, his dad is a Hollywood movie director, I'm not kidding. I made friends that I'll keep for the rest of my life. . . .*

What was wrong with me? Now I was lying in my imagination.

I hadn't spoken to Penelope since the day that neither of us explained why I was crying. She didn't accuse me and I didn't confess. Kirsten and Percy patted my back and felt sorry for me and the master plan worked. Matt had broken up with me. They were sympathetic and no one asked awkward questions. But how could they be my friends—for the rest of my life—if the only me they knew was a fake?

*   *   *

Tom knew who I was. Possibly the only person in the world. But I'd stopped calling him because he was never there. How many messages had I left with roommates? And he'd never called back. What happened to my promised weekend at Sheffield? Never the right time. Was it *Tom* I missed?

Tom. And Matt. Home the way it was supposed to be. Thanksgiving *after* the meal, when Matt came over and we stayed up later than late, joking around, playing charades, eating leftovers at two in the morning. It wouldn't be like that, not anymore, maybe not ever. . . . Tom would be in England until the war was over, and Matt . . . Would Matt come home?

And now I was going back, without them, and without . . . Maybe I'd been hoping for a miracle, but I thought I'd be someone else by now. I thought at least that I'd be . . . *someone*.

I lifted the lid of my trunk. Nothing ever got folded unless it had just come back from the laundry, where fairies packed it all in a tidy net bag every other Monday. Each week, there were more clumps missing from the fringes on my sweaters and T-shirts, probably clogging the pipes of the washing machines.

I scooped everything out and dumped it on my bed. The trunk bottom was dusted with sweater lint and a pinkish stain from where my hair conditioner had leaked. I began to sort and fold. The checklist, sent to Philadelphia by Isobel—before I knew who she was—was taped to the inside of the lid, each item carefully marked off to show what I'd brought so I'd be certain to take the right things home again. *Vests, V-neck sweaters, dark skirts, collared blouses.* Tatters at this point. Useless, really, anywhere else.

I'd arrived with high hopes, my trunk bursting with the ingredients to become a new person. A person who—I ran my fingers over the cut edges of the skirt nearest me—who didn't need parents or a brother telling her what to think. A person who was daring and intriguing. Funny and carefree. Sure of herself.

What a bleeding joke, as Penelope would say.

Don't think about Penelope.

If I were lucky, the next three weeks would pass with no more Penelope drama.

The Austen door banged open, Kirsten and Brenda bustling in.

"Off-day with Penelope?" Brenda was saying. "She *can* be a bit of a cow, just like my sister, Kath."

"This is more than a *bit*," said Kirsten. "She did something so stupid it was evil."

"What did I miss?" I said.

"Penelope and Kirsten," said Brenda. "Hammer and tongs on trolley duty."

"Not open for discussion," said Kirsten. "Brenda, stick your bag on Caroline's bed."

Brenda had a paper bag, its top folded over a bulging middle.

"We don't have an overnight case at our house." Brenda

laughed, cheeks pink. She didn't seem embarrassed to carry her belongings in a grocery sack. "We've never been anywhere, my old dad or me."

"This is finally your night?" I said.

"Yeah, I'm dead tickled!"

"Good timing, with Caroline gone home for the weekend."

Brenda wore such a grin. "It looks different, me knowing I'm sleeping over, not just popping in."

"What's with your new decor?" Kirsten meant my piles of clothing. "You're not *packing*!"

"My semester's nearly done."

"But you're not leaving," she said. "Right? You're coming back after the break?"

"I . . ."

"Shouldn't we all be getting to Games?" said Brenda. "We still have to change."

Who invented field hockey anyway? Some girl-hating sadist with a perverted addiction to reddened, wind-chafed thighs and bruised shins. At Ill Hall we had Games instead of PE, usually quite benign: running laps around the playing field or smudging the dirt to obliterate poor effort in the broad jump. But when Fran and Kirby rounded up girls and handed out hooked wooden mallets and shin guards, normally tame females were transformed into gladiators. Hockey sticks became brutal weapons in a battle to the death. It was the end of November, drizzling and *miserable*.

Looking at the other girls, you'd think we'd been promised a chocolate cake for the muddiest participant. They
went crashing up and down the field, banging sticks at the
stupid ball, ruddy-cheeked, shouting, *Hooray! Good show!*
and twirling their soggy pleated skirts with every darting
smash.

It had taken Fran two minutes to plunk me in one of
the nets as goaltender; she'd seen that otherwise I'd be
trampled among the sheep droppings. Meaning I was the
farthest from the road when Oona started hollering, "Oy,
Penelope! Where the hell are you going? Our goal is at the
other end!"

Penelope trotted along the boundary line and then off
the field through long grass, toward the road where someone . . . a boy . . . it was *Tom*! I set off running too, only I
had on bulky goalie pads, so my pace was a waddle. Fran
blasted her whistle. The game stopped, sticks frozen.
Kirby blew *his* whistle and charged after Penelope, catching her on the verge of the drive. I clumsily unstrapped a
shin guard while I ran, and then the other, leaving them in
the scrub.

"Jenny!" Kirby held Penelope's arm and now reached out
to grab mine. "What's happening?"

"It's my brother. I just . . . it's a surprise, him being
here."

"I dig that." He untucked his ponytail from the collar
of his jersey and wiped his damp forehead with a sleeve.
"But you can't just split. We're in the middle of a game,
right?"

I didn't answer.

"No relation to you?" Kirby asked Penelope. She pouted and kicked the grass.

"Jenny, say hello to your brother and make arrangements for his visit to begin *after* lessons." He put a hand on Penelope's shoulder. "*You.* Stick with me." He steered her back to where the girls were tearing around again, clacking their swords.

By the time I'd plowed through the spiky stalks that rimmed the field, Tom was holding out his arms. The hug was flannel and warm and weedy, until I remembered I was mad at him.

"You suck," I said. "You got off with Penelope on Visiting Day and then left with Mom and Dad and I never heard from you again."

"That was *weeks* ago!"

"Yeah. *Weeks* ago!"

"You can't be bummed about *her*. She . . . made me. I told you that."

"She *made* you? That's the weakest crap I've ever heard."

"Jesus, Jenn, I'm here now." He sounded exhausted, as if he'd walked the forty miles from Sheffield. "Happy Thanksgiving."

"How did you get here?"

"I hitched."

"You look terrible." Kind of shrunken.

A whistle blew on the field. Two whistles. The players jogged off, hair whipping, skirts flapping in the wind.

"I've got lessons until three-thirty. It's not okay to just

262

show up." I sounded prickly, but he deserved some flack. I should be hoofing it to catch the others.

"But I came to tell you . . . I just wanted to see you. There's some stuff going on. . . ."

"What?"

"Trouble. And stuff. At school."

"What do you mean, *trouble*? What did you do?"

"More about what I didn't do. I've . . . missed a few classes . . . not shown up for seminars, that kind of thing." Tom blinked his pink-rimmed eyes. "I've been *warned*."

"You're high," I said. "You get high and don't go to class. You're always effing high, aren't you?"

He shrugged, rolling his eyeballs back like I was Mom or something. He'd come looking for me but he wasn't ready to see me yet. *People*, I thought, *are in and out of each other's orbits every minute*. Often we don't even notice. Once in a while, we collide, knock ourselves into new territory. Here on the grounds of Illington Hall, Tom was so vividly an alien from another place, it was like one of Percy's movies.

"Why are you messing up?" I couldn't control the pissy shake in my voice. "You're at school to stay out of the *army*, for god's sake! What are you *thinking*?"

"Jenny!" called Fran. "Time's up!"

"Come on, it's raining." I grabbed his hand, pulling him along.

I stuck him in the library, said I'd be back after Art. When I got to the Girls' Changing Room to peel off my drenched and yucky hockey togs, most of the others had

263

already disappeared to class. But in where the loo stalls were, a furious dispute was going on.

I didn't recognize Kirsten's voice at first, because I'd never heard it mad before.

" . . . so bloody thoughtless!"

"How was I supposed to know? I only said it as a joke." Penelope, defending herself.

"How is it amusing to spread malignant rumors about someone?"

Penelope took in a deep breath. "It's not a rumor, though, is it? What I said was the truth."

Was this about me?

"There are certain true things"—Kirsten, terse as hell—"that should not be said. You don't tell the Nazis that someone is hiding under the floorboards just because it's a *fact*! That's what you did! There's no prize for telling the truth if it leads to someone getting seriously hurt."

"Remind me," said Penelope. "Since you and your family live in emotional hibernation, avoiding reality. Next time I go around telling the truth, remind me to shut my gob."

"You should shut your gob before you say pretty much *anything*!" Kirsten shouted.

"Stop it!" I stepped into the doorway. "I utterly guarantee that I did *not* get off with Luke! There is *nothing* to fight about!"

They stared as if I were speaking Chinese, looked at each other and back at me. They shook their heads, slowly, as if they'd practiced doing it together.

"I . . . saw him . . . ," I said. "Down the woods. But we didn't . . . We never . . ."

"Obviously," said Penelope.

"This is something else," said Kirsten. "Not about you."

"Not everything *is* about you," Penelope added. "As shocking as that may seem."

"Jenny," said Kirsten. "All she meant was . . ."

"Sorry," I said. "Didn't mean to butt in. Just wanted you to definitely know that I didn't—"

"We get it," said Penelope. "Saint Jennifer. Saving yourself for your boyfriend. Oh! Excuse me! Your *ex*-boyfriend!"

"Shut it, Pen." Kirsten's voice went shrill. "Why do you have to be so nasty all the time?"

"And why do you have to be so *nice*?" Penelope snatched up her shoulder bag from where it sat in one of the sinks. She pushed past me, but then turned back to Kirsten.

"If it *was* me," she said. "My fault, what happened . . . well, I wouldn't do that on purpose, I *never* would. I hope you know that, Kirsten."

She made her exit, hair bouncing.

"Not exactly an apology," said Kirsten. "But the closest she'll ever come."

"Wait," I said. "What just happened? I thought you were talking about Luke. And me. The rumor. Who got hurt?"

"A boy in town."

"Brenda's friend?"

"His name is Robbie, as it turns out."

"Is he also . . . a friend of *Luke's*?" Finally the pieces were clicking together.

Kirsten breathed on the mirror and drew a little circle with the tip of her finger.

"It's . . . none of my business," I said. "But . . . I saw . . ."

There was no mistake about what I'd seen. It wasn't misinterpretation, like kids "seeing" Luke and *me*. If I hadn't seen the boys together . . . all this would have been behind my back, out of earshot. Someone else's secret, one of the million or two that lingered like ghosts within these old walls.

"Just chance," I said. "I saw him . . . *them* . . . down the woods. Luke knows I know. He knows I'd never tell."

So then it came out. Luke was shy, he'd never had a girlfriend even though they all thought he was a heartthrob. He'd never said a word, even when Kirsten guessed a while back and dropped hints. "You sort of know, right? Your own brother." But Luke never said, just went quietly along. Turned out he'd met this boy in town, oh, did I remember meeting him, that first day in the chip shop? That was before Kirsten knew anything. But then the boy got beaten up and horribly hurt. Being queer might be legal but it wasn't liked. Luke had skived off lessons and gone to see Robbie in hospital. Back at school, he'd found Kirsten and told her everything. He'd cried. She hadn't seen her brother cry since he stepped on glass at the beach when he was nine. So she'd cried too and they'd had this big moment.

"Robbie seemed fine when I saw him." I hoped she didn't ask for details.

"He's much better," she said. "Scars, but otherwise fine."

"How is it Penelope's fault? Is she . . . she's not against them, is she?"

"She opened her big fat mouth and said something. To the wrong somebody. Luke found out at the weekend, at a wedding. But he only told me today."

"You mean the somebody who . . . hurt Robbie?"

Kirsten turned to look at me. "Where's *your* brother, speaking of Penelope's big fat mouth?"

"I left him in the library after Games."

"What do you bet Pen's with him by now? I'll cover for you," said Kirsten. "We've missed half of Art already."

Penelope jumped up to wave me off when I came into the library.

"He's sort of pathetically messed over," she whispered, blocking my way.

Tom lay on the library sofa, shoes kicked off, feet dangling over the end, familiar holes in the toes of his gray sweat socks.

"Move, Penelope. He's *my* brother."

"You just hate me," she said.

"You start galloping across the playing field like a deodorant commercial, with *my* brother as the *hero*. Did you . . ." I hated asking her this. "Did you *know* he was coming?"

Her curls tumbled forward as she dropped her face.

"No." Finally. "But . . ."

But?

"But there was this tiny hopeful crappy stupid bit of me . . ." She glanced over her shoulder to check Tom. His eyes were closed. "I had a minute's worth of fantasy, while I was running, that he *had* come . . . to visit *me*. All right?"

I stared at her. There was a tiny crappy stupid bit of me still worried that Pen was right. He'd hardly ever called, let alone traveled forty miles for *my* sake, other than Visiting Day when our parents brought him. Maybe he *was* here to find *her*?

"Happy now? That you've seen into my pathetic heart?" She stepped aside, letting me in. "He's passed out."

"He's faking." I jounced his foot, watched his eyelids flutter.

"I'm off," said Penelope. "Precious family moments are not my favorite entertainment." One of Pen's guilt-inducing remarks that we all ignored. Except that . . . family moments—or Tom and Matt moments, anyway—*had* always been *my* favorite entertainment. Maybe Kirsten felt that way about Luke. I watched Pen go, surprised at how not mad I was.

Tom spent half his life with his eyes closed. When someone asked an irritating question, Tom's eyes went *click* shut, like the snap of a lens cap on a camera. Was he hiding? Or giving the other person a chance to slink away into the undergrowth? And what is *undergrowth* anyway? We all grow underneath what people see, right? Most of life happened out of sight, as it turned out.

"Jenn." He patted a spot next to him for me to sit close. "I know I'm stoned. I know I've made a total cock-up of the whole semester. . . . Don't you love that word? *Cock-up*? Best thing I've learned in England."

"Have you been kicked out?"

"Not quite," he said.

"But almost?"

"Really, really almost." He shuffled himself to a sitting position. "All Matt's fault," he said. "Every day I wake up, I think about where Matt must be waking up. It's making me crazy, Jenn."

I thought about Matt waking up, going outside to find a dead barber's body. It made me want to kick Tom.

"I never noticed," I said, "how selfish you are."

He closed his eyes.

"I know he's your best friend. But he . . . I . . . Matt's my . . ."

"Brother." Tom, still shut-eye. "He's our n'other brother."

"Kind of," I said.

"Now you're up to where I have to smoke a pipeful to forget."

I whacked his arm. "That's the dumbest thing I've ever heard *ever*. Total bullshit!" I punched the sofa cushion to stop from hitting him. "How can you waste time being guilty? How dare you? Don't make me scream. How will it help Matt if you're drafted and get your pot-wasted head blown off?"

Tom sat up and looked at me. I'd never yelled at him before. I'd hardly even disagreed with him before.

"Change of plan." He cleared his throat. "That's what I came to tell you . . . I came here for a reason, you know. Not to whine or collapse or . . . bonk your friend."

I tucked my legs under me. Listening.

"There was an academic hearing. Three ancient professors grilled and reprimanded and scolded and chastised. I had to wear a *tie*!"

"A tie is not a *helmet*!"

"I know that, Jenn."

"Did you have to tell Mom and Dad?"

"Not yet. Never, if I can avoid it. Pray that the college holds off. And that includes you, unless you want your tongue sliced and fed to pigeons. Listen to me. There's an outcome. If I never get high again—"

"Ha! What are the chances of that?" I'd say zero. "You're high right now!"

Click. Eyes again. "I'm ignoring your negative vibes. If I chill on smoking. If I can possibly manage to chill on smoking. Which I really, really mean to. Today is my farewell stone. If I go to every lecture. If I miraculously pass my exams next week with gold stars. If all that happens, I get another hearing instead of expulsion."

"Instead of the army, you mean."

"Right."

I lay down with my head on his knee. "You better," I whispered. "You really better, Tom-Tom."

He laid a hand on my head and patted ever so gently.

The bell rang for the end of lessons.

"And!" I popped back up. "You write to Matt. Right away."

He sighed, sort of a moan. "Matt wrote to me," he said. "That's what killed me. Him being plucky as hell, telling me plans for after."

"Or, better yet, *ten* letters."

"I get it. I hear you. It's a deal." He lay back against the lumpy cushions. "Do you think I could stay on this sofa tonight? It's not in me to hitch back."

"It's called thumbing." Maybe he could pull off his plan, gold stars and all. He was lazy but also crazy smart. "We're having baked beans for tea. It's the worst food you'll ever eat. Wouldn't you rather sleep in one of the boys' dorms, if there's a bed?"

"Seriously, no. I'd have to participate in a schoolboy ritual or something drastic. Can't I just stay here?"

"I'll have to ask Richard. The headmaster."

"Jolly good."

A church bell in town chimed on the hour. We heard midnight and then waited at the top of the stairs for another many minutes to make sure. Four of us from the girls' dorms, plus Percy, converged in the corridor outside the kitchen with only one flashlight among us.

"You're bleeding useless," whispered Penelope, aiming the beam at the door. "Brenda will come with me, since this is her big adventure. You others wait here to receive the goods." They were back in under a minute, giggling like maniacs, balancing two baking trays covered in foil.

"Come on, come on, come on!" Percy hopped up and down in socks.

"Did you get cutlery? Napkins?"

"Jesus, do you think we're at the Buckingham Hotel?"

271

Tom was not thrilled at first to have a party land on his sofa, but we soon won him over. The flashlight battery died after a few minutes, making the library grow in size, especially with a half-moon glimmering through the window.

"I count twenty-six baked apples," said Kirsten. "Enough for six of us, do you think?"

Not having spoons or plates, we hovered around the pans, slurping sugary apple flesh and trying not to touch anything else with sticky fingers. We finished off about half before they lost their appeal.

"We'd better return the leftovers," said Brenda. "Think how ticked Vera will be at dinner tomorrow to find some missing!" She volunteered to tiptoe back with the trays, and I helped her put things away.

"It's just how I fancied it would be." Brenda's voice was eerie in the unlit kitchen hallway. "Staying in the dormitory, mucking about all night, being silly. Dream come true."

"It's not always like this. Usually we sleep."

"For me, it's my one go. It'll be this way forever, noshing stolen apples in the dark. Like one of Richard's poems, you know? 'Gather ye rosebuds while ye may' . . . ?"

I laughed. "I never thought of you as the poetry-reciting type."

"One of my hidden talents," said Brenda. "Learned at Ill Hall."

We crept back, feet getting bloody cold on the stone floor.

"*Oi!*" Penelope whispered urgently from partway up the stairs. "Hairy Mary on the prowl! Percy made a racket so she's trailing him to Kipling. Kirsten's gone up. Come on!"

Barely swallowing laughter, we tore upward, completely breathless on the Austen landing, peering over the railing to the dark depths below. All quiet. Brenda crept back into the dorm, but Pen and I settled our bums on the top step, not ready for the night to end.

"Hot gossip out of Brontë," said Penelope. "Oona got off with Nico *again*! According to her, anyway. Can you imagine? After all that remorse about betraying Sarah. It's just too foul."

"Speaking of betrayal . . . ," I said.

"It's nothing," said Penelope. "Your brother and me. Don't turn it into drama."

"That's not what I meant," I said. "I was wondering about Kirsten. She was a bit chilly tonight." With good reason, seemed to me.

Penelope did that shrugging thing, lifting her hair and letting it settle in rippling waves. "She'll forgive me eventually. She always does. I truly didn't mean . . ."

Was it that easy? Would Pen be so forgiving if given the chance? Was it trusting, or blind, to assume that a friendship would go on even when the truth came out?

"I have to tell you something," I whispered. We were side by side, snug on the step, so I didn't actually have to look Pen in the eye.

"Matt is not my boyfriend." There. I'd said it. "When you asked me, that first day, I said yes, because I . . . I think I

273

wish that he was . . . Because I love him. But he's not my boyfriend. That was a lie."

"Surprise, surprise."

"That's it? No evil comment?"

"I'll think of something. Before you leave." She slipped off a sock, scratched an ankle. "We're all hiding something, you know."

"What if I don't leave? What if I . . . tell my parents I want to stay?"

"That would be . . . grand." *Grand* means "grand." "Is it scary? Having Matt over there?"

"Scary as hell," I said.

Tap, tap, tap . . . Hairy Mary's shoes clicked and echoed on the lower stairs. We scrambled for the Austen dorm.

My bed was still covered in neatly folded piles of rags. I shoveled them into the empty trunk, not minding how they landed. I wasn't leaving. One semester wasn't enough. I'd ring my parents tomorrow, after I told Tom the plan.

He would write to Matt. He would pass his exams. We would go home for Christmas and send a huge care package to Vietnam. Peanut butter, *Star Trek* comics, jelly beans . . .

We would *both* come back to school. Tom not stoned, but straight. I'd make him. And me, straight too, no lies.

I'd pack a ton of regular clothes. Bell-bottom jeans. A peasant blouse. A miniskirt.

I brushed the lint off my pillow, peeled the checklist

274

from inside the lid of my trunk. What you arrive with is never what you take home anyway.

I crawled under the flannel sheet and gray wool blanket. The first few minutes in bed were always freezing. I would bring a duvet too, after the break. I lay for a long time, my cheek in a perfect hollow of the pillow, listening to the others breathing, letting myself get warm.

Acknowledgments

Thank you to Martha Slaughter, Hannah Jocelyn, Michele Spirn, and especially Catherine Nichol, for early input.

Thanks also to the short story workshop of Paulette Bates Alden as part of the Key West Literary Seminar, and to the Access Copyright Foundation for funding my attendance there.